WHEN THE PELICAN LAUGHED

Alice Nannup with
Lauren Marsh and Stephen Kinnane

The next morning when I woke up I remembered their dance and I said to my mother, 'Ngangka, do you think I could be a Brolga?'

'No,' she said, 'you Wari, you're a jutarrara (pelican), and you can't change that.'

When the Pelican Laughed tells the remarkable story of Alice Nannup. Deeply informed by Alice's battling spirit and her particular voice, it is a story of learning to be strong in who you are.

Born on a Pilbara station in 1911, of an Aboriginal mother and European father, Alice Nannup was taken South at the age of twelve and trained in domestic service. After a full and eventful life, including many battles with authority and raising ten children, she returned home sixty-four years later 'to make peace with my country'.

Whilst very much a personal account of Alice's life story, *When the Pelican Laughed* compellingly illuminates many aspects of the experience of Aboriginal people taken from their family community in the nineteen twenties and thirties.

Alice Nannup was born on a Pilbara station in 1911 to an Aboriginal mother and white father. She was taken from her community at the age of twelve and sent south to work as a domestic servant. After her marriage in 1932, Alice raised ten children. Known as 'Nan', she lived in Geraldton surrounded by her friends and extensive family until she passed away in November 1995.

Lauren Marsh is a writer and researcher born in Kalgoorlie, Western Australia, in 1961. She co-wrote and co-produced *The Coolbaroo Club*, an ABC Television documentary.

Steve Kinnane works as a researcher and writer, he has also collaborated on a number of community heritage projects. His people come from the East Kimberley of Western Australia. He co-wrote and co-produced *The Coolbaroo Club,* an ABC Television documentary.

WHEN THE PELICAN LAUGHED

ALICE NANNUP
LAUREN MARSH STEPHEN KINNANE

FREMANTLE ARTS CENTRE PRESS

First published 1992 by
FREMANTLE ARTS CENTRE PRESS
193 South Terrace (PO Box 320), South Fremantle
Western Australia 6162.

Reprinted 1992, 1993, 1996.

Editor Wendy Jenkins.
Designer John Douglass.
Production Manager Linda Martin.

Printed by McPherson's Printing Group, Victoria.

National Library of Australia
Cataloguing-in-publication data

Nannup, Alice, 1911-.
When the Pelican Laughed

ISBN 1 86368 020 9.

1. Nannup, Alice, 1911-. [2]. Aborigines, Australian - Western
Australia - Mixed descent - Biography. [3]. Aborigines,
Australian - Western Australia - Social conditions.
[4]. Aborigines, Australian - Western Australia - Moore River
Region - Reserves - History [5]. Aborigines, Australian -
Women - Western Australia - Biography. I. Marsh, Lauren,
1961-. II Kinnane, Stephen, 1967-. III Title.

994.0049915

In memory
of my mother,
my family,
and for all of us
who were taken
from our people.

Alice Nannup

ACKNOWLEDGEMENTS

We would like to thank the following people: Wendy Jenkins for her support and insight, Mark Turton for many things over the past four years, Uni Parker for Aboriginal language words and for helping to hunt down family photographs, Girlie Clarke for the photographs on pages 19, 43 and 129, Joan Gray for her support and the photographs on pages 188 and 199, and Penny Taylor from the Australian Institute of Aboriginal and Torres Strait Islander Studies, Margaret Florey from Wangka Maya Pilbara Aboriginal Language Centre, and Dr Alan Dench from the Anthropology Department of The University of Western Australia.

We also wish to acknowledge the Australian Institute of Aboriginal and Torres Strait Islander Studies and the Aboriginal Arts Unit of the Australia Council for their financial assistance with the preparation of this book.

The creative writing programme of Fremantle Arts Centre Press is assisted by the Australia Council, the Australian Government's arts funding and advisory body.

Fremantle Arts Centre Press receives financial assistance from the Western Australian Department for the Arts.

INTRODUCTION

In the course of researching material on Stephen Kinnane's grandmother, Jessie Argyle, Stephen and I met many elderly Aboriginal women who knew his nanna, and were willing to talk to us about their experiences under the repressive 1905 Aborigines Act (WA). We came to meet Alice Nannup through one of these ladies, Aunty Jean Hill. When Stephen explained to Aunty Jean that he wanted to understand more about his nanna's life, her immediate advice was, 'Go ask Alice.'

Alice Nannup (Nan) and Jessie Argyle had met, and formed a friendship, during the late 1920s. Both women shared the bond of being Nor'westers, had been taken from their families as children and, under the control of the Chief Protector of Aborigines, were contracted to white households as servants.

Our first meeting with Nan was in Geraldton Hospital, where she lay flat on her back in a hospital bed, surrounded by visitors. We approached her bedside to introduce ourselves, and when Stephen explained he was Jessie Argyle's grandson, Nan was both surprised and welcoming. Although she had other visitors that day, Nan made the time to tell Stephen about how she came to be in Perth when she met Jessie, and explained how important their friendship had been to her. When we left Nan, we promised to keep in contact and to visit again — when she was back home — and bring with us a collection of old photos that belonged to Stephen's nanna.

A couple of months later, Stephen and I drove up to

Geraldton looking forward to meeting Nan properly and spending time talking and hearing stories. Towards the end of 1989 we started working with Nan, recording an account of her life experiences on tape, with the intention of including her story in an anthology.

Over the next three years we made regular trips to Nan's, and as our friendship grew, so did the size of Nan's story. Our main method of working was for storytelling sessions to be taped in the morning and big lunches to be eaten in the afternoon. In between trips to Geraldton, Stephen and I transcribed tapes, carried out research at the J S Battye Library of West Australian History, collected photographic material, and I began organising material from the transcripts into a single story format. Central to this working process was Nan's involvement and editorial control over her emerging story. I believe this was an essential part of our working relationship as it ensured that the written version was in a language style Nan felt comfortable with, and that any stories told to us privately during a taping session would not turn up in print twelve months later unbeknown to her.

In January 1991, Nan, Stephen and I discussed the idea of publishing Nan's story separately from the anthology. By this time, the content and scope of our work together had well and truly out grown the original concept. Nan was very enthusiastic about having her own book, so from this point on *When The Pelican Laughed* started to take shape.

Now that the book is finally finished we are all feeling a mixture of things: satisfaction, relief, pride and amazement. This book means different things to each of us, but to all three of us it is as much a product of the valuable friendship that developed between us as it is our response to the need for more Aboriginal women's perspectives on the history of this country.

Lauren Marsh
December, 1991

CONTENTS

Radio Theatre: Geraldton, 1950

I used to take my kids every Saturday afternoon to the matinee in town. We'd all go in, sit down and try to enjoy ourselves, but there were a few white kids in town who were really terrible. They'd turn around and poke their tongues out, or sling off at us with 'Nigger, Nigger, pull the trigger — BANG BANG you're dead.'

On this particular day a Tom Mix picture was on. Tom Mix was a cowboy, and he'd be going 'bang, bang' too, you see, so those kids would just turn it on to us.

There was one boy, and he was the main one. On this day he had chewing gum and he went and stuck it on my son's seat while he was out of the room. I didn't see him do it, of course, and I was that cross because these were brand new melange pants. They were the only pair in Wright's and because they were a bit damaged, shop soiled it was, they let me have them cheap.

The kid that did it thought it was a great joke. I said to my daughter, 'I've had enough of this Pearl. You tell me when the picture is nearly over.'

'Why, what are you going to do?' she asked.

'I'll show you what I'm going to do. You just tell me.'

'Well, it's just about finished now, Mum.'

Right, I thought, and I got up with my baby and I walked outside.

Out in the foyer, near the place where you buy the tickets, there was a rail running right to the other end of the room. There was a break in the rail where the audience goes in, so I went and stood there with my little bloke on my hip.

Before long they all started coming out, but I was blocking the way see, so some of the little kids started slipping under the rail. I was holding on to one baby, and I had another one of my kids at my feet clutching my dress, when I put up my hand. 'Just a minute, I've got something to say — and I want you all to listen.'

Everyone just stood there and looked at me, and there were quite a few of them too; the foyer was full.

'Look,' I said, 'I've been coming here every Saturday afternoon, bringing my children to enjoy the matinee, just like you people, and what do we get? Nigger, nigger, boong, boong, pull the trigger, this, that, and the other. Well I've had it. I want you people to try and understand how that feels. Why don't you bring your children up, don't drag them up — it's a disgrace!'

Well, they were all standing there, not saying anything. They were shocked, I suppose, that the likes of me could get up there and dress them down.

'You know,' I said, 'it's not fair. We're all the same, we're all human beings; we walk, we talk, we eat the same kind of food, we are all just made the same. Colour is skin deep and I think we should all be treated as human beings.'

Pearl was standing next to me and I said to them, 'I'll send my daughter next door to the tearooms to get two saucers. Then whoever of you is willing to come up here can be blindfolded. I'll take blood from me and from you, swirl it around in the saucers...then you come and tell me which is your blood.'

While I was saying all this two policemen came in, broke past and went and stood in front of me. I saw them there but I kept on telling them. I said, 'When we come into this theatre we don't throw off at you people, yet we're called everything. I'll tell you another thing too, there were three of your goody-goody boys across the road the other day and an old lady came out of the butcher's shop. She had two bags of groceries and every time she went to step off the kerb a car would come, and she'd have to step back. Well, those goody-goodies would laugh their heads off. That's shame,' I told them. 'But my son was with me, this "boong kid", and he walked across the road and carried that old lady's parcels home for her. That's what a "boong boy" does. And why? Because I brought him up to respect other people, not like you people. You're dragging your children up.'

They were all quiet, all just looking at me. The police were looking too and I tried not to look at them. But you should have seen these police, grinning from ear to ear, and one of those policeman didn't like Aborigines much either.

Then I said, 'I'll be back next week, don't worry about that. And I want to be treated as such, no names called, because we want to enjoy the matinee as well. Furthermore, before I go, if any of you can defend yourselves, come out here and tell me if I'm wrong. You come out here and tell me.'

But they didn't tell me, they just stood there.

'Right,' I said, 'you haven't got anything to say. You can go.' And I just stepped aside.

PART ONE

WARI, a young girl

1911–1925

Kangan Girl

'You, Wari, you're lucky to be with us, because you nearly got drowned one time.' This is a story my mother told me about when I was very young. She told it to me in language. She said, 'We went to Bamboo Springs and it started to rain very heavy. So we started back to Hillside where we were staying. The water was rising so we had to leave the cart and horse on the bank and wade across the river. You were only a little baby. I was carrying you along and the water was up to my waist. There was a hole in the middle of the riverbed and I put my foot down it and fell, letting you go. You went floating down the river and I was screaming and screaming. Just as well there was somebody near and they were able to pull you out. We shook you and got the water out and made you cry. It made us know you were really alive. Then we kept on going until we reached the station and dried you out properly. We were lucky to still have you.'

I always used to ask my mother to tell me stories about what happened when I was little. She was a good storyteller but she never really told me many stories about herself. She did tell me she had me on Abydos Station, out from Port Hedland. She was very young, just fifteen years old, and we left there when I was a baby. My mother never told me who my father was but I knew he was a white man because I was fair like my grandmother.

My mother's name was Ngulyi, that's her Aborigine name,

Dot (Ngulyi), Alice's mother, c. 1928.

and her European name was Dot. That's like me, my mulba name is Wari, and I've got a European name too. She was born on Pilbara Station, which is between Roebourne and Marble Bar, and she belonged to the Yindjibarndi tribe. My mother spoke five languages, as well as English — Nyamal, Palyku, Kariyarra, Ngarluma and Yindjibarndi. I spoke Kariyarra and Ngarluma the most, and, of course, English. Mother had two brothers, Sambo and Chubby, and a sister, Aunty Minnie or Inhabun, but she had lots of other brothers and sisters in the tribal way.

I don't remember much about my grandmother except that she was a lovely lady, and she came to stay with us once. Her name was Mary and I wasn't allowed near her much because she was very sick.

I had other grandmothers too, grandmothers in the mulba way. One old granny I remember was named Mulla, or Dinah. I always remember when she came to Kangan because she'd never seen billygoats before. She'd seen the female ones but not these big males. She was really amazed by these goats and she was shouting at me, 'Nganabalu, nganabalu!' That means, what's that? I didn't know what she was so excited about, but she was going, 'Walyaaril! Jurnda barni nanigut thumbubi jawardaala.' That means, hey, just like that nannygoat but with a bare behind and a beard! I tell you, I just laugh when I think back to the way she was carrying on.

I never knew my grandfather, but his name was Sam Singh, and he was Indian. He was a hawker and he had these camels to travel around hawking from place to place. So that makes me a real marda marda: I'm Aboriginal, English and Indian — a real international person. You hear people run down the English but I never do, because that's a part of me, just like having Indian blood.

After leaving Abydos my mother took me to Kangan Station just out of Roebourne. I think she must have worked there before I was born. She worked on lots of different stations, in the kitchens and doing housework. All the Yindjibarndi people did, that was their country up there and they travelled from station to station and worked.

Kangan was owned by an Englishman, Tom Bassett. I didn't

know it at the time but he was my father. He was from Roebourne, from the Bassetts of Roebourne, and he originally started out as the mailman. He had a four-in-hand; four grey horses and a covered wagon like a Cobb & Co. He used to deliver the mail all around, but he wanted to get out of that so he started up a station of his own.

I see Kangan as my home because that's the main station I grew up on. Mother would work for other station owners but we always came back to Kangan.

My mother really ran that whole place. She used to keep house for Tommy and his brother Lou, and cook for all the working men. She used to go back and forth into Roebourne and that's how she met up with Old Roebourne Ned. See, the elders reckoned she shouldn't be living there without an Aboriginal husband; that was law.

Those old ones, they were very strict on the law, like with the skin groups. There's four to a group — four on the mother's side and four on the father's side. Everyone fits into these and you've got a 'straight', like you can't marry just anybody, you've got to marry straight. My mother was banaga and Old Ned was burungu, her straight.

They were very strict laws all right, but it was good law really because everyone knew where they fitted in and what they could and couldn't do. Things like, a woman wasn't allowed to talk to her son-in-law, she'd have to turn her back. No one was free to do whatever they liked, they all had to go by what the elders said.

Not long after Mother and Old Ned got together they had a daughter, Mangkayurangu, or Ella. As well as having a skin group we all have totems too. I am a pelican, the fella with the big beak, and Ella was a scorpion. I tell you what, she could be a real little scorpion too. Her and I used to fight. She used to give me beans, but I couldn't fight back because Old Ned wouldn't let me. He'd tell me off if I did.

We stayed living on Kangan, and Old Ned worked for Tommy too. There was the main station house, where Tommy and Lou lived, and then there was our little house just away from it. My mother still used to go up and cook for Tommy and Lou and clean house for them, but we all lived in our own place.

21

Old Ned and me never really got along. In my memories he was an old grumbler and he'd always be on my back. It was: ' Wari, bring me this; Wari, get me that; Wari, ask your Ngangka (Mother); Wari, do this. Well, Wari got fed up! '

When I was really little I stayed in the house with them, but when I was a little bit older and Old Ned started up, I used to ask, 'Tommy, can I come and sleep at your place tonight?' He'd say, 'Any time you want to come it's all right. You've got your room.' I think my mother must have had a talk to him and asked if I could go up there from time to time, and that's what I'd do for some peace.

See, I think Tommy tried to make things easier for Mother because he didn't want them to leave the station and take me with them. But as I said, I didn't know he was my father until I was a bit older, and I always called him Tommy. He knew he was my father, and everyone else knew, but me being a little kid it never really occurred to me. I just thought I had no father. I didn't think of Old Ned as my father, but I used to call him mama, because he was my step-dad and mama can mean father or uncle.

Kangan was only a little station. Tommy started off with a couple of sheep and he had a lot of wild goats that he tamed. All that he used to have to do at night time was call coooeee, and all the sheep and goats would come in. He ended up with about ninety goats, most of them milking goats. He was very good to us, and Ella and I had our own nannygoats. Ella had Lena and I had Nancy, they were ours, the milk from them was just for us.

I learnt to ride when I was six years old. I had my own horse, saddle, bridle, everything, and I used to help muster the sheep in with my uncle, but that horse was old. When my pony was born he was born in a claypan, so I called him Clay.

I was a real little tomboy, I only ever wanted to be where Tommy and the men were. I used to be in boy's clothes all the time. (But today I wouldn't be seen dead in a pair of pants.) I used to get around in these little safari suits with a hat on my head, and I'd have these knee-high boots that buttoned up from the ankle. I had a big long plait right down my back, and when I'd go past Lou Bassett used to pull on it and say, 'What's this, a little chinaman!'

I used to have such trouble getting on my horse that I'd have to take him over to a stump or climb a fence post. I was just too bottom heavy, I couldn't lift myself up in the stirrup. I'd say to Tommy, 'I don't know how you get on that horse, Tommy.'

'Well, you've gotta have spring heels,' he'd say.

I'd try and try until he'd say, 'Get on a post, or go over there and find an anthill.' It was the only thing that I couldn't do.

When my mother wasn't working, she used to try and teach me how to read and write. But I was too keen on my old goat cart and things like that. I had a big old goat named Togo, and a cart that Tommy made for me, and I used to put the halter on Togo and drive him around the place. Ella and me used to love going up to get the wood for Mother in the goat cart. We didn't have a stove or anything like that. We had a long pole thing with bars across it that hung by chains. That's what Mother used to cook on, over a big open fire. It used to get really hot so it was built right away from the house. She used to cook beautiful things in the camp oven too: brownies, rock cakes and these marvellous rainbow cakes. She certainly was a wonderful cook.

We had a big boughshed where we used to eat and where the cooler was. To keep the water and butter and stuff cool we had a safe with a tray on top filled with water. The water would drip down hessian or old blankets on either side. You wouldn't think it but it used to keep everything lovely and cool.

Tommy had two houses in Roebourne and every now and then we used to go in and stay. Roebourne was just a little town of mud houses then, and all the other Bassetts were scattered around the place.

Tommy had one house up on the hill, a big iron bungalow, and that's where mother, Old Ned and us kids stayed. His other house you could see as you came into town, and his sister lived there. Tommy's sister was married, and some people say her husband was a gaol warden, others say he was a magistrate. I don't know which one he was, but they lived in that house all the time and Tommy would stay with them when we came to town.

While we were staying there, my mother would wash and iron for the other Bassetts. She used to take me and Ella with her, because some of the families had kids and we used to play with them.

Sometimes we'd get a sovereign to spend and we'd go down to Sam Comealong, the Chinaman, and buy lollies. Ella used to love these moon-lollies — they were hard boiled ones, as big as a tom bowler marble. Whenever Tommy went into Wodgina, which was the nearest town, he'd ask us girls what we'd like. Ella would always ask for moon-lollies and I used to ask for seed jam. That was raspberry jam, only I didn't know the name of it.

I remember staying in the house on the hill so well, because at around half past five or six o'clock every morning there used to be these prisoners, Aborigines from Roebourne gaol, coming along all chained together by the neck. I used to go down really early in the morning and watch these poor fellas go past.

When I saw them I used to run back up to my mother and say in language that I felt sorry for them and that. She'd say to me, 'You shouldn't look, you shouldn't look. Don't go back down there.' But I couldn't help it. I'd know exactly when they'd be coming and I'd have to go and see them. There was a big rock that I used to sit behind to watch.

There would be about sixteen of them, eight on each side, and they'd all be walking in a line carrying a pick, shovel and water-bag. There would be a policeman at the front, and one at the back, and those chains around their necks. I used to just cry. I'd sit there and cry for them because they were my people. They were treated that way just because they'd killed a bullock or something like that. Then they'd be put in this gaol and fed on something they couldn't survive on, and brought out to work on a chain-gang. They used to come back around sunset, all filing past, not speaking. It was so cruel, and I couldn't get away from them, couldn't get away. I used to enjoy going in to Roebourne except for this one thing, and it's a story I've told my own kids time and time again.

When I was about seven, Old Roebourne Ned got very sick. Tommy took us all into Roebourne to get him medical attention but Old Ned ended up dying. I suppose when it happened someone must have gone around and let everyone know. I remember the funeral and going up to the Aboriginal cemetery in a horse and cart with Mother, Ella, and all our relations. During the funeral me and Ella stayed a bit back from it all, but we could see them running around and throwing themselves around. We could hear the wailing and talking in language, and we saw the women scraping stones on their heads and bleeding.

Not long after Old Ned was buried we all went back to the station, but this time we moved up into the station house with Tommy and Lou. Lou Bassett lived there most of the time but him and Tommy used to take it in turns to be away from the station. I don't think my mother was with Tommy because he had his own section of the place and we had ours. I think they must have come to some arrangement that she'd look after him and the house but they'd keep separate lives.

I remember they got on quite well together and they played a lot of cribbage. They had this long bar of soap that they'd made all these little sections in for crib. At night I'd hear them laughing and growling at one another, you know, cheating and things like that. One would say, 'Oh, I don't think you made a proper count there,' and they'd start growling about it. Mother would end up chucking the cards in and going to bed, but next night she'd be ready to play again.

Then one night one of the Aborigine scouts came and saw Tommy. He said that Mother had to be at the Yule River by a certain time. You see, it's law that when a woman's nyuba (partner) dies she's got to have all her hair cut off to make herself ugly for somebody else. But mother didn't do it. I think she must have known why they came for her, but she didn't explain why, and the next morning Tommy packed her and us kids into the sulky with some food.

We got to the meeting place, and that evening they made a big fire at two sites. The elders were all there waiting and Mother had to kneel down in a circle of men. We were sitting back from it with the women. They started asking her questions and rattling their spears — Kata-kata-kata-kata-kata — and asking her in language, 'Why didn't you carry out the law?'

Mother wouldn't talk, she just knelt there quietly, and they kept jabbing her in the leg. She was sitting there with her feet tucked under her and she had points of spears all in her legs. Ella and I were afraid to look. We were so scared for Mother, we thought she was finished. They'd rattle the spears and say, 'Nyinda wanyjabarri,' which means, do you understand?

She told them that she didn't think it was necessary to cut off her hair, and they were really cross with her. They said to her she thought she was white because she had Tommy behind her. But Mother didn't think that at all and she was very upset.

Later that night the women came and cut Mother's hair off. She was allowed to keep it, of course, because if anybody got hold of it they could sing her with it.

We were only supposed to be there for a few days but the next morning Mother had gone blind. See, her and Aunty Winnie had gone out walking and they'd walked across sacred ground where the men were having a meeting. They reckoned she went blind for doing that. So we had to stay there for a week, and I used to go and get hot water to bathe her eyes. People used to cook food for us and we just stayed in the camp and looked after Mother.

After about a week she woke up and she could see a little bit. She said, 'Where's the horse?' I told her he was over there and she said, 'Can you get somebody to bring him to us. We're going home.'

When we got back and Tommy saw the way Mother was looking he said, 'Oh, they don't miss a trick!' But he never said anything about it because, well, he couldn't really. He would eat bush tucker quick and lively, but he always stayed separate from law. He never ever learnt to speak any language either. Sometimes when people came, like the shearers or just visitors, they'd be sitting there talking in English, then they'd switch to Aborigine. They'd be having a good old laugh and jabbering away there. After, he'd say to me, 'What was all the laughing and talking about?' Well, I couldn't tell him if they'd been talking about him, but mostly they weren't, anyway. I'd just say, 'Oh, they were just talking about how well shearing went,' or whatever.

I had to be very careful about speaking in lingo around

Tommy. One day Mother said, 'Come on you kids, we're going to get ready for a drive.'

'What horse are we taking?' I asked

'Old Kelly,' she said, just like that.

Then quick as lightning I said in Aborigine, 'Old Kelly! He's no good, he'll bog and we'll be there all night.'

Well, Tommy was coming around the corner and he overheard me. 'Alice, in my presence you speak English!' he said.

I said I was sorry and all that because he didn't like me speaking in my language. He never really minded about Ella but it was different for me.

Tommy had his ways like that, but really he was very good to me. He was a religious man, a Salvationist. I don't remember if he ever went into Roebourne to go to church, but I do remember the services he held on Kangan. Every Sunday morning he'd read from the bible and we'd sing a couple of hymns. He taught us bible stories and prayers, and he and I would sing ''Tell Me The Old Old Story'' together.

Mother used to take me and Ella to meetings and ceremonies all the time, and I really liked it. We used to dance too, us girls, like in little kid's dances. We'd be singing and dancing away, all us little girls from around. There'd be me and Ella, my cousin Uni, Doris, and quite a few others. It was really great, we really enjoyed life.

There were also ceremonies that women weren't allowed to go to, like initiation time. Then the men used to be on one side of the river. The women had the other side and they couldn't pass on the men's side. To walk on it would be crossing sacred ground because that's the business side. See, that's what my mother did that time, and they reckoned she went blind for it. That's just the way of the law; they tell you not to do things, and if you do, well, you're disobeying.

Every year Tommy would leave the station and go away for a holiday. This was usually after the shearing. He'd go and stay with his sister in Roebourne or down to Perth. Len Houghton, Uncle Alf Lockyer and Uncle Aubrey Lockyer were the three main ones who used to stay on the station and manage it for him. When he'd go, Mother would take us to another station or to visit some of our relations. We'd go for a few months until Mother felt like coming back.

I remember one of these times we went to Tabba-Tabba. I would have been about eight years old and Aunty Winnie and my cousin Uni were staying there too.

We used to play with all the other kids, and one day we were up playing on the hill when my mother and Aunty sung out for us. Uni and I grabbed hands and came scooting down as fast as we could. But there was this Empire meat tin laying on the ground and I put my foot on it and got cut very deeply.

When Mother saw all the blood she got a basin of water and put some kerosene in it to soak my foot. I put my foot in the basin and all the blood went underneath and the kerosene came up thick. Then Mother bandaged me up and they took me into Port Hedland.

I don't remember the trip because I must have been sick with the loss of blood. But I do remember there was a causeway at Port Hedland then, and it was very white, like it was covered with crushed shells. They got me to the doctor to treat my foot, and then we stayed in Hedland for some time. We stayed out in the bush on the reserve, the One-Mile they called it. Then when Mother was ready to move we went to Wodgina for a bit, then back to Kangan.

My mother used to be kept pretty busy looking after me and fixing me up with home remedies. I used to suffer from earache a lot and to cure it she'd get some cooking salt, warm it up in the camp oven, then wrap it up in a cloth and place it on my ear. These were the kind of cures we had way out in the bush and they used to work too.

Croup was also something I used to suffer with, and it used to make me nearly choke. Mother would get an onion, slice it up, place it in a cloth and lay it on my pillow. It wasn't the most pleasant thing, to sleep with an onion on your pillow, but I tell you what, breathing in the onion fumes used to really work.

Aside from those things there were lots of cuts and accidents she had to fix up for me. One time I put Togo in the goat cart and went to get wood. On the way home I tried to ride him and he threw me in the rubbish tip. When I picked myself up I trod on a rusty nail sticking out of a packing case strip. The nail sunk right into my foot and I had to stand on the strip with the other foot to pull the nail out. I limped back to the house and Mother soaked my foot in kerosene to get the rust out, then bathed it in salt water and bandaged it up.

Well, there was no wood carted that day, and I was put straight to bed. When Tommy came home my foot was swollen up, so he suggested soaking it in hot water every hour and putting a linseed poultice on every other hour. My poor mother did everything she could but I cried for two days in pain. Finally Tommy said, 'This is useless, we're going to Roebourne.'

Out in the bush you had to do the best you could because the doctor was so far away. It took us three and a half days to get into Roebourne from Kangan, and mother applied the poultice and soaking treatment all the way there.

They got me to Dr Mansell and we ended up staying for two weeks until I was well and truly over it.

I have such great admiration for my mother because she was always having to do the best she could to patch me up. I was a very clumsy kid. I'd fall over nearly everything I came across, or hurt myself in some other way. My mother said I was a real bumble-foot, and the nickname stuck. When anyone wanted me they used to sing out, 'Hey bumble, where are you?'

One time we went off to De Grey Station. Mother had a job working up at the house, and while the men went out mustering cattle they'd take us kids with them. They'd put planks of wood up in the fork of a tree for us to sit on because some of the cattle were very wild and we might get in the way. So we'd sit up there with water and something to eat for the day, and watch them bring the cattle in across the river.

It was terrible work, really dangerous. Some of those wild bullocks used to charge at the stockmen and try to gore them. My uncle was lucky to live through one day when his horse fell and a bullock came for him. All he could do was lay on the other side and wait for the bullock to have his satisfaction goring the poor horse. I was up in the tree watching and I was that worried for him.

After a day of this, to relax, everyone would go down to the river and make a big fire. There were quite a crowd of us — men, women, house-girls, kids — and we'd all gather together

29

to have our tea. When we'd finished eating they'd say, 'Come on, let's move back and watch the corroboree.'

Well, the first time they said that, I thought to myself, there's going to be dancing, so I went and made up a bed and got myself set up. Next minute all these birds came swooping down. The sun was just setting and these beautiful brolgas were calling to one another, swinging and dancing and swaying their heads. They'd bow to one another, swing their necks back, lift their wings, fly away a bit, then fly back. It was the most amazing sight and I was absolutely glued to them, glued to these birds making corroboree.

The next morning when I woke up I remembered their dance and I said to my mother, 'Ngangka, do you think I could be a Brolga?'

'No,' she said, 'you Wari, you're a jutarrara (pelican), and you can't change that.'

I was a bit disappointed at first but I just had to remind myself that pelicans are beautiful birds too.

Another place Mother would take us to was Wodgina. That's where Aunty Winnie and Uni mainly stayed. It was also where the tin mine was, and where we used to get all our mail from.

Wodgina is in a basin with hills around it, hills that look blue from a distance. Up on the side of one of these hills was where the mine was built.

The plant manager was Mr Dobson, and Mother used to do washing and ironing for his wife. One time when we went there we went across with Mr Dobson to have a look at the plant working. It was really hot and there was this thud, thud, thud, of engines knocking rocks to bits. Water was running through machinery and these big belts were spinning around. Mr Dobson said, 'Keep your clothes close to your body, because if you get caught in the belts you'll be whisked away.' We went right down into the mine and all around. It was interesting, but sort of eerie.

Tommy was friends with the Dobsons, and they had a chinaman cook in the mess for the men. It was a big long mess and they had a big long blind with a rope hanging down. There were two of these in the dining room, and while the men were eating they used to pay me and Ella a shilling each to pull the rope and fan them. We used to enjoy doing it because we thought that it was really good to get a shilling each.

As soon as I got that shilling I used to go across to old Jimmy's shop and buy whatever I wanted. One time I bought myself a mouth organ and I learnt to play songs like, "It's a Long Way to Tipperary".

I had such a great life on Kangan, it was really beautiful country up there. I can remember when we used to come into Roebourne from the station from time to time. Just out of Roebourne, between Whim Creek and Roebourne, the vegetation was beautiful in those days. There's nothing there now, it's as flat as a table. Through the years that I've been away they've just cleared it all out. But when I was a kid that place was alive and flourishing.

There were lots of these little low trees and they used to have bardies in them. Us kids used to only have to pull one up and in that root there might be about three of these bardies clinging. We'd pull them out, then we'd have to lay that root back to where it was, because that way it'd knit together and grow again.

In the wet weather the silvergrass used to be waving out on the land like a big crop. Out near Roebourne, that flat country would be covered with wild turkeys. You'd see them walking along, proud as anything, looking this way and that. Sometimes, on our way into town, Tommy would stop and shoot one or two of them and the rest would keep going. He'd take that turkey in with him to give to his brothers or his sister. The place just used to be so alive, it was really and truly beautiful.

On our property we used to have plenty of wild fruits, bush tucker and bush medicines. There were wild plums, wild mandarines, ngarlgu (wild onion), and a fruit that's like a coconut. It's called wagarlu, and you get it, chop it in half, and the inside tastes like coconut. There were galubu (bush tomato) too, but they didn't turn red. They'd be green, and then they'd go a little bit yellowish, but the flesh tasted just like a tomato.

We used to go out and dig for mardarra too — that's the wild potato — with our wanas. Wanas were big sticks that could be used for walking sticks, but mostly the ladies used them for fighting with. There were other sticks for digging too, but you could use a wana as well. When they made the sticks for hunting they didn't just get them off a tree, they'd roll them around and around in the fire to harden them up.

My mother used to take me out hunting with her, and one day when we went out for a kangaroo, she saw this goanna. He was a barnka, a race-horse goanna, and he ran into a hole. She said to me, 'I'm going to get him,' and she got off her horse. I got off my horse too and stood there just watching. As fast as Mother was digging down after him, this little fella was digging up to get away. She said to me, 'Oh, he's starting to climb. You better move away from there because if he comes out he'll think you're a tree and run up your leg.'

But instead of moving away properly, I just took a few steps back. I stayed standing there, and the next minute this bloomin' thing jumped out of this hole and ran straight up me and stood with his back legs on my shoulders and his two front feet on my head! He was very upright and looking around, puffing away, while his feet were really squeezing me.

Mother started growling at me in language, 'I told you to get away, I told you, but you never do as you're told.'

I was shocked, and I just stood there as still as anything with this thing on my head.

'Now,' Mother said, 'just shut your eyes and keep still.'

So I did, then I heard this great WHACK. She'd crept up and whacked him under the neck with her stick.

Well, eventually he fell off — he clung to me a bit, then lost his balance and down he went. I was glad of that, I tell you, glad that they made those hunting sticks so hard.

Another time when Mother and I were going out to get a kangaroo, a thunderstorm came up. Tommy said, 'I don't think it's safe for you to go just yet. You better wait for about half an hour, otherwise you might go in the line of it.'

Next minute, after he finished saying this, there was a POW, and off in the bush lightning had struck the ground and fire shot up. Mother was watching and she said, 'We're going there because that means there's steel where it hit, and I want steel for my knives.'

Tommy laughed at her and walked away. So Mother waited for a while, then we went out. She had such good eyes she saw exactly where the lightning had struck the ground. She got off her horse, dug down, and dug up a piece of steel. She took it back home and Tommy was really surprised. 'Never in a hundred years would I have found that place,' he said.

But see, Mother was a really good tracker, and she rode beautifully too. She used to ride side-saddle. She'd wear these riding skirts that her and Aunty Minnie used to make. They'd get denim, same as they have today, and make their skirts for riding in.

Up in the Pilbara they have just the two main seasons: one is called the wet season, when the rains come, and the other is called the dry. Before the rains come it gets very hot and everyone is just waiting for the relief to come.

One time it was very hot and dry, and Tommy went to see Old Tom Santi who was a rainmaker. 'Tom,' he said, 'it's about time we had some rain. You reckon you can go and make rain for us?'

'Oh, I think so, maybe boss,' Old Tom said.

They were talking about this outside and I was just going off to do something when I heard them. 'Ngangka,' I whispered. 'Old Tom's talking about making rain. He says him and Mary are going off to make rain. Can I go with them?'

'No,' she said, 'they don't want you with them.'

'I won't be a nuisance. I'll be with Mary.'

'Oh...all right,' Mother finally said.

So Old Tom got two billy cans of water and we were off. We went right down to this place that had these big rocks, like Devil's marbles, two or three of them. There was a big hole there. Old Tom got down into it with one billy of water, and Mary and I sat in the bush a little bit back from him.

Old Tom started talking in Aborigine and chucking sand up in the air. He was going "Baba, baba," because baba means water. He called out in his language to send water down, send water down. I could hear him going Brrrrrr, ohhhhhh, he was really going off and dancing around and around, shouting, throwing water up, then sand would come flying up.

I whispered to Mary, 'So that's how they make rain?'

'That's how they make baba, yeah,' she said, and it was a real experience for me.

Old Tom kept on going and going and going until the billy was empty. Next minute he was tossing himself around and he called out, 'Mary, Mary! Quick, make a fire, I'm C-O-L-D-D-D,' and he was shivering like anything.

Mary said, 'Come on, come with me sister,' and we made a fire for him.

He came out and he was shivering and dancing around this fire getting warm. He got water from the other billy and washed all the sand off his face and arms, then we walked home.

When we got back Tommy said, 'How'd you go?'

'Oh, might be rain,' Old Tom said. He wouldn't say there would be, he'd just say might be.

Then, for a few days after, we could see clouds gathering and Tommy said, 'By gee, I think you're right. There must be rain coming.'

Well, I tell you what, within the week he didn't bring rain, he brought a cyclone! One day it just hit — lightning, thunder — it killed five of our goats. Old Tom and Mary had a little mia-mia and my father called, 'Come on, quick, into the saddle room.' So poor Old Tom and Mary had to go and stay there the night.

I got up early the next morning and all I was worried about was our garden. Ella and I had two banana trees that Tommy had brought us back from Carnarvon. I ran up the hill to see, and not a banana tree in sight. No tomatoes, nothing. It was all gone.

Our garden was on an island in the middle of a creek. The island wasn't big but we always had our garden there because we could run pipes from the well to water it. But the rain had flooded the creek and washed everything away. I went back down the hill and I said to everyone at home, 'No bananas.'

Tommy went out and saw Old Tom. 'Tom,' he said, 'I asked you to make rain!'

'Yeah boss, must be bit too strong. Big strong fella willy-willy.'

They went up to the stockyard and found all these goats sprawled around. Five of them had been struck dead, and Old Tom was sad. 'This time boss,' he said, 'no more, no more make rain.'

Well, the way he carried on in that hole it's a wonder he didn't make a tidal wave! Poor old fella, I can still hear him going, 'Wooorrr...baba baba baba,' singing away in his language and throwing up the sand.

When I was born they gave me to an old man. My group is garimarra, and halyirri is my straight. They did it by the men picking who they wanted as their mother-in-law. Like when this old fella was around fifty, and mother was having me, he said, 'If that's a girl, that's my woman.' Well I was born a girl, worst luck.

It was never the old women that chose, it was only ever the men. They had it all their own way. A woman used to walk about four or five yards behind her man, carrying a baby on her hip, a bundle of wood or something on her head, another bundle on her back, and have children walking along with her. She'd do all that while the man was walking along carrying a couple of spears! I tell you what, the men had it made.

Anyway, when I was about nine going on ten, this fella I was promised to used to come over to the station to see me. He was waiting until I was old enough, however old that was, and he'd say, 'When you're ready to come with me, you're coming, whether you like it or not.' This was all in Aborigine of course, and he'd come over demanding a feed.

When he'd come, Mother would go off and hide herself because she was forbidden to mix with her son-in-law. She used to say to me, 'Make it, make him a cup of tea. Go on, give him what he wants.'

He'd be saying to me, 'You my woman, you feed me.'

I said to him, 'Mirda, nyinda buga,' That means, no! you buga, you stink.

'Never mind about the buga,' he said. 'You my manga (woman).'

Sometimes he'd come around and Mother would have made a loaf of bread, one long loaf, and he'd just break it into four bits and gobble it down.

'He's just greedy hungry,' I'd say. Mother would say, 'Never mind, never mind, you just feed him.' He'd eat everything, like if we had any cold meat or anything he'd eat it.

He always used to come when Tommy was away from the station. How he knew that I don't know but that's when he'd come. So when Tommy came home one day I told him this fella had been carrying on and bullying me around. 'He wants to take me away. He reckons I'm going to be his wife,' I said.

'Huh, over my dead body,' he said. 'If he comes around while I'm here I'll shoot him.'

My mother was a bit upset and she said, 'Oh, you can't do anything like that!'

Thinking about it now, I think this must have been one of the reasons why my mother decided to leave. Another reason was, after Old Ned died, the Aborigines reckoned my mother shouldn't be living on the station without another husband. I think they'd been on at her for awhile, threatening her about breaking the law, and she got that way she just wanted to leave.

She had the urge to take Ella and me back to Abydos to see our relations, the Lockyers. This was the station I was born on and she wanted me to see it. Tommy came with us on this trip and I remember it so well. We took the wrong track and it was just a spinifex blur. The poor horse went down a hole and broke the shaft on the dray. Tommy said to stay there while he went and found a tree to make a shaft. By joves, he used to carry everything with him; he had axes, chisels, and goodness knows what else in this cart. So, anyway, he fixed it and we were on the road again.

We couldn't reach Abydos that night so we camped out on the road. We had tea, then pulled all the gear off the dray and slept on top of it. The dingoes were really bad and there were a lot of snakes around too. It's an experience I've never forgotten. Those dingoes were howling around but Tommy wouldn't shoot them. He just kept them away. He and Mother took it in turns — Mother would sleep while he kept watch, and then she'd keep watch while he slept.

One time I peeped over the side of the dray, and in the

moonlight I could see the white of this dingo's chest. He went, ' Woooooooooooow, ' and I jumped back under the rugs. Those dingoes were that game they'd sneak up and try to pull food away.

After we returned to Kangan my mother got really restless. One night her and Tommy were playing crib when I heard him break down and start crying. I was in bed and I didn't know what they were talking about, but I just buried my head because I didn't want to hear him cry.

The next morning when I got up he said, 'Come on, we're going into Wodgina today...did you know your mother is leaving?'

'Is she?' I said.

'Yes,' he said, and I could see he was upset.

'Well, I'm not going.'

'Look,' he said, 'you've got to go where your mother goes. You can't stay with me.'

So he took me into Wodgina because he knew he was going to lose me. We ended up staying the night and the next day we went back home.

A couple of days after our trip, Tommy packed us up with the sulky, two horses, some food and things, and Mother, me and Ella went off to Mallina Station. It took us about three days to get there, and on the way we stayed with Mr Ben Hewitt for the night. He was prospecting with another man, Mr Wilson, and they had a gold mine on the Yule River. The next morning we crossed the Yule and stayed at Mount Satirist for the night. Then it was on to Mallina.

Mallina Station was owned by Mr and Mrs Campbell and it was one of the bigger ones around. There was Croyden, Satirist, Mallina and Munda, all big stations up there. Aborigines would live down at the camps or in cottages, and the station owners lived up in their homesteads.

My mother, Aunty Minnie and Aunty Silvie Lockyer all worked up in the kitchen and the house. They had a chinaman cook there and Mother used to be like a kitchen maid. There was another woman too, and she worked in the house cleaning. There was always work on Mallina, you'd never ever come there and just sit around. Mrs Campbell would make sure of that.

Always plenty to be done, like cleaning windows, cooking, gardening or watering fruit trees.

Women worked as musterers and stockworkers as well, not just charwomen and cooks. Aunty Minnie, Aunty Silvie, Miss Greenwood, myself and a couple of others used to ride out mustering sheep. My mother would stay back in the kitchen. We'd go way out to bring the sheep back and it would still be dark, just as the sun was breaking. The earlier you went the better, because if you left after sunrise it'd be a bit too hot for the sheep to travel in.

We used to take our breakfast with us and eat it out there on the way back. It used to be really beautiful, with all the colours changing going from browns to reds around us, and I just loved it.

It wasn't long after we got to Mallina that I went with Aunty Minnie and Uncle Bill to Balla-Balla Station. We were there for awhile — until Tommy got in touch with them because he was going droving. Aunty and Uncle always went droving with him, so they went off and I went back to my mother.

When I got back to Mallina Mother had got together with a man named Captain. He was a marda marda like me, except his father was Ceylonese. Captain was working on Mallina when we first got there but I don't remember much about him; only that I didn't much like him because he took Mother away from us.

Captain decided he wanted to go over to Munda Station to work, so we all went with him. Mother worked up at the house and us kids used to stay in the camp all day, waiting for her to come home. This camp was by the river. We were with a lot of other Mulbas and we'd just swim nearly all day.

It was when we were back on Mallina that the scouts started to come around. They were sent up from the Aboriginal Affairs in Perth to come and look for the half-caste kids. My mother would say, 'The scouts are back so you'd better be careful,' and she'd tell us to stay in the bunkhouse all day. She was working in the kitchen so she'd bring down a sandwich and a bottle of water and say, 'If they come around, get under the bed and don't talk, just keep quiet.' So we'd get under the bed and stay there until we couldn't hear anything. Then Ella would jump

38

up and have a look and say, 'No, he's gone now,' and we'd be able to come out. Really, because Ella wasn't fair like me she didn't have to worry, but Mother would hide her with me in case they got hold of her and asked questions.

Because we used to hide they could never catch us. Then, this one time, and I remember it as clear as daylight, the Aboriginal Affairs man ended up staying the night. He stayed up at the station house with Mr and Mrs Campbell. They had a conversation together and that must have been when they made all the arrangements.

After his visit the Campbells talked to my mother, my aunt, and my Uncle Paddy about me and Doris. Doris was another fair one like me, and they told them they were going to take us down South to educate us, then bring us back home to our family. I was really excited about going, it sounded like a real adventure. Besides, I thought, it was a good way for me to get out of marrying that old fella I was promised to. But I didn't know, I never even thought of it really, that there were other plans for me.

And it is my belief, too, that if my mother had known what was going to happen she would never have let me go. But she had no reason to think anything other than what they said, because, when she was a young girl, the owners of Abydos Station took her, Aunty Minnie, Aunty Silvie and Aunty Louise down to Bindoon. The station owners went on a holiday and took these four girls with them to help out, and while they were there they went to school. Then afterwards, they all came back to Abydos, and I suppose my mother just thought it would be the same for me.

So, as soon as it was agreed upon, they took me and Doris from the camps and put us up in the station house with the Campbells. We both had to work while we were there — washing dishes, sweeping the verandahs, scrubbing out the bathroom and toilet, things like that. They used to say to us, 'You're our children now,' but they didn't treat us like that. Doris and I shared a room in the house, but we ate on the verandah where we washed up and not with them.

Now we were up at the house we weren't allowed to go past the gate or leave the yard any more. I wasn't allowed to play with Ella either, but she used to come and sit on the other side of the gate. There was a big garden up at the station yard and we used to pull up radishes and things and push them through the wire to her and talk.

I was very lonely up there at the house and I was missing my mother and my life on Kangan. Now that I look back on it, I think if I'd stayed with Tommy on his station I would never have been taken.

When Aunty Minnie had finished droving, she came back to the station and was working with us up at the house. For a

Alice's Aunty Minnie (Inhabun) and cousin Uni Parker holding their nephews, c. 1955.

while my mother was working there too, and at night, after the washing up was done, she used to come and see me. My mother made sure she never went home without coming to see me first. I was at a bit of a loss to know why I had to be drafted away like this, but she used to say, 'Don't worry, don't worry Wari, you'll be all right.'

Aunty Minnie was younger than my mother, probably only about eight years older than me. One day she had to be rushed to Roebourne to have an operation because she was having a baby and something went wrong. She had to have a caesarean, which was a dangerous operation in those days, and she ended up losing that little baby.

Then one day Tommy came over Mallina way and Mother got to hear of it. I was up at the house with Mrs Campbell and she came over and spoke to her. Then she came to me and said, 'Tommy's down at the mill and we're going down to see him tonight. Then you can tell him you're going to school.' So I was all excited and we went down to the mill where he used to camp by the creek. It was sundown and he was cooking his tea, curry and rice, and he offered us something to eat.

We stayed and ate with him and then we sat around talking until Mother said, 'Well, we better get back now. But you must tell Tommy what you're doing.'

Of course Tommy pricked his ears up and said, 'What's going on?'

'Well,' I said, 'Tommy, I'm going South to school.'

'Who says!'

'Oh, Mr and Mrs Campbell are taking me down and Doris is coming too. We're going to go to school down there and when we're finished we'll be coming home.'

He was very upset. 'Well,' he said, 'that's the finish of it then. What's the good of me living out there, hanging on to the station, if you're not going to be around.'

'Well, Mrs Campbell's promised to bring them back,' my mother said.

But he wasn't happy about it, and he did go and see the Campbells himself, and they assured him everything would be all right and I'd be coming back.

We said goodbye to him after that, and on the way back to

the house I was thinking about what Tommy said about wanting to toss it all in. I was really baffled so I said to Mother, 'Ngangka, that's funny. Tommy reckons he doesn't want the station because I'm going South. But when you said you were leaving I wanted to stay, and Tommy said I had to go where you went, and now he doesn't want the station any more!'

'Well,' she said, 'that's because you are a part of him. It's a big shock to him that you're going South, because he thought when you grew up a bit more that you'd go back and look after him.'

When she said this I didn't really understand what she was getting at, and I don't know why, but I just didn't take it any further.

When it was getting close to the time we'd all be leaving, Miss Greenwood, who was Mrs Campbell's niece, took me with her over to Portree Station. She had friends over there and she wanted to have a farewell party with them before she left.

While we were there she stayed up with the station owners, and I stayed down at the Aborigine camp. One night I was sitting with everyone around a big camp fire when I felt something crawl up my back. I put my hand up to grab it, and it grabbed me — twice!

This big bloke named Paddy said, 'What's the matter, what's the matter?'

'I don't know,' I yelled. 'Something is biting me.'

I thought it was a snake, see, but it was a big long centipede. Paddy looked and there were two big bites, so he got some safety matches and broke two of them on my back. He reckoned the sulphur would go in and do something about the poison.

Well, I ended up sick, and Miss Greenwood went back to Mallina and left me there at the camp. We'd ridden across by horse but they took her back in the car. They could've taken me back in the car too but they didn't. I had to stay there until my Uncle Sam rode across to get me.

When I got back to Mallina my mother had had a baby daughter to Captain, and she was only a couple of weeks old. They named her Myrtle, and not long after I got back they took Ella and went to work on Croyden Station.

Some members of Alice's family. Standing: Silvie Hall (Lockyer),
Lilla Whalebone and Ella (half sister). Sitting: Margery Whalebone
and Ron Captain (half brother). The photograph is from the late
1920s after Alice had been taken South.

I was very upset to see them go, but now I'm older I
understand that it was getting close to the time when I'd be
leaving, and I don't think my mother wanted to see me actually
leave. I also wouldn't be surprised if the Campbells had told her
to go so I wouldn't be so restless.

When it was very close to when we'd leave, Mr and Mrs
Campbell's son, Noble, and Miss Greenwood, took me over to
Croyden to say goodbye to my mother. My dear old Uncle Paddy
had given me a tin of cling peaches and I said to Mother, 'Uncle

said to take this and remember him.' It was a big tin of peaches so she said, 'Well, you can't take it with you, so we might as well eat it.'

So I spent time with them, and my baby step-sister was a bit older then and she was really beautiful. Then, when it was time for me to go back to the station, I said goodbye to everyone, not realising that this would be the last time I would ever see any of them again.

Garrgarra, to The South

There were three of us kids that went with the Campbells down south; two girls and a boy. The boy was from another station and he was brought over two or three days before we all left. Now that I'm older, I often think back to this time and I think everything was arranged before we ever left the North. It was a cunning way to get me, to trick my mother by telling her I was going off to be educated, then brought back to be with them when I turned eighteen.

Doris, Herbert and I were taken from Mallina Station to Point Samson on the coast to catch the boat down. Herbert would have been around twelve years old, the same age as me, and little Doris would have only been nine or ten. It was a bit of a journey to get to Point Samson, and first of all we went to Whim Creek to spend the night so Mr and Mrs Campbell could say goodbye to all of their friends. Miss Greenwood and Noble were travelling with us too, and while they stayed in a hotel with the Campbells, Doris, Herbert and I had to sleep out in the open. Lucky for us though the constable helped us out. He went and got three mattresses, cyclone-wire beds, rugs and sheets from the police station. We slept out under the stars that night, and the next day we went into Roebourne and stayed at the hotel for two nights.

When we were in Roebourne the Campbells took us three kids up to the hospital to see Aunty Minnie. We sat up there on the verandah with her for quite a while, and she was that

45

sick after the caesarean she couldn't even walk. We stayed with her for quite a long time until they came to pick us up and take us back with them to the hotel.

After Roebourne we went to Point Samson and when we got there Tommy was there too. I said to him, 'You come to see me off Tommy?'

'No,' he said, 'I'm coming with you.'

See, when he found out that I was going South he decided to sell up and come with me. So he sold his station to Mrs Campbell's brother, Jack Noble. When my father told me that, I thought to myself, well that's marvellous. I was pleased to see him because my mother had no hope of coming with me. However, when the Campbells saw him there they weren't too happy, but that was just too bad.

On the boat Doris and I slept on the floor of Mrs Campbell's and Miss Greenwood's cabin. Herbert was in another cabin with Mr Campbell. I can remember the nights so well because of the humming sound of the boat in my ears, and the boom, boom, boom, that kept us awake. It was real agony for us.

During the day us three kids would get up onto this big box, the life jacket box, and sit there crying and talking in our language. We kept on wishing we'd never come. If we'd only known what it was going to be like we would have run away. Herbert would say something like, 'Oh, it's too late to be worrying now,' and we'd tell him to quieten down. Then he'd start up with us, crying for our mothers.

This boat we were on was called the *Charon*. It was only a small boat and, by joves, it was rough. We'd sit out on that box all day, watching the sun come up and go down. The funniest thing about that was the way we used to see the sun coming up over here one morning, or over there the next, and setting either in front of us or behind us. We couldn't believe it! But of course it was just the way the boat was facing at the time. We didn't know that, being kids — we just thought they were getting lost.

The whole time we were on that boat they never took us into the dining room once. We had to sit on the deck outside the kitchen door and they'd bring us a round bowl with food in it. The waves would be coming up and going down, and ohhh, it was awful. I'd just put one mouthful of food in my mouth and I'd have to go and feed the fish. The Campbells never once came to see how we were, or see if we wanted anything like a biscuit or something. We were just little nobodies. The only time we saw them was at night. If it wasn't for Tommy, I don't think we would have survived it. He used to go and buy fruit for us and sit with us whenever he could.

It took us eight days to get from Point Samson to Fremantle, and every day it was getting colder. One good thing the Campbells did was give us a rug, and we'd sit outside with it around us.

Doris wouldn't sit next to Herbert because by law he was her uncle. That meant she wasn't allowed to mix with him, and certainly couldn't touch him. She was the littlest and she'd always sit at the end and we'd give her more blanket.

Herbert was nyuba to me, like my straight, so I could sit in the middle and we'd pull our bit of blanket around and all talk about home.

As the sun was setting it used to be the worst. Soon as we'd come back from having tea, and the sun was going down, it was the time when we'd think of home. Tears would be flowing, and we'd be jabbering away in our language. Then bed time would come and we'd say goodnight to Herbert. He'd be wiping his eyes walking away from us and we'd be wiping ours going to our little cabin.

This boat we were on was a State boat which used to stop off along the way. But Doris, Herbert and I were never allowed off at any of the ports. When we got to Mauds Landing — which is halfway between Onslow and Carnarvon — the boat anchored out on the sea, and these luggers came out and put bales of wool on and took things off. We thought it was great watching the boats getting loaded like that, with these big winches going up and down.

I can remember we stopped off at Carnarvon too, because Tommy went to see his brother who had a banana plantation, and he came back with all these bananas for us.

One day we were travelling along — and this wasn't far out of Fremantle — and I saw the longest fish I have ever seen. He was skinny, like streamlined, and he was travelling along with

47

the boat. He had people nearly falling out of the boat to have a look at him. He had a funny little tail, and he was long like a submarine, with a head no wider than his body. But he was beautiful. We always used to look out for the fish to occupy ourselves. There were other fish too, beautiful flying fish that jumped out of the water and were pretty like rainbows.

When we finally got to Fremantle we had to anchor out for a while, until a boat with a doctor came out. He came aboard and examined everybody's fingernails to see if it was all right for us to get off. When everyone had passed quarantine the boat was allowed to come in.

Doris and I were both wearing little white blouses, green striped skirts and long black stockings right up to our knees. There were people everywhere and I was madly looking for Tommy, but somehow the Campbells managed to get us right out of it without me even seeing him.

They took us to the railway station to catch the train to Perth. From Fremantle to Perth was a bit of a trip, and there were hardly any buildings along the track — it was all just bush and flat country. There wasn't a Subiaco as such, just saleyards and cattle. This is 1923 I'm talking about, and that's a long, long, time ago now.

One of the funniest things I remember about this trip is I just loved the smell of Perth. There weren't any diesels in those days, and I just took to the smell of the coal engines.

Perth was like nothing I'd ever seen, and as soon as we got there Mr and Mrs Campbell took us up to an office in Murray Street. This was the Aborigines Department, and we waited outside while they had a conversation about us. Then when all of that was finished we left for Belmont.

To get out there we caught this bus — it was an old fashioned looking thing with big windows and shaped like a pot belly stove. We got there and went to a hotel owned by Mr and Mrs Ball. They were friends of the Campbells and their son, Stan Ball, worked on Mallina Station. I think Stan must have made arrangements for us kids to be left with his parents while the Campbells did their business before going to the farm at Beeginup.

We had a sad time staying there at Belmont, and we cried

every day and every night. We were all missing our mothers and family back home. The three of us slept in this little cubicle-like room. Now that I've grown up and I'm thinking back over these things, I think this room was where they tossed the drunks for the night.

At bed time we used to go and lay on a straw mattress, pull up the blankets — no sheets of course — and I'd say a prayer for us that Tommy had taught me.

> Dear Lord, before sweet slumber comes
> to close our weary eyes
> up to thy throne of heavenly grace
> our voice in prayer we rise.
> Forgive us Lord for Jesus' sake
> for all our naughty ways
> and as thou lay us down to sleep
> do thou an angel send
> to watch beside us all the night
> for Jesus' sake, amen.

Then in the morning we'd get up and go into the pantry to get our plate of porridge. After we'd finished we'd have to go out for the day. We never saw lunch the whole time we were there, never saw it. We used to go over to the racecourse and look around hoping to find money. Sometimes Herbert would find some, so we'd take it and wash it in the Swan River, then go and buy some biscuits or lollies.

The only time we came inside was in the evenings. We'd have our bath, then have some tea and go and walk around in the big garden for a little while. Then it was off to bed again.

From time to time, Mr and Mrs Campbell came over to the hotel to spend the night. One time when they stayed, Mrs Campbell told me Tommy had been in contact with them and wanted to take us kids out for the day. I thought that sounded really great, and I was talking away about Tommy when she interrupted me. 'Look here, isn't it about time you stopped calling him Tommy and addressed him as your father? Because that's who he is.' It was only then that the penny dropped and I realised who Tommy really was. It made sense then what my mother had meant when she said I was a part of him, and I was really sad that she wasn't there to answer all the questions I had about it.

After I found out, I really wanted to call him father, but it just didn't feel right. Perhaps if the information had come from him I would have been able to say father, but because it hadn't I went on calling him Tommy. He came to see me three times and brought my cousin Mary with him. Mary was my father's sister's daughter, and we really liked each other, never mind if I was a little brown cousin.

The first time we went out he took us to the Museum. When we walked in the door there was this great big gorilla standing with his hands out ready to pounce. We all got a fright and jumped back. But Tommy explained that he was dead and only a stuffed one, so we quite enjoyed it all when we knew this.

I remember too, we walked right through this big whale. The bones were all standing up and it was as long as a house. We had a really good time, even though I got a terrible shock when I backed into a stuffed camel. See they had all these stuffed ducks, and rushes, and it must have been mirrors because it looked like water. I was busy looking at these foxes sneaking up through the grass when I felt something tap me on the head. I looked around and saw this big camel standing there and I just about hit the roof.

On the other times Tommy took us out we went to the pictures, which were silent movies in those days, and on a visit to the zoo. I also remember one time we were in town and he took us to meet Mr Boan. That was Harry Boan, of Boan's department store, and he and Tommy were old friends. Mr Boan really fussed over us and we had our photos taken there in the store. He was a real lovely old fella, Mr Boan.

Then, everything changed. Mr and Mrs Campbell came over to the hotel again to spend the night, and the next day Mrs Campbell said to me, 'Your father rang this morning. He wanted to take you children out but I had to say to him that he isn't allowed to.'

'But why?' I said.

'Because Mr Neville forbids you to see him again.'

At the time I didn't know who this Mr Neville was, so I couldn't understand why he was denying me seeing my father.

But it wasn't much further down the track that I found out he was the Chief Protector of Aborigines, and he had a lot of say over what I could and couldn't do.

As soon as Mrs Campbell told us that Tommy couldn't come any more, the three of us just went outside, sat under a tree, and howled. I think this is the one main thing I'm bitter about today, depriving me of my father. It just makes no sense. They wanted me to have white people's ways, yet they denied me my father. How does that make any sense?

Well, that was the end of that, and not long after, Miss Greenwood came and collected us from Belmont and took us even further South to the Shannons' farm in Nyabing.

What I remember most about staying with the Shannons is Colin. In all, I think they had about three children, but it was Colin who was a good friend to us.

Their farm was in the fruit growing area of the South-west, and they had a big orchard that Colin took us all to see. We walked through the orchard, it was summertime, and we were surrounded by beautiful fruit; peaches, apricots, and plums.

As we were walking along I saw a quince hanging on a tree. I said to Colin, 'What sort of fruit is that?'

'Quince, but it's no good to eat,' he said, 'so don't touch it.'

Now when I think of this, I think of the story about Adam and Eve, and how Eve was tempted with forbidden fruit. Well, Eve, little Eve here, had to get to that fruit!

'But Colin,' I said, and I went up to the tree and smelt the fruit. It smelt so beautiful, and looked so lovely hanging there.

'All right,' he said, 'you take it — but you won't eat it.'

I pulled it off the tree and had a big bite. 'Yow,' I cried, 'errrgh.'

'Now what are you going to do with it?' he asked.

'Um...throw it away?'

'No you don't. Mother will kill me if you throw it away.'

So I had to take it home and tell her what I'd done. It ended up she cooked it for me, but it just shows you about being easily tempted.

Another of the things I remember about being there was we used to go around pulling up sheets of corrugated iron to see if there were any snakes underneath. That place used to be covered with snakes, and it's a real wonder we never got bitten. We used to trample all over these sheets of iron and you'd see them all wriggling out. All colours they'd be too.

We stayed down at Nyabing for about a month I suppose, until Mr and Mrs Campbell sent for us. Mr and Mrs Murray owned a farm at Beeginup and, while they went on a cruise to Singapore, the Campbells managed their place. So Miss Greenwood came again and took us all on the train to Broomehill, then out to the farm at Beeginup.

Beeginup was hard work. Doris worked in the house because she was a dainty one and didn't like working outside. But I was an outdoor girl, I'd rather work out in the paddock with Tommy than inside helping my mother.

So Herbert and I used to work outside. We used to have to milk sixteen cows. We'd milk them, take them out to the paddock and bring them back in the evening. I'd have to separate the milk, and then Herbert would take it off to the pigs and poddy-calves. The poddies are the babies, and they weaned them off their mothers.

Looking back, they didn't have us there as kids, they had us as slaves. We had a little room, not much bigger than a laundry, and all three of us slept in it. It had three beds pushed in there and just enough room for us to crawl through. To have our bath we used the tub down in the laundry, which was away from the main house. There was a big underground rain water tank and we used to pump up our water for baths and things.

We got paid for working there; two shillings a week. But if we did anything wrong they'd take that two shillings off of us and put it in the Lady Lawley Cottage Fund. They had this tin with Lady Lawley Cottage written on it, and they'd give us the two shillings and make us slip it in. See, we'd have ten minutes to wash up the dishes, and if we didn't do it in time we'd lose that two shillings. All our chores were like that, if we didn't do it by a certain time our money would go into the tin. That way they made us realise that things had to be done properly and by a certain time.

While we were in Beeginup we all went to Toolbrunup school. Mr Burridge had a farm out at Toolbrunup and they were short of kids for the school. See, if they didn't have enough children they'd have to close the school down. I think they had to have about nine kids and with us three it made up the right number.

In the mornings we'd get up and milk the cows, then I'd do the separating and wash the separator, while Herbert shut the cows out in the paddock. Then we'd go off and feed the poddies. After that was all finished, we'd rush off to get ready for school, then rush up to the house to have our breakfast, and then the three of us would head off.

To get to school we used to drive a sulky. We had a horse named Dinah, but some days when they used her for the team we'd have to walk there and back, which was four miles each way.

We were the only three Aborigines at the school and we were aware of that. The other kids were a bit funny at first, a bit cheeky, but most of them got better as it went along.

We didn't quite finish the school year and on our last day the kids made a plan for me. Herbert used to go and water the horse before putting her in the sulky for us to go home. On this day he was doing something else so I went off to get the horse. Well, these boys — one was a Burridge and the other a Hulland — they were standing around while I watered the horse. Then just as I was going to take her out of the yard they came rushing in. They got one each side of me, wrestled me until they got an arm and a leg each, swung me up and threw me into the water. Splash, I went. I got up and I let a few Aboriginal words go, and they ran away laughing.

Miss Markham, who was the schoolteacher, came running out and told them off, but they just laughed. I suppose it was my last day so they thought they had to do something, but I was pretty upset about it. I was the biggest kid there — some of the boys might have been around my age, but I was the biggest — so they picked on me.

We were still down in Beeginup when Christmas time came, and we were all feeling the cold so we had a big open fire in the loungeroom. See, all of us, coming from the North, hadn't adjusted to the cooler climate yet. Anyway, we had Christmas stockings hanging up, we all got some little presents, and we

53

thought it was just marvellous.

But really Christmas was nothing new to me. Back home Tommy used to provide all those things for me and Ella, and there was always a gift for us when our birthday was on. We never ever went without. He'd say to me one day, 'Well, your birthday is next week. What would you like?' I'd say what I'd like and he'd say, 'Oh yeah.' Then he wouldn't go to Roebourne or anywhere, you know, but that doll would be there when I woke up on my birthday.

Now, if we thought it was cold at Christmas time, imagine how we felt when it came winter. It got so cold that when Herbert and I used to go and get the cows to bring them in, the ice used to freeze our feet. We didn't have shoes to wear, so we used to wait for the cows to let their droppings down and fight for every cow that dropped so we could stick our feet in it. We had shoes but they were only for going to school in. They wouldn't let us wear our shoes for anything other than that.

Anyway, eventually the Murrays came back from their cruise, so the Campbells moved on to another farm and took us with them. Mr Burridge was most upset about it because we were the ones keeping the school open.

They moved to a farm at Pallinup, but there wasn't a school so we had a year without any schooling. Not long after we got there, we went up to where the school was but it was just all dead sticks and dry flowers. The windows were closed and everything was shut up. It must have been unused for years.

No school meant more chores for us. The Campbells decided to start up a garden, so we worked clearing the bush to make the fences, digging up the beds and getting it up and running. Every morning we'd have to go down and wash the leaves on the lettuces and tomatoes to get the frost off so that when the sun came up it wouldn't burn the leaves.

We had to go out sucker-bashing too, because the Campbells decided they wanted to put a crop in. They bought us three little axes and we'd go out chopping down the scrub. Mind you, they never did grow a crop, not while we were there anyway.

Another one of our jobs was to go and pick up the mail. It was about a mile away, and if they thought we were worthy of riding, we could ride. But if they thought we'd been naughty, then we'd have to walk it.

We picked the mail up from the Moores' farm. Mr Moore was a member of parliament down at Gnowangerup, and he also had a store. When we'd come Mrs Moore would take us into her kitchen and give us a cup of cocoa and a piece of brownie. Her kitchen had a dirt floor, and she used to make these big cakes and things. All three of us used to want to go and get the mail, especially if we were allowed to ride, and we'd fight to get down there.

One day I was sick and Herbert was sick as well. Doris was the only one still floating, so Mrs Campbell said to her that she'd have to go and get the mail. So off she went and saddled up the horse. On her way down there a calf came through a fence and her horse shied. Doris wasn't expecting it and she fell off.

She'd been gone for a couple of hours when Mrs Campbell said to me, 'Doris is not back yet. You'd better go and get her.'

I was too sick, so she went in to see Herbert, got him out of bed and told him to go. He rode off just a little bit and then came back to the house calling, 'Missie, Missie.' (We never called her Mrs Campbell, we always addressed her as Missie.)

'What's the matter?' she said.

'Doris' horse is at the gate,' he said.

Well of course there was great panic, and Mrs Campbell said to him, 'Well, you better get on that horse and go look for her.'

Herbert galloped off and he came along the road to where Doris fell. The calf was still there and his horse shied too, but Herbert's reflexes were good and he didn't fall off. He looked around and saw Doris laying on the side of the road, just coming to her senses.

She'd been there for nearly two hours. He got down and said, 'You all right Doris?'

'I dunno,' she said, and she was all confused.

'Well, I'd better go for the mail, so you just wait here for me and I'll get you on my way back.'

So off he went to the Moores', and when he came back he put her on his horse and brought her home.

Doris was really groggy, she must have fallen off full force onto the hard road. Poor little thing, she was only about eleven

55

years old. Anyway, she got into bed and I got up and got her a cup of hot cocoa, and she started to cry.

Everytime something went wrong, or we did something wrong, it all flashed back to our home. We'd get upset and want to be home with our mothers.

Herbert came in and we all sat on Doris' bed crying. Then Mrs Campbell came in and roared at us, 'Get back, get back to your beds.'

When things like that happened we used to curse those Campbells. We used to say to each other in language that they were terrible for taking us away from our home, and we wished something would happen to them. Oh, we used to be nasty, but we just wished they'd never made a promise that they didn't keep.

Not long after her fall, Doris was sent back to Beeginup to work for Mr and Mrs Murray. We still got to see her though, because we used to go and help the Hornseys on their farm near Beeginup, and we'd call in and say hello to her. Sometimes, too, the Campbells would go and visit the Murrays to have tea, and they might take us with them.

While we were with the Campbells I got four letters; one from Tommy, two from my mother, and one letter from my Aunty Minnie. Mrs Campbell read the letters to me because I never really had much schooling and I couldn't read well enough. Because I couldn't write either I asked Mrs Campbell to write back to my mother for me. She said she would, but when my mother wrote the second time she said she hoped I was all right, and why hadn't I answered her first letter. See, she never got an answer to that first letter, and probably not to the other one as well. I doubt Aunty Minnie got an answer either, so back at home they wouldn't have known how I was, whether I was alive or dead.

When Easter time came around Tommy got in contact with the Campbells.

'Oh Tommy rang this morning,' they said.

'Yeah?' I was really excited.

'He wanted to come and have Easter with you, but we said he couldn't because he's not allowed to.'

'But why?' I cried.

'We told you. That's what Mr Neville wants, that you don't see him any more.'

I was so upset I howled for nearly a week. He'd come to visit me and he'd got as far as Broomehill, got in touch with them to tell them he was coming, and they'd said no, he wasn't allowed to. That Easter he sent me two parcels: one full of Easter eggs and the other full of clothes, shoes and socks. This turned out to be the closest I would ever get to seeing him again. Just talking about it today makes me feel so sad that we never got back to one another, and the last I saw of him was when he came and took us out from the hotel in Belmont.

On Easter day Mrs Holthouse came over — she was Mrs Campbell's sister — and so did the Campbell's son, Noble. Noble said I was walking around like a chook with it's head cut off, or something like that, you know, very sad. So they took Herbert and me with them into Gnowangerup to see this show. It was like a vaudeville show and Madame Melba was in it. She was singing, and oh, she was beautiful. She had a beautiful green frock on and it glittered when she breathed in and out. She had a tiara on her head and she sang all these songs like ' Home Sweet Home ', and a few others. It was really great and I sort of settled down and felt a bit better.

But after Tommy hadn't been allowed to come and see me, and after the schooling they'd promised me wasn't happening, I started feeling really bitter. I just stopped caring if I did anything or not. Mrs Campbell would have to talk to me two or three times before I'd do what she wanted, I was really rebelling. She could see that I wasn't happy because I used to be willing to do whatever I was told to do, nothing was ever too much for me.

Then, and I don't know who made the arrangements, we were gone, on our way to Moore River mission. All I remember the Campbells saying to us was, 'Mr Neville says you've got to go to school. There's no school here, so you'll have to go away to a mission.'

PART TWO

ALICE BASSETT, a young woman

1925–1932

Moore River Native Settlement: The Walls Have Eyes

Mrs Campbell took Herbert and me into the Broomehill Station, to put us on the train to Perth. On the way there we went to Beeginup and picked up Doris. Mrs Campbell didn't come up on the train with us so I suppose the guard or whoever looked out for us.

The night before we left for the mission she drummed it into my head about boys, gave it to me with both barrels. Then when we were getting on the train she told us when we got to the mission to tell them we were Church of England.

When we arrived in Perth, Mrs Mulvale picked us up in a Cobb & Co cab and took us to West Perth. Mrs Mulvale looked after all the kids who went to Mogumber or came down from Mogumber to Perth for medical treatment. Mogumber is really the name of the railway siding near the mission, but we all called the settlement Mogumber for short.

I think we stayed with her for about three or four days, and I remember we used to go down and visit this chinaman's garden. It had high walls around it, and he used to poke beetroots and carrots and things through the fence to us, and we used to eat them raw.

Anyway, the time came for us to catch the train to Mogumber and we all felt really excited. We knew nothing about Moore River, hadn't heard much about it. All we knew was what they told us; that we were going to a mission. To us, we thought we were going to a place where there'd be lots of

Moore River Settlement, 1922.

lovely little kids and that we were going to be really happy. Well, what a joke that turned out to be.

We got to Mogumber siding at about one or two o'clock in the morning. We got off the train and onto this old truck to go the eight mile ride out to the settlement.

When we got there they unlocked the dormitory to let us in, then showed us to our beds. Doris and I had the two beds in the middle. When we got in we could hear all this whispering, like little kids talking. We didn't see Herbert again for a while because he was stuck over with the boys.

The next morning when I woke up I could hear birds singing. I peeped out from under the rug and all I could see were these little faces looking at me. I thought, ooooh, what's this. I'd never seen so many faces.

Anyway, we got up and went to have a wash. We never wore nighties in that place, we just slept in our shimmy and pants. We went off to wash our face and comb our hair, when all these kids came across and asked, 'Where you come from?' I told them we came from Roebourne and they didn't much care about us, just walked off. See, they were South girls, they were all from country in the South.

Then these other little girls came around and said, 'Where you come from?'

'I come from North,' I told them.

'Oh well,' they said. 'We come from North too.' So the North took over then and looked after us.

On the very first morning we were there we were taken up to the office. Mr Brodie was the superintendent then, and his wife was the matron.

They spoke to us for a while about the rules and things like that, then Matron asked me if I knew who my father was. I told her yes, I did. Then she asked me, 'Do you know the Flinders?' and certain other people from Roebourne. I told her yes because they were all my father's friends. In fact, Mrs Flinders said that if she had known I was going to be taken away I could have stayed with her and gone to school with her three daughters in Roebourne.

Anyway, this questioning went on for a while, and then they let us go. But afterwards they always called me Cassit. Matron would be coming along and she'd say, 'Cassit! Cassit! Cassit! Don't you go past me when I call you.' I'd look at her and say, 'I'm not Cassit, I'm Bassett,' but she'd never call me by my proper name.

It used to eat me a little bit, but then I found out that Mr Brodie had been a policeman up in Roebourne. See, they probably didn't like me having my father's name because he came from such a big family up there.

Well, now that I saw for myself what the settlement was really like, I just gave up all hope. I thought, there's no way I'll be going back home now.

Moore River was split into two main parts; the compound where all the kids and older girls were, and the camps, where all the married people and old people had to live.

The compound was set up just like a little town. At the bottom end of the main street was the Big House — that's the superintendent's quarters — and this faced the church which was at the top end of the street. In between, on either side, were all the other buildings, like the dormitories, dining room, sewing room, bakehouse and staff quarters. It was built up on a ridge, and down on the flats near the river were the camps where all the campies built their little places.

The superintendent and his wife were the head workers there. They had five sisters: one for the surgery, one for the dining room, the sewing room, the school and the girls' dormitory. There was also a second boss who was in charge of the stables and fencing, outdoor things like that, and a third boss who went out with the woodcutters.

There were black trackers for policemen too, both Nor'westers and Sou'westers. But mostly they were Nor'westers because if they did anything wrong up on the North, like killing a bullock, they'd be sent down south away from their country. Their main job was to catch anyone who ran away, and they used to wear these old police uniforms with the brass buttons pulled off.

Us kids were all put up in the compound and it was a rule that we weren't allowed to go down to the camps. They always tried to keep everything separate there. There were separate dormitories for boys and girls, and even to go into the dining room we were kept separate.

The dining room was shaped longwise, with the boys having steps up one way, and the girls having steps up the other. It was really horrible to eat in there because the cups and things were that dirty, and we had all these old tin mugs and plates left over from the First World War.

The food was terrible; that's the food we ate, not what the superintendent and white staff had. They had beautiful food; roasts, lovely stews, curries with rice, food like that. I know because I ended up working at the Big House, and they certainly didn't have to eat like we did.

At dinnertime we used to have this soup, only I couldn't eat it because it was just like dishwater. None of us could eat it, we'd just try and pick through the best of it. We used to make up on the semolina — that's what they used to give us for breakfast — no sugar on it of course. We'd have semolina and a piece of bread'n'dripping for breakfast. Well that would be our fill for the day because we couldn't eat the soup.

One day I was asked to go up to the kitchen to relieve because one of the girls was sick. Luckily I only had to do it twice; I couldn't stand what I saw there. The food for the compound was cooked by the girls. They'd have one of the nurses — well, they were all called nurses — up there instructing the girls. There were two coppers: one for the soup, and one for the tea. The water would be all boiled up in a copper, and they had this great big shearer's teapot, with tea stewed and stewed up in it.

For the soup they'd cook up these awful sheep heads. First they'd skin them, but never take the eyes out, then they'd split them down the middle, give them a quick rinse and throw them in the copper. Sometimes those sheep heads had bott-fly in their noses but they wouldn't worry about that. They'd just throw it in and we'd see that in our soup.

It was all so dirty. You'd think those nurses would have been more alert, could have done things properly. But they didn't care. I suppose they were told, 'Just anything will do those natives.'

I couldn't eat the soup before I worked there, but when I saw this I definitely couldn't eat it. See, I wasn't brought up like that. My mother was a beautiful cook and we ate lovely meals back home. I think they did things like this to deliberately lower us; well, degrade us really.

The girls' dormitory was an old weatherboard place with a verandah halfway around. It had all different wings under the one main roof. The mothers' wing was out on the verandah at the back, and around five or six of them would be there at a time. See, most of the older girls that went out to work were pregnant when they came back in.

Inside the dormitory was the little kids' dorm, the washroom, and the other two parts were for the rest of us girls. We were all locked in at night but the doors between each wing were left open.

In the girls' dormitory we had an old matron-mother, old dormitory mother they called her. We called her Nanna Leyland, and she was a beautiful old lady you know, but strict too.

She'd be next door in a room to the side, and she wouldn't yell at us if we made any noise, she'd use her stick. She had a big stick, and she'd hit the wall three times. I tell you what, you'd hear a pin drop. Then you'd hear her coming across the floor, walking stick going; toong toong toong.

When she got to the door she'd say, 'Galahs live outside — people live inside. I'm looking after little kids next door and they need their sleep. If I hear another word I won't hit the wall, I'll come in and crack every head in this room. So just keep quiet.' And she would have done it too!

Just off the side of our dormitory was the pan-room. In there they just had the one night pan for all of us, and we had only enough room to wriggle our way in and sit down. It was in our part of the dorm and sometimes girls used to come in a hurry and mess the floor trying to get there in the dark, poor things. It was usually the little ones, and for the rest of the night we'd have to walk on water.

On the windows of the girls' dormitory they had wire mesh to stop you from getting out, and a trellis around the verandah. Although they always locked the girls' door, the boys were left free. The boys used to come and talk to the girls at night through the window, but if Matron or someone came along they'd run underneath the building to hide. When the superintendent woke up to what was happening, he had a stone wall put around the bottom of the girls' dormitory to stop the boys from hiding underneath.

Even though Nanna Leyland was really strict, she was a lovely lady to us too. When I got in favour with her I used to live like a queen. See, she used to give us her dog, Brindle, to go bush and get a kangaroo for her. There'd be me, Melba, Ruth and another Melba, and we'd go out along the river hunting, just us girls, taking the butcher's knife and everything. Then after we'd given her the brush kangaroo, she'd make a beautiful big stew and a damper for those girls that did the hunting for her. She'd bring in that special food at night, because even though she had her own camp outside, she was always locked up in the compound at night.

Sometimes, too, we used to go across to old Bill Kimberley and old Mary — that was the policeman and his wife — and they'd have a bit of brush kangaroo or something. The boys' dormitory was built up high, you could walk right under it and sit down, and that's where Bill and Mary lived. They just had a few sheets of iron put this way and that, and they'd have their fire out in the open. See, where the girls had Nanna Leyland as a dormitory-mother, the boys were kept in line by one of the trackers.

Besides old Bill Kimberley there was Bluey, Ginger, and Paddy Darby, who were all Kimberleyites like old Bill. And there was Bob Allen — Uncle Bob we used to call him — he was a lovely man from around Port Hedland.

There is a story to Paddy Darby being in Mogumber, and it was told to me not long after I got there. It goes like this: Paddy did something wrong up in the Kimberley and was sent to Fremantle prison. All these fellas they had in there were a bit rebellious, you see, and they used to give the screws a rough time. So these screws thought, oh well, we'll fix them. We'll take them out to Rottnest Island Prison and put them out there. They've got no chance of escaping or causing trouble there.

So anyway, poor old Paddy was one of the fellas who was taken out there. They were all told, 'If you try to escape from here you won't get to the shore alive because there's sharks out there, big sharks, and they'll eat you.' They were allowed to roam around Rottnest because there was no escape, and that was their life, these poor fellas, to die out there.

But Paddy, he was a strong young man and he made his mind up he wasn't going to be a captured bloke. He'd rather feed the sharks than be treated like that. So one evening, before rollcall, he stripped off, and into the water he went. When rollcall came they were calling, 'Paddy, Paddy,' but no Paddy. So they went around to look for him and all they found were his clothes. I suppose those gaolers thought, 'Oh well, Paddy's gone in the sea. We won't see him any more, he's feed for the sharks.'

The next day the police from Perth went up and down the coast when they saw this black heap lying on the beach. They walked up and it was Paddy thawing himself out in the sun. He'd swum that twelve miles to the other shore because he was that determined to get away.

So they took him to Fremantle gaol. Then, after he'd been

there for a while, they said to him, 'Paddy, you're a brave man. You've done your punishment, you're a free man now. We'll send you to Mogumber.' So they gave him one of those old police uniforms to wear and they made him a tracker.

Well, some freedom. But at least when he got to Mogumber there were people he could speak his language to, and his sisters, Julia and Minnie Darby, were there too. In the end, after he'd done his time, he was freed, and he went up to Marble Bar to work.

Some people liked the trackers and some didn't. It's just the same as every other place I suppose. My mate Dorothy didn't like Bluey, they just couldn't see eye to eye. He used to stand at the door to the dormitory and usher us girls in, and Dorothy would have a go at him, you know, give him a good stir. So she'd be there stirring him up, and one day he said, 'Dorothy Nannup, get in that formatory or I'll hit you over the stick with a head!' Well, look, we just roared laughing, she didn't have an answer for that. I tell you, we used to have funny little instances like that. It never used to be running smooth at all.

That old Bluey had a vegie garden and he used to supply the compound with soup vegetables. The girls used to sneak down, get in there, and pinch a few of these vegies. They'd tie their belts tight and stuff carrots, turnips or whatever they could get down their tops. Then they'd crawl through the fence, get across the river and wash them, then have a good old feed. They'd bring some back to us too, to have in the dormitory when we were locked in at night. See, we were always hungry, but I'd never do anything like that — I just couldn't.

Life in Moore River had a real routine to it. Every Saturday morning Sister Stewart would line us all up, boys on one side, and girls on the other. She'd stand at the top of one line and another sister would stand at the other. They'd have these big chemist bottles full of Epsom salts and everyone would get a big glass full. It'd be down with the Epsom and then you'd get a lolly to wash the taste away.

We hated it, and instead of getting in the front of the line we'd all push to get at the back. But sooner or later it would be your turn, and I tell you, they'd make sure you swallowed it all before you got your lolly.

Girls' Drill, Moore River Settlement, 1923.

We also used to have drill down on the playground. That was just like the aerobics they do today. The playground was just a big sandy area on the flat, behind the church and next to the boob. The boob was the prison. We'd wear the same clothes for that, nothing special, and usually it was the schoolteacher who took us. I don't know what the big girls did, whether they did drill somewhere else, but this was only for us younger ones.

We had to play sports too, and I used to like playing boys' hockey. We never had proper hockey sticks though. We used to go down the river and find crooked sticks, then put them in the fire so they'd tighten up. Sometimes we'd get wire and tie it on the end to make it look like a real hockey stick, and we'd run around having a good old time.

Doris, Herbert and I were sent to Moore River in August, and the first Christmas we had there was in 1925. I always remember that Christmas morning because these beautiful voices were singing, coming down from the church. I woke up and heard these beautiful voices floating down over the compound. 'Doris, Doris, quick, wake up,' I said. 'The angels are coming!' I really thought it must have been angels to sound like that.

All the girls in the dormitory jumped up and went to the verandah. The dormitory was all blocked off with a trellis but we could just see through to the outside. I looked and saw these girls standing out there in the middle of the street, between the two dormitories, singing.

It was the girls' choir, and I could see the two Darby girls, Dinah Hall and several others. They sang, ' Christians Awake ' and ' Oh, Come All Ye Faithful '. They really made the ranges ring, and that's the only time Mogumber was ever beautiful.

I was going to school in the settlement up until that Christmas, and for a couple of months after. But I can truly say that they never taught me anything in all that time.

I'd finished up to grade three at the school in Toolbrunup, and that was as high as Moore River went. So when the teacher was busy she'd get me to go out and keep the infants occupied while she taught the bigger class.

Moore River did nothing for me by way of schooling; I had to learn through experience and picking up little bits here and there on my own. Really, all I ever did there was work. I had chores to do before school and chores to do after. I tell you, they never allowed me to be idle.

I was still going to school when they decided to show us a movie. We all went up to the church, men and boys on one side and girls and grown up ladies on the other. This was a Charlie Chaplin movie and you know how funny he is.

Nanna Leyland used to always wear this hat and her and a couple of the old ladies were sitting in front of us. A lot of the people there had never seen a movie before, especially these old ones. Anyway, the thing went on, flickering away, when this motor car came full ball down the street towards us. Poor old Nanna went, aaarrrgghh, and ducked right down. Oh, look, it was such a laugh, funnier than the movie. Every now and again this motor car would come around the corner and Nanna and these old ladies would duck. Us little girls sitting behind her were killing ourselves laughing, but we couldn't laugh out loud or she would have thumped us.

That's the only movie I can recall them ever showing us. We had a couple of slide nights too, religious ones, but those soon fell by the wayside.

I hadn't been at the settlement long when I got a letter from Jessie Hornsey. Miss Greenwood had married while we were with the Campbells and her name became Mrs Hornsey. When we were at Pallingup we used to ride over to her place and do odd jobs. Anyway, she wrote to me and asked if I'd come and work for her. Mr Brodie knew all about it, because everybody's letter that was written into that place was read before it was given out. He didn't say anything to me when I got the letter but he called me into his office a couple of days later.

'Do you really want to go and work for Mrs Hornsey?' he asked.

I said that I'd like to because she'd written and asked me.

'But,' he said, 'you can't go because we've got another job lined up for you.'

Well I don't know what that job was but I never went to it. I think they just wouldn't let me go to Mrs Hornsey's because they wanted to disconnect people from their past. I was still at school at this time, but not long after they needed girls in the sewing room so they put me there to work. So whether that was the other job he was talking about or not, I don't know.

All the girls who were taken out of school and sent down to the sewing room, were started off on button holing and things like that. We had no choice about working there and we were never paid for it. We'd work a full week, then we'd go down every Saturday morning to clean the machines, brush them and oil them up ready for Monday. Then they'd come along with a little block of chocolate for us and that was our pay.

Every so often, Mr Neville, or an outside visitor, used to come up to the settlement. Whenever Mr Neville came everything had to be spit and polish — we'd have to really clean the place up, and sometimes we had to get into lines for when he arrived.

The best thing about someone from the outside coming was we'd get to eat better food, something special, in case whoever it was came into the dining room and had a look around. But this was only once in a blue moon. I remember hearing around the place that the Prince of Wales wanted to come up to the settlement but Mr Neville put him off. 'No,' he said. 'You don't want to go there. They're cannibals.' I don't know if this is true — it's just what I heard.

One time when Mr Neville came we were all in the sewing room, and he was standing talking to the sewing mistress. They were talking about education and other things, and I heard him say, 'Ohh, it's all right, as long as they can write their name and count money...that's all the education they need.' Well, I think that tells you all he thought of us.

When I think back to the time I spent at Mogumber, I think about how they always had me working, never left me free. Every morning I'd get up and go to breakfast, then I'd go straight over to the office. A boy named Edward and I used to work in the store weighing up the rations — like sugar, tea, flour — and handing it out to the camp people.

When Nanna Leyland came to get her rations I'd always put a little extra in and hand it over myself. I gave her a tin of baking powder once, just a little tin. I stuck it in with the flour so you couldn't see it. Sometimes I'd give her a little bit extra rice or salt or whatever, because that's how we would work it. She'd have extra and then she'd cook something to bring into the dormitory and feed us at night.

After I'd finished up in the store in the mornings I'd go straight down to the sewing room. Then at around five o'clock I'd be finished there, and I'd go up to the office to trim the lamps. I used to do the lamps for the girls' dormitory — they had to be trimmed every night and put in each wing before tea.

One night I finished trimming the lamps and I took them off to the dormitory. When I got there a girl was standing on the steps waiting for me. She was deliberately blocking my way, so I looked up at her and asked her to please get out of the road. She moved aside, but when I walked into the room she shoved me in the back. I didn't take any notice of that, I just walked into the dormitory and took all the lamps to their different places. But as I was walking out she stood in the doorway.

'You've been talking about me,' she said.

'You?' I was surprised.

'Yeah me, and what have you got to say about it now?'

'Oh,' I said, 'tell me what I said about you then?'

71

'I know what you said about me.'

'Well then, you tell me.'

But she wouldn't tell me, so I told her to get out of the way, and she hit me. So I up and hit her back, I gave her the works. She was a bigger person than me, too, but I just lost my block.

There was another girl sitting there and she said, 'Come on break it up, you two.' But I was angry and I wouldn't stop.

When I did let her go I said, 'You tell me who told you I was talking about you?'

'Ruby Windy told me,' she said.

'All right,' I said 'I'll go and bring Ruby back.'

As I was walking down the steps to go and get Ruby I said to her, 'Are you going to face Ruby?'

'No,' she said.

'Why,' I asked her, but I knew why. 'Well,' I said, 'you've got to face her,' and I walked off around the corner.

When I found Ruby and told her she was furious. She came back with me to the dormitory, walked up the steps and said to this girl, 'When did I tell you this?' Well of course she couldn't answer, so Ruby lifted her too.

Then the girl who had told us to let off fighting butted in and it was a free-for-all. It ended up us telling them that if they wanted to find anything to make a fight over, they'd better make sure they knew what they were talking about. See Ruby was a Nor'wester — she came from Carnarvon — and all us North people stuck up for each other. It was that kind of a place, you just had to stick up for one another.

The North and the South would have many a fight you know, they were terrible. They'd fight rather than have a feed — just like the Irish and the English. The two sides were a very strong thing. Northies were anyone from Carnarvon up. See, someone would make up a story that wasn't even worth talking about and it'd spread and spread, until it was way out. Then that would be passed around and, before long, there'd be a fight over it.

Another time it happened was when I was sitting on the edge of the bed one night. A girl came up to me and said, 'What have you been talking to my man for?'

'I don't know, what man?' I didn't even know who she was

talking about.

'You know, you were talking to Tom. You want to try and take him away from me.'

'I don't know Tom,' I said, 'and if I want a man, I'll get one of my own.'

Well, she hit me. Knocked me clean off the bed, and I tell you, I saw a million stars. So I got up and we got into it, and talk about fight! You don't only fight one of them either, somebody else will get in and then there'll be about a dozen of them.

This was all going on when this girl from Derby stepped in. Her name was Alice like me, and she just pushed this one back and that one over. Oooooh I tell you, she had arms about three feet long and she really laid those girls cold, she really did. She hit like a mule kicking, and I thought to myself, why did I go and bust my knuckles when I could have just waited for her to come? That girl, Alice, none of them used to give her any lip. She was about five foot ten, and muscles! — full of muscles she was.

Unfortunately, as much as you didn't want it, fighting was a part of your life at Moore River. With everyone all thrown in together they always found something to growl about and you just had to stand up for yourself. When I was working in the store they didn't like me because they reckoned I was the boss's favourite or something, just things like that.

It wasn't only the girls from the compound that used to fight with one another either. One time there was a terrible fight right outside the superintendent's office. I wondered what was going on so I asked one of the other girls what she knew.

'Oh, that camp woman came up and smashed into her because she's running around with her husband.' This used to happen from time to time because there were more women there than men. But still, I don't see why men should have had two or three women.

But girls were fools, they'd answer these men's notes. See, everything was done by notes. Some man might like you so he'd write you a note and send it over with one of the kids. Women were never supposed to send notes, they just answered them.

A boy wrote me a note once saying he wanted to see me,

but I didn't want any part of it so I just ripped it up. A few days later he came over to the sewing room. We were all having our morning break and I had just run across to visit someone. I was hurrying back through the fence when this chap happened to come along.

'Just a minute,' he said. 'I want to talk to you.'

'What do you want?'

'Did you get my note?'

'Yeah,' I said.

'Well, what did you do? Why didn't you answer it?'

'I ripped it up,' I said, 'I don't want you.'

Well he grabbed hold of me by the neck and pushed me down onto the fence. He was nearly choking me and I couldn't get away. 'When I write notes to girls I expect an answer,' he said, and I could hear how angry he was.

'You don't get one from me,' I said.

But the boys didn't always have it their way. One time this nice young man came into the settlement. He was one of the Little boys, you know, that was his name. He was all dressed up like a million dollars because he'd been out working. Well look, all these girls were running around everywhere looking for a pencil and paper. They reckoned, 'Ally owns him*, Ally owns him,' and, 'he's solid,' you know, 'ooooh he's a killer, cruel killer!' Oh, it was a laugh to see them all rushing around after him.

One thing I was lucky about at Moore River was I never got a beating. Lots of girls got a thrashing but I never did. They used to take them down to the storeroom and the superintendent would belt them until they weed all over the floor. They never spared them, and in the afternoons I'd have to go down with a mop and mop it up.

So for those that got punished, the punishment was harsh. If girls ran away they'd send the trackers after them and they'd be brought back and their hair would be cut off, then they'd do time in the boob.

There was this beautiful girl named Linda and she was as fair as anything. She had long curly, wavy hair, right down her

*Ally owns him — Moore River lingo for, I want him.

back. She had a boyfriend named Norman and they used to see one another. Norman lived down in the camps, and she lived up in the compound.

One day they decided they'd had enough of Moore River and they ran away together, but they were caught. They brought Linda to the middle of the main street right in front of the office. They made her kneel, then they cut all her hair off. It was falling down in big long tresses and we were made to stand and watch. We watched it fall onto the ground around her, and we all stood quietly crying for her.

Then they took Norman down to the shed, stripped him and tarred and feathered him. The trackers brought him up to the compound and paraded him around to show everybody. He was covered in feathers and all you could see were his eyes. Linda just sat there, said nothing, but most probably inside her heart she was very bitter.

It was a dreadful thing they did, and when they'd finished they took Norman away and locked him up in the boob. It took hours and hours for that poor boy to get the tar off, and it took a lot of his skin with it.

For extra punishment Linda had to do more chores around the place. It was a harsh punishment they got for trying to be together, and it's especially wrong because those two ended up getting married a couple of years later.

When this happened Mr Brodie was in charge, but not long after the tar and feathering he left the settlement. We didn't know it at the time, but he lost his job over what he did to Norman. He should have too — there was a lot of cruelty that went on in those days and mostly they just turned a blind eye to it.

So Mr Brodie left and a new man was sent in his place. It all happened very quickly — one day it was Mr Brodie and the next Mr Neal was in charge. But even though they brought in a new superintendent nothing really changed, people still got the same strict treatment.

When the new superintendent came I'd been working at the sewing room for the good part of a year. The superintendent's name was Mr Neal, and his wife was the matron.

At the sewing room we used to make clothes for Forrest

River Mission, and for Moore River as well. They never had to buy clothing for us, we made it all. It was terrible material too. But if you were a good worker, at Christmas they'd give you a piece of good material and you could make yourself a frock. Me and another girl, Dorothy Nannup, were really favoured — we used to get a piece and we'd make ourselves something nice to wear.

One morning me and Dorothy stepped outside to get into line for church and all these boys looked across and wolf-whistled and shouted. We had our new dresses on and they reckoned I was a butterfly and goodness knows what else. My dress was a plain one, but Dorothy, she made a flarey, flouncey one. When she'd spin around it would all twirl out. Mine was more of a plain Jane sort of thing, but still, I made a good job of it.

There were two churches at the settlement, the Catholics and the Church of England. We'd have our Sunday school every Sunday morning but the Catholics would only have theirs when their priest came over. Our church was lovely, and I was christened there. I put my head over and they made the sign of the cross in holy water.

What the Catholics used to do, though, was try and draw our congregation away. They would try and entice the Church of England girls by giving them boiled lollies after Confession. Three or four of our girls went across there, and when we asked them why they went they said, 'Oh, their priest is lovely, he gives us lollies.' And they stayed on the lolly side.

When our minister couldn't come one of the sisters and Tom Bropho would take the service. Tommy lived down at the camps with his wife Bella. He was a beautiful lay preacher, and his voice, it was wonderful. We used to love it when Tom took the service.

Tommy would also take some of the funeral services. There was a cemetery just for Mogumber people and it was about a two-mile walk from the main compound. When someone died they'd wrap them up in a blanket, and when they were going along in the cart their head would be moving around. It was wicked, you know, for the family, because they'd be all walking behind the horse and cart and they'd have to watch the one they lost bump around like that.

They reckoned they didn't have any material to make a proper coffin, and that's the way it was for most of the people that died there. That's if there weren't some old fruit boxes or kerosene cases around. Us girls would try to make the best of it though. There was bougainvillea at the settlement and we used to make wreaths out of it, twirl it around with any wild flowers we could get, and take them along to the funerals.

Although there were awful things that went on at the settlement, and once you were there you were there until it suited them, good things used to happen too. I used to really enjoy going to church, and I loved swimming down at the river. Another one of the things I liked was going to the dances they held once a fortnight. The compound would have our dance on a Wednesday night, and the campies would have theirs on the Saturday.

Everybody looked forward to these dances. We'd wear the dresses we made, and get electric wires and do one another's hair. Olive Harris was a good friend of mine and we used to go off to Nanna Leyland's, or down to old Aunty Pat Rowe's, and sit by the fire warming up our electric wires. When the wire gets hot enough you curl your hair around it and you end up with ringlets or lots of curls. Matron used to give us some hair clips, and we'd all get dressed up for the dance.

These old fellas from New Norcia — Charlie Bullfrog and Ben Jedda — used to come over. Old Charlie played the piano accordian and Ben played the violin. Oh, Ben was beautiful, he used to make that violin talk, and we'd all just get stuck into it. We used to love square dancing too you know. Four here, two over there and two there, and you promenade, and do this that and the other. Oh, it was beautiful. We enjoyed it so much we'd be saying, 'Oohh, come on Wednesday night.'

One dance night this old lady, Aunty Pat, was sick. We used to call them all Aunty, all the old ladies. Anyway, she used to live in the dormitory up next to Nanna Leyland.

On this night she was so sick she asked me to make burlgu for her. Burlgu is made by chewing up tobacco, then rolling it in ashes, chewing it some more, and rolling it again until it is ready. I did this for Aunty Pat and I got drunk from it, you know, it made my head go all whizzy-whizzy.

My friend Olive came over to me and asked if I was coming to the dance. 'I've got a headache,' I said. 'I made burlgu for Aunty Pat and now I feel giddy.' I really didn't feel the best but I didn't want to miss the dance so I went off with Olive.

Mr Neal was at the dance. He used to be my partner sometimes because he reckoned I was easy to teach. People thought I was Mr Neal's pet and all this, that and the other, but what could I do?

Anyway, the Garden Waltz came on, and Mr Neal came over and said, 'Come on Alice, this is our dance.' Everybody else would be dancing around doing the ordinary waltz, but this Garden Waltz was my favourite.

To do it you go a few steps forward, then two steps back, then swing your legs this way and that, and waltz around, and around, and around, and around. Well, by the last spin I was so giddy, and Mr Neal was saying, 'What's wrong. What's the matter with you?'

'Oh, I've just got a headache, Mr Neal.'

'Well, you better pull yourself together,' he said.

Whether I'd swallowed a bit of that tobacco or what I don't know, but I felt really terrible.

After that year I spent in the sewing room they put me in the Big House. This was working for Mr Neal and I suppose it was to have a bit of training, but I knew most of it already from doing it all at Mrs Campbell's. I knew how to wash up, I knew how to set tables, do the ironing — none of it was new to me. But I was cracking dumb see, I didn't want them to know that I knew all of this. Their idea of training was to take us up every Thursday and give us a cooking class. But I already knew most of that because I used to cook at the Campbell's.

Dorothy was working there too and on the first night, when we were serving up the meals, she said to me, 'Watch it, the walls have eyes.' Mr Neal, Matron, and their children were all sitting in the dining room around the table when she said this to me.

'What are you talking about?' I asked.

'Well, just walk in there and look to the door, you'll see.'

So I walked into the dining room and moved around the table

serving when I saw what Dorothy was talking about. Matron was sitting with her back to us but up above her head was a mirror so she could look straight towards us into the kitchen. That way we couldn't see her, but she could see us and watch to make sure we didn't pinch any food.

I went back to the kitchen. 'Yes,' I said to Dorothy, 'I see what you mean,' and I had to resist the temptation to pop any little bits of meat into my mouth.

The Big House was exactly that — it had about five or six bedrooms. Mr and Mrs Neal had their own room, the children had one each, and there was a spare for when anyone came up from Perth. It was our job to keep the place clean and tidy and do all the cooking.

The Neals had four children but they were only home occasionally. The three younger ones went to school in Moora, but Eileen was bigger and she used to be around a bit more. They were kept pretty separate from the compound kids, but sometimes one of the nurses would take Eileen on a picnic with the compound girls.

Dorothy and I were always kept busy there, Matron saw to that. One day I had just put a batch of bread in the oven when Mr Neal came and said to me, 'I'm going to pick up the mail and you two girls can come in for the run.' The mail used to come up by train from Perth to Mogumber siding.

'Well,' I said, 'will you tell Mrs Neal?'

'No, it's all right, it'll be all right. She won't mind,' he said.

So we went into the town with him and a couple of blokes he brought along to help.

Anyway, there we were, having a nice old time, Dorothy and I, sitting at the railway station, legs swinging, talking and laughing with the men who'd come in with us. One of the men said, 'You know, you girls are going to get into a big row tonight.'

'Why?' we asked.

'Because you fellas never told Mrs Neal you were going in with Mr Neal,' and they started teasing us.

All of a sudden I jumped up, grabbed Dorothy and ran around the corner with her. 'Dorothy, I'm going to get into trouble all right, I'm going to get into BIG trouble.'

'What are you talking about?' she said.

'Dorothy, the bread's still in the oven!'

'Oh no!' she went, and we raced off to find Mr Neal.

When we got back to the settlement it was about nine o'clock at night. Mrs Neal was supposed to be in bed but she was on the doorstep waiting for us.

'Please explain where you have been,' she said.

'We went for a drive with Mr Neal.'

'Yes, and left the bread in the oven.'

She'd come back to the house, gone to the oven and found the bread. The fire had gone out and the bread had turned to jelly. She was really cross about it and didn't speak to me for a good two days. I made some more bread up for her, and some scones, and just waited until she was ready to speak to me again.

After working for the superintendent I was sent to work at the second boss's place. I was a bit wary of working there at first, but when I knew Eva was going too I felt better. I'd heard a few stories about the second boss, so I thought I'd have to keep a bit of an eye on him. I would have preferred not to go but we had no choice about it. Different ones worked there for a time, then they'd be sent out to work and somebody else would be pushed in.

The second boss's quarters was like a little house and when you worked there you had to sleep there as well. Eva and I shared a little room that opened into his dining room. He might have made advances towards other girls in his time, but we were lucky — we never had any trouble like that from him.

Working there we were kept fairly separate from the other girls, but we'd still manage to get away from time to time. The second boss's house was just across from the compound dining room, and the dining room girls used to get off every day at about one o'clock. When they got permission, they used to go down to the river for a swim and be back at work by four. They'd always come across to us and say, 'Come on, come for a swim.' We'd ask the second boss if we could go with them, and sometimes he'd say yes. But if he was going any distance and wouldn't be back all day, he'd say no.

Anyway, this day he said that he didn't want us to go

swimming or anywhere, because he was going out for the day. We told him yes, yes, we wouldn't go anywhere. But when the dining room girls came across, and it was so hot, we found it hard to refuse. They asked us where he had gone. We said we didn't know, but he was going to be gone all day. 'Oh,' they said, 'he's gone to Moora. Come on, we'll be back before he comes home.' So I looked at Eva and said, 'Come on let's go.'

We were down swimming at Almond Pool, having a good old time, when I looked up at the sun and saw it was getting low. I said to Eva, 'I think we better start making it back, or he might get there before us.'

To swim we used to take off our dresses and go in in our shimmy and pants. I'd taken off my dress and put the key to the quarters on a safety pin on my belt. Anyway we had to walk across this log, over a murky pool, to get to the clean water where we'd been swimming.

On my way back over I wasn't thinking and I shook my dress out, and what happened? The key fell off the safety pin, bang into the water.

'Oh no,' I cried, 'the key, the key!'

'Where is it?' said Eva.

'There!' and I was pointing to the murky pool.

Just when we were going to do something about the key, Ginger the tracker came around the corner and saw us. 'What you girls doing here? You not supposed to be here! When you get back you go to the office.' The second boss must've warned him that we weren't allowed to go out.

'Look Ginger,' I said. 'I've lost the key.'

'Where?' he said.

'Down there!' and I pointed to where it had plopped in.

'All right,' he said, 'we'll get it, see.'

So Ginger wadded in carefully and asked me to point to exactly where it fell. He spoke in his language a bit — he was a Kimberleyite — and he dived down.

He came up and said, 'Nup, nothing there.'

'Yes it is, it's down there,' I said.

'You show me.'

'DOWN THERE!' I was starting to get really worried.

So down he went again, and this time he was a bit longer,

when all of a sudden he came up with the key. I took it off him and said, 'Oh Ginger, thank you, thank you.'

'Don't you talk good to me,' he said. 'You going to the office.'

We were walking along back to the compound and I was racking my brains to think of how to get out of going to the office. 'Ginger,' I said. 'If I give you some mandu, will you let us off?'

'What sort of mandu you going to give me?' he asked.

'Bardurra,' I said.

'Bardurra, you got bardurra!' He was very excited.

'Yeah.'

'All right, but I want martumirri too.'

As we got close to the house I whispered to Eva, 'You go inside and get that half a loaf of bread he wants, and the turkey.' Mandu means meat — the boss had shot a turkey coming into Mogumber a couple of days ago, and he'd had a few meals of it so I didn't think he'd miss it.

I stayed on the back verandah talking to Ginger, keeping him sweet, while Eva went and got the food. 'Now Ginger,' I said, 'you promised me you won't go and tell on us at the office if we give you the mandu, so you can't turn back on us now.'

'No,' he said. 'You give me that mandu and martumirri and I won't put you in to the office.'

So out came Eva with this big parcel, and his eyes went, 'Ahhhh, what a feed.' These fellas were as hungry as what we were, you know.

We gave it to him and he just walked off around the corner. Eva and I ran to the kitchen window to see what he was doing. As he was going along he was unravelling this parcel and he was really and truly shoving this food down his neck.

Eva said to me, 'Gee Alice, I never would have thought about doing anything like that to get out of going to the office.'

I never smudged my slate the whole time I was there. I don't think I did anyway. I tried to keep the straight and narrow all the way. So anyway, no more was said about this, and the second boss never got back that night until around nine o'clock.

Although us girls were pretty much supervised, the boys were free to roam around as they liked. Eva and I sort of had boyfriends, well friends really, they were our dancing partners. They were both milk men, cowboys that looked after the cows.

One time they came to the second boss's looking for a feed. We were the only ones there at the time and I was shocked to see them. 'What do you want to come here for?' I asked.

'We're hungry,' they said.

Well, Bluey the tracker must have spotted them because he started coming towards the house. We didn't know what to do, so we pushed them into our room and told them, 'Don't make a noise.'

Just then there was a knock, knock, knock, and Bluey was at the door. 'Where are them boys?' he said.

'What boys?'

'Don't bide me, you know where them boys.'

'I haven't seen any boys,' I said.

'You seen them. They come here.'

'Did you see them come in here, Bluey?' I asked.

'No,' he said, 'but I seen them come this way.'

'Well, they never came in here,' I said, and I was standing there with my bare face hanging out telling a lie. I wasn't happy about the whole thing, but I couldn't have refused them food when they were so hungry.

Anyway, Bluey turns to Eva. 'You telling truth, Eva?'

'Yeah,' she said.

'Are you sure?' he said, but he believed us.

Then I said to him, 'Now, Bluey, don't you come here looking for boys. We don't know where the boys are.' And we watched him as he took off down the street, out of sight.

These boys were still in there, so we just let them sweat for a while longer. We made them up some food, put some meat in some bread, and some tea in a fruit tin. Then we called out to them, 'Come on, come on out, you two.'

My mate was named Willie and Eva's was called Harold. She ended up marrying hers, but I didn't marry mine. Anyway, they came out and they were that worried, because they would have got really punished if they'd been caught.

'Here's your food,' we said. 'Now get!'

Those boys ran off and hid behind this little clump of bushes in the back area. They were sitting down there eating when this bloomin' tracker came back to the house.

'Them fellas not down there, where are they?' he demanded.

'You want to have a look in here?' I said, and I was being cheeky now. 'You want to have a look, go on, see if they're here. Go on, come and have a look!'

'No no, all right, I believe you,' he said.

Eva got even cheekier than me then — it wasn't always that you could get away with something with him. 'You got a cheek coming back here,' she yelled.

And while he was there talking to us those two boys scooted for their lives. That was just lucky that we hadn't all got caught.

The camps were off limits to us up in the compound — well, the girls really, because boys were much freer. Some of the girls had relatives down there and they would ask to go down to see them. They might be allowed, but if they weren't they'd sneak down.

Up in the compound was the bake-house and a few of the compound boys worked there making bread for the settlement. One day I got talking to one of the blokes and found out we were related. That was my Uncle Jack Doherty, from Marble Bar. He only had half his eyesight, but what he could do was really terrific.

When I was working up at the Big House, Aunty Jean came into the settlement. Of course she wasn't my Aunty then, because her and Uncle Jack hadn't married yet. All of us used to notice when anyone new was brought in, everyone would have a good old stickybeak. So I remember her when she came.

Aunty Jean was having a baby, and they put her to work at the maternity hospital as a midwife helping the sister. It was after she had her baby that her and Uncle got together and were married.

The maternity ward was a little tin place at the back of the mother's dormitory. This was before the new hospital was built. A woman would be in there a few days having her baby, then she'd go into the mother's dormitory. If it was summer time those poor women would roast in that tin place.

Well, anyway, Aunty was living in the mothers' dorm when

her and Uncle Jack got together. I heard around the place that he pinched a bit of her hair and sung her to him. Then, after they were married, they moved down to the camps and Uncle built her a good little place to live in.

Down at the camps people had to build their places out of whatever they could get their hands on. It's amazing really: things like kerosene tins, sheets of iron, hessian sacks, would appear from nowhere. They'd build these places with low rooves, and whitewash the hessian for walls. Uncle Jack built a really nice little camp, and it had a separate room for the baby.

I used to say to Matron that I was going down to help look after the baby for Aunty Jean, and sometimes she'd let me go. It was good to spend time there away from the compound, and Aunty Jean used to make a few little things and give me something to eat.

It was much freer at the camps, and there was much better food too. People would go out, kill a brush kangaroo, make a damper and have a good old meal. Sometimes Aunty Jean and Uncle Jack would take a couple of us on a picnic along the river to Long Pool, or down to Elbow. So I used to really look forward to getting down there.

At the camps there were Nor'westers and Sou'westers all mixed in together like up at the compound. So people spoke in different languages, and if you were from the North you'd pick up lingo from the South. See, us from the North, we'd call the bosses Nyambali but the South had different words. Like we would say marndamara for policeman, and the South would call them menarch, that sort of thing. I picked up quite a bit of South language and I used to be able to talk in my language with some of the Nor'westers. But in those days they didn't like us speaking in our language, we all had to keep to English, and that way they stamped a lot of it out.

Moore River ran right through that country, and the camps were built near one part of it. There were lots of different places we used to go along the river, like to Round Pool, Elbow, Long Pool, and Almond Pool which was where we used to go swimming. But there was one pool where no one was allowed to swim because it was the water for the whole settlement. The pumping station was down at this pool and a couple of the married men from the camps used to look after it.

One night there was this funny noise, Errrrrrrrrrr, coming from the pool, and the engines stopped. The blokes looking after the pumps went and asked old Moses if he knew what was wrong.

'What do you reckon stopped that engine?' they said.

'You know what stopped that engine', old Moses said. 'That big fella down there.'

He was talking about the big water snake you see. The Sou'westers call them Waugals, but we call them Warlu. He reckoned the snake had coiled itself around the pumps to stop them from running, and was making that noise because he was getting sucked up.

'How are we going to get him out?' they said, and they were scared stiff.

Well this went on for a bit. No water was coming up to the tank in the compound so they went and told Mr Neal.

'The engine's seized,' they said.

'Well you better get down there and have a look,' he told them.

But I tell you what, none of them would get down there. So they had to undo all the pipes and bring them up and set it all up again. But that snake was still down there. You see, they reckoned that at a certain time you've got to give in, because you're draining all the water out for the Waugal, and he gets cross and stops you. I suppose it's feasible too, when you think about it.

When Uncle Jack got married he left the bake-house and worked as a woodcutter. The woodcutters used to get paid. They'd go a long way out with the third boss and a team of wagons, cutting. When Uncle was away I'd go down and keep Aunty company.

Then, towards the end of 1927, I was sixteen and Matron Neal came and told me I was going out to work. I had to pack up my things, but all I had to take with me were the dresses I'd made myself. I did have a suitcase of things when I first got there, but somebody had taken it from me. When the girls left to go out to work they didn't care whose things they took. So

I lost all my treasured things, things that I treasured from my father and that reminded me of home.

To Williams

I left Mogumber by train and was met at Perth station by Mrs Mulvale. She took me to West Perth to stay, and when the time came took me back to Perth station.

I didn't know who I was going to work for, and when I asked Mrs Mulvale she said, 'Oh, you'll find out when you get there. It's all fixed, everything's fixed.' Then she put me on the half past seven train and handed me a sandwich.

In those days the trains crawled, and I sat on that train all day in a carriage that was more like a dogbox. I didn't know where I was going, what was waiting for me, and I just sat there like a little blind lamb.

As we were coming into Collie I was dry for a drink of water. The guard came along and he said to me, 'Are you all right?'

'I'd like a drink of water, please,' I said.

'Haven't you got one in there?'

'No.'

'That's funny,' he said, and he came inside to have a look. I suppose he thought I was a fibber, I don't know. Anyway, he went and brought the waterbag down, hung it up for me and gave me a big glass. I had a drink then and felt better.

When we got to Collie, the station master was walking up and down the platform. He came over to me and said, 'Hello Miss, how are you?'

'All right, thank you,' I said.

'Did you get a cup of tea?'

'No,' I said.

He wanted to know why, so I explained that I didn't have any money.

'You haven't got any money for travelling! Where are you going?'

'Well, I don't know,' I told him, and I explained about going out to my first job.

'Just hang on a minute,' he said, and he went over and got a cup of tea and a plate of food for me. I was really starving.

The next minute the train whistle blew and I called out to him, 'Hey Mister, I can't eat this because the train's going now.' I was worried about what to do with the cup and plate.

'Look,' he said, 'all that belongs to the government, so you just leave it on the train after you've finished your food. I'm going to look into this. Sending kids out without any money!'

Anyway, we got to Williams and it was about nine o'clock at night. The train stopped and a different guard came along and told me, 'You're getting out here.'

'Oh, am I?' I said.

He went and got my case off the rack and climbed down out of the train with it. I stood there out on the platform, thinking to myself, who's going to come and get me? and, if this train pulls out, what am I going to do. I was really worried.

Next minute I saw this headlight coming towards me. A motor car pulled up and a tall man came across to me.

'Are you Alice Bassett?'

'Yes,' I said.

'Then come with me,' he said, and picked up my case.

We got into the car and as we were driving along he asked me, 'Are you tired? What time did you catch the train?'

'Half past seven,' I said. I knew that much.

I was feeling very, very nervous as it was, and then when we got there it was a police station. I walked down the passage into the loungeroom. He put my case down, and I saw this lady in a wheelchair. I nearly fell over! I didn't know that I was going to work for an invalid lady. Furthermore, I didn't know it was going to be a police station either. But I was as smart as anything. I glanced around quickly to see what was going on, and on the side board was a policeman's tunic, coat and cap.

Looking at all this made me feel...doomed, you know, as though I was caught.

Mrs Larsen, who was the lady in the wheelchair, said, 'Are you hungry?' I was, so she said, 'Oh, then, Mr Larsen will get you something to eat.' When Mr Larsen went out she turned to me and asked, 'Would you like to have a wash?'

'Yes please,' I said, and went into the bathroom and had a bit of a clean up. Then I went into the kitchen and Mr Larsen had a lovely tea for me. He sat there for a minute and talked to me.

'Did you know you were coming to work for me?'

'I didn't know who I was going to work for,' I said.

'Do you know I am a policeman?'

'Yes,' I said, 'I saw your cap and coat.'

'Did they tell you that you had an invalid lady to look after?'

'No,' I told him.

'Well, what sort of people are they!' he said, and he just left me there and went off to speak to Mrs Larsen.

When I had finished my tea, I washed up the dishes and just left them there to dry. Then Mrs Larsen took me and sat me down and started firing questions at me.

'How old are you?'

'Sixteen,' I said.

'Oh,' she said, 'I wanted a woman.' She was a seamstress before she married Mr Larsen. She was a big woman, about six feet tall, and broad.

'What religion are you?'

'Church of England,' I said.

'I wanted a Roman Catholic girl. Can you cook?'

'Um...no.' I wasn't letting on too much.

'I wanted an experienced woman,' she said. 'You're too young for a start.'

I piped up then and said, 'Look, Mrs Larsen. I'm here now and if you're willing to give me a chance, I'll do my best.'

She changed then. She said, 'That's what I like to hear. I'll give you a month. You've got to bath me, put me on the commode, and you've got to cook — but seeing as you can't cook, I'll teach you.'

90

'Thank you,' I said. I was humble because I didn't want to get thrown out and sent back to Moore River, that would be the last straw. I was just glad to get out and I was determined not to go back.

The next morning I got up and sponged Mrs Larsen and put her in her chair. I went out into the kitchen and Mr Larsen prepared breakfast for us. One of his jobs was to collect statistics in those days, and he had to go out to the farms. I wheeled her in and we ate breakfast. She looked at me and said, 'Ooh, you're a strong looking girl. I think you'll be able to cope.'

After breakfast Mrs Larsen sat at the end of the table and she started teaching me. 'You always serve on the left, and take away on the right,' she said. At Moore River they never trained us at all. I'd learnt a lot of cooking and how to do washing from my time with the Campbells when I was only a kid. But Mrs Larsen liked everything to be done in the correct way. She was a very upright and strict lady to work for, but looking back, I am grateful to her for training me the way she did in my first job.

Anyway, I started to sort of settle in there. I don't think I could ever have felt homesick for the settlement, but I used to have my little tears for my family back home.

The Larsens lived a quiet life and sometimes in the evenings Mr Larsen would play the gramophone. Also they were bridge players and they'd have people around for a bridge night.

I always slept in the same room as Mrs Larsen, just in case she needed me in the night. Sometimes I sat up nearly all night and the only way I could keep awake was to do embroidery work. I'd be that tired I'd just fall over onto the bed asleep with my sewing still in my hand. Then I'd hear her sing out for me, 'Alice, Alice, I need a drink of water,' or she might ask for the pan in bed.

The Larsens never asked me anything about where I came from but Mrs Larsen told me a little bit about herself. Mr Larsen was a country boy, but Mrs Larsen was from the city. She was ten years older than him, and early in their marriage she had a baby but it died, and she never had any more children. She'd had a business of her own in Perth but when she got sick with rheumatoid arthritis she had to give it up.

Little by little, during my time with the Larsens, I started to lose my language. Now that I was separated from Doris and Herbert, there wasn't anyone to keep it going with. There'd been people to jabber to in Mogumber, but that was all gone now.

On the nights the Larsens played bridge, I'd sit in the kitchen and practise my handwriting. Doris and I were writing letters to each other but it used to take me hours to write one page. After she'd left Moore River, she'd been sent to work for the manager of the flour mill in Merredin. I wanted to keep writing to her so I'd take every opportunity to try and get my hand going.

The police station where we lived was on the side of the ridge nearest to Narrogin. I used to walk into town to pick up the mail or buy bread, or do whatever needed doing. Williams was very small in those days, there were only a few houses scattered here and there. The doctor didn't even have a car, he used to walk everywhere. I got to know most of the people who had shops in town. The bakery shop people were Mr and Mrs Keeley, and they were beautiful people. When Mrs Larsen had her niece come to stay for a holiday we used to go and sit in the shop with those lovely old people.

One day I was out picking plums, because we used to make plenty of jam, when I saw this big buggy full of coloured people coming along. I heard this whistling, and when I looked up they were whistling and shouting at me. I jumped down from the tree and I ran towards the house. This old woman, Benji, shouted at me, 'Come back, come back, I only want to talk to you,' and she chased after me. She came into the yard and asked me for a box of matches. I said to her, 'You know this is a police station, don't you?' She said that she did, so I told her to wait outside and I'd go and get the matches.

I came back with them and we stood there talking for a while. She said, 'One of the young fellas wants to take you to the pictures tonight.' I was a bit surprised, and I told her that I couldn't go. We talked a bit more because she'd been in Mogumber too, and then she left me to go back to my plums.

I wasn't allowed to go out with anyone, and besides, I was scared of boys myself. Also I knew I wasn't supposed to mix with other Aborigines. It wasn't something I was told but it was the feeling I got. Also, I didn't know Benji that well and it wouldn't have been a good thing for Mrs Larsen to see me talking to her in my working hours.

I'd been with the Larsens for a little while when Mrs Larsen and I were sitting talking one day. I was about to go up to Keeleys to get some bread and things, when she gave me two and six. I said to her, 'What's this?'

'Oh, this is your pocket money,' she said. It was my first pay, but I didn't even know I was going to get paid. Mrs Larsen said, 'You know your wages are five shillings a week, and that two and six is your pocket money, and the other half goes to Mr Neville to put in the bank.' Well I didn't know. They never even told me when I left the settlement where I was going, let alone anything about wages.

When she gave me that money I thought I was really well off, earning five shillings a week, because when Mrs Campbell had us we were only getting two shillings.

I used my pocket money to buy my personal goods and things with, and it was up to the mistress to keep me in clothes like frocks and aprons. So I was given all of Mrs Larsen's beautiful dresses and skirts that she couldn't wear any more and I cut them down to fit me. Because she had been a seamstress, she taught me how to do it really nicely, and I suppose it saved her from having to buy anything new for me.

After I'd been with them for awhile, Mrs Larsen had to go to Perth to visit the doctor. So Mr Larsen took me to Kojonup to his sister's farm and left me to work there for them.

I worked in the house and as soon as the housework was finished I went down to the farm to help with the harvesting. They were cutting wheat at the time. They take the heads off and put them through a thing called the winnower. The winnower throws all the cocky chaff out and all the seed goes into a bag. I had to stand there and do that from about ten o'clock in the morning, through to about five in the afternoon. We'd break off for lunch at midday, then get started again. Mrs Yates, gave me a big hat, but that wasn't the problem — it was my arms and legs that ached from all the standing.

Mrs Yates had three children and one day Phyliss said to me, 'Come on, we're going to pick blackberries because Mum wants to make a blackberry pie.'

Under the blackberry bush there was an old carpet snake — he'd lived there for years. Well, they knew about him but they wanted to have a joke with me. So I was off picking, picking, and going right up to where this old fella was. My foot was getting closer to him and he was going, ffffff. I said, 'There's a funny noise somewhere.'

'Oh, that's nothing, that's nothing,' they said.

So, pick, pick, pick, pick, when I heard it again: ffff.

I looked down, saw him, the bowl went up in the air and I hit sixty!

Mrs Yates said, 'What's the matter, what's the matter?'

'They didn't tell me there was a snake,' I cried.

'Where's all the blackberries?' she said.

'Oh', I said, 'they're gone.'

So we had to go back and pick them all up. But this time I went on the other side, and I kept looking to see if he was coming after me. He was only a docile old thing, you know. But still, a snake's a snake, docile or not, I say.

Another of my jobs was to go and clean house for Mrs Yates' mother and father. That was Mr and Mrs Larsen senior, and they had a place at Muradup. The old man was ninety-six and the old lady was eighty-four.

Once a week, every Thursday, I left the farm and went down to their little place which was about twelve miles west of Kojonup. I had to leave the farm at half past eight to get there, because it was a three mile walk. When I arrived I'd have morning tea and then get stuck into the washing. When all that was hung out I'd go back and do two or three rooms before lunch. Then I'd do the kitchen last, and all the scrubbing and polishing. After that, I'd bring in the clothes and fold what had to go away, and do the ironing. When it was four o'clock, or sometimes a bit later, I'd worm my way back home to the farm.

When I'd get back to Mrs Yates it would be time to help with getting tea, and then the next day all my chores would be the same as the other days.

I don't know if anyone was paying my money into the department at the time, but I never got any money while I was down there. It might have been coming out of Mr and Mrs Larsens' pocket, I really wouldn't know. But still, I used to look forward to going to that old couple's house because they were such old timers, and besides, it was a bit of a break from the farm.

I had Christmas at the Yates and then Mr and Mrs Larsen came and took me back to Williams. I'd been with them for about a year, and at school holiday time, Phyliss, from the farm in Kojonup, came to stay. I don't think I will ever forget that summer because all these things happened.

The first thing was when Phyliss, Ivy and I went up to the post office one day. Ivy was a farmer's daughter from Darkan. When we got there this bloke who was working as a farm labourer started talking to us. 'Hey, you girls, how about coming to the pictures with me tomorrow?'

I remember he had the most beautiful red hair, all wavy.

'No I can't,' I said, 'because I'm looking after an invalid lady.'

'Well, what about you other girls?' he said.

'No, we can't come out with you,' they told him, and I think he was very cross about that.

Then one night Phyliss and I were washing up when the train came in from Collie. I looked out of the window and I could see the light coming.

I cried out, 'Phyliss, quick, quick, this is what I came on, the nine o'clock train, right on time.'

Just under the window they had this big peach tree. We were standing there looking out at the train when Phyliss said to me, 'Grab a peach for me while you're there.'

'All right,' I said, 'you hang on to me and I'll lean out.'

So I leaned right out and started picking some peaches, when suddenly a bloke jumped right up and grabbed me. He started pulling and he nearly pulled me through the window. He ripped all my apron and my dress. I slung right back and hit him on the back of the head with the peaches. Then I managed to quickly pull the window down. I looked around and Phyliss was gone, she'd left me.

I ran into the lounge where Mrs Larsen was sitting up at the table reading. I looked over and saw the loungeroom window was open, so I raced over to pull it down. It was one of those old fashioned ones, with the big ball hanging on the end. Anyway, I was pulling at the window, and as I nearly got it closed this bloke tried to pull it up at the same time. So I just pulled it down as hard as I could and I fell back onto the floor. I jumped up and shouted, 'Phyliss, quick, quick, help me.'

Mrs Larsen didn't know what was going on. The front door was open so I raced up the passage to slam it shut. But as I shot past Mrs Larsen, I brushed her chair and knocked her onto the floor — poor lady. Once I got the door closed I ran back and got Phyliss to help me get her back into her chair.

Mrs Larsen wanted to go to the bedroom so I wheeled her in there. I bent down to put her onto the bed, but as I lifted her leg I fainted.

I don't remember any more, except that as I was coming to I heard, 'Get the brandy, get the brandy.'

Then Mrs Larsen put brandy on my lips and I came to. 'You all right?' she asked.

'Yeah,' I said, but then I went into hysterics. I started crying like mad, and she was saying to me, 'Pull yourself together, pull yourself together.'

Eventually I calmed down and, between us, Phyliss and I explained what had happened. There wasn't anything much we could do about it now — this bloke had taken off — so we got Mrs Larsen into bed. That night Mr Larsen was away, and I went to bed feeling very nervous.

The next day, when Mr Larsen came back, this story was there waiting for him. We didn't know who it was, but I had this feeling that it was the same bloke who'd asked us girls to the pictures.

Not long after all this happened, Ivy's two brothers went out digging field mice. One had a pick and the other was digging. The one with the pick said, 'You'd better stand back and I'll give it another couple of jabs.' But no, the little fella dug his hands into the ground, and the other brother swung his pick at the same time and put it through the back of his neck.

I was at home when the phone rang so I answered it. I wasn't a very good writer, see, so I used to take a piece of paper, quickly write down the message, then come into the kitchen, sit down and write the message out again. I'd be writing it out and — nup, that wasn't good enough — so I'd rip it off and keep going until I got it understandable.

When Mr Larsen came home I told him, 'There's a message for you, Mr Larsen, to ring Darkan. There's been an accident out there.' Well, he rang Darkan police and everything, but the little fella was dead, you see. It was really terrible. Later on Mr Larsen said to me, 'You did a good job, Alice. You're doing all right.'

Only a few weeks after that, maybe a bit longer, Ivy and the remaining brother were going to school. Ivy made her lunch and everything, and she just walked a little bit behind her brother. The brother, he got there, but Ivy never got to school. A man waylaid her.

See, the farmers were all burning off, and there was this bloke who was working on a nearby farm. He killed Ivy and put her body in between some rocks, piled wood on top, then found he had no matches. When he went away to get some matches he didn't have the stomach to go back and set the pile alight. So he went to the pub and got drunk.

The phone rang at the station and they told me to get in touch with Mr Larsen as quickly as possible. The publican at the hotel had this bloke locked up in the upstairs bathroom until the police arrived. There was a big crowd gathered at the hotel and they all wanted to lynch him.

They brought that bloke back to the police station to put him in gaol, and it turned out he was the same bloke that had asked us girls to go to the pictures with him that day.

I was that terrified having him so close to the house. I used to have to go down the back to get water from the rainwater tank outside. I'd get two buckets of water and quickly take them up to the house. I used to go in the day time but I switched to night, because in the day he'd watch me. He said, 'If I get outta here — you're next.'

When I had to go to the toilet I used to try and wait as long as I could before going. We all had to use the same toilet, and they used to take him on a chain. They'd take him to the toilet, and he'd be standing there, and then he'd come out and he'd look towards the house. I'd be watching him through the window, but carefully, so he couldn't see me.

Sergeant Broun said to me, 'Look, don't let it worry you. He can't get away.' But he didn't know that for sure. I used to be the one that had to take his meals to him, and I'd stand right back. I wouldn't let him see me because he was really cross with me.

It had been terrible for all of us, all those things happening in such a short space of time. My nerves were really cracking up — I had big responsibilities as it was, looking after the poor invalid lady. During that year Mrs Larsen's health had been deteriorating, so they decided they'd had enough, and we left Williams and moved up to Perth.

The Move to Perth

We drove up from Williams in Mr Larsen's Buick. All the furniture and household goods belonged to the police station, so all we had to pack up were our clothes. When we got to Perth, Mr and Mrs Larsen moved into a house in Daphne Street, North Perth. This was a half-house, and Loftie Larsen and his wife lived on the other side. Loftie was Mr Larsen's nephew and he was a detective. Sometimes he and his wife would come and have tea with us, but apart from that it was pretty quiet.

I'm not sure how long we stayed at this place, but it wasn't long before we moved to Dunedin Street in Mount Hawthorn. This was a new house and we got the garden looking really lovely. I remember planting the grass out the front there, and it's still alive today.

Down on Angove Street there used to be this big open vegetable market. It was quite a walk from our place but one day Mrs Larsen said to me, 'I feel like going out. We'll go and visit the Mannings, then go to the open market.' Frank Manning was a detective too, and they were good friends with the Larsens.

Going all this way meant I had to take her in the wheelchair. She had a lovely chair, a leather one with a big high back. So off we went with me pushing her, but as we went along, the road got more and more uphill. It was getting very hard for me to push and I was puffing and carrying on.

Halfway up this hill I thought, I'll just slow down and have a bit of a spell. Well, I don't know how it happened but my foot slipped and I went crashing down on my knee. Of course the wheelchair came rolling back full force, so I was on my knees trying to stop it from speeding away, holding it with my back.

I was all scratched and bleeding and my stocking had a hole in it — but I just got the giggles. A man happened to come out of the hotel and he came running across yelling, 'You all right Miss, you all right?' Mrs Larsen was sitting up there in her chair wondering what's going on, and all I could do was just shake my head because I was killing myself laughing. I was trying to giggle quietly so Mrs Larsen wouldn't hear me but that was only making me worse.

The man helped us on our way up the hill until I could push the chair again by myself.

We got to Mrs Manning's house and shot through the gate. We all went off to the market but I tell you what, this was the first and last time we ever had that idea.

I'd been with Mrs Larsen for well over a year now and I really needed to go for a break. As her health was getting worse it was getting harder for me to look after her. By the time we'd been in Dunedin Street for six months my nerves were terrible. What I really wanted to do was leave for good, but she talked me out of it and we agreed on a three-week break.

Mrs Larsen had interviews for a girl to replace me, and about six girls came for the job. They were all white girls and some of them were really good.

Mrs Larsen said to me, 'I want you to be present so that you can pick the girl you'd like.'

'Ohh,' I said, 'I'm not going to pick anyone on my own. But if you decide which one you think is suitable, and I say yes too, then all right.'

So Mrs Larsen picked this girl, a big one, big stable girl. She said to her, 'Oh yes, I think you'll be suitable. Would you like to work?'

'Yes,' said the girl. 'I want a job.'

The girl went home and came back with her case and two or three other little boxes. She put them all out on the front verandah and came inside with me.

I was so excited, I was going away for a break. But first I had to teach her the run of the kitchen and how to look after Mrs Larsen. I showed her around and I put the kettle on for some tea. She asked if there was a shop around as she thought she'd go and get something for us for that night, something to chew on. I told her how to get to the Hobart Street shops and she went to find them.

About twenty minutes later Mrs Larsen asked me where the new girl was. I told her that she'd gone to the shops. Mrs Larsen frowned and said that she should have been back by now, so maybe she was lost. She told me to go and look down the street to see if she was coming.

I went out on to the verandah and the case and everything was missing. She'd picked them up and kept on marching. I went back inside and I just looked at Mrs Larsen. 'She's gone,' I said, and I walked slowly back into the kitchen. I was so disappointed. If only that girl had said she didn't want to stay, because there were other girls to choose from.

The next day Mrs Larsen was writing a letter, and she said she wanted to go to the commode. I took her, and as she had left the letter on the table I went and stickybeaked. I really wanted to see what she was writing because I had a feeling it affected me.

She was writing to her brother who lived in Sydney. She told him that she'd found a girl, but she had run off. She said to him, 'My little black girl has been with me for such a long time and she's worth a hundred of those others that I can't trust, so I've decided to keep her on for awhile.' You know, I think it's terrible that she called me that, her 'little black girl' . I mean, she wasn't thinking about my feelings to say that.

Anyway, after I finished reading I went back to see if she was ready to go into the lounge. She was, so I took her there, and then went straight outside and howled my eyes out. I couldn't go away now. See, I couldn't leave; it was Mr Neville's strict orders that you're not allowed to leave. When you are there, you are there for good. The only time you could leave was when they didn't want you any more.

Dr Cohen used to come and see Mrs Larsen, and he wanted to put her in hospital which would've given me a break. But she wouldn't go: 'No,' she said.

So I was there to stay. I never had a day off in all the time I worked for Mrs Larsen. I never, ever, went to Perth or anywhere by myself. When they went out in the car, I went with them. They used to go out to City Beach to get firewood. There were no houses there then, only scrub. Mr Larsen and I used to bag all the wood up and put it in the boot of the car. Sometimes we went up to Kalamunda for a drive, but that was all. The only time I got out of the house was when I went driving with them. When Miss Ryan came to stay she took me to the pictures a couple of times, but that was really the only outings I had, and I never had any friends at that time in my life.

I can honestly say the only time I ever had any trouble there was with Miss Ryan, Mrs Larsen's niece. We were in Mount Hawthorn when she came over from Sydney for a holiday. She was only supposed to stay for a short while, but she liked the place so much she decided to stay. She went and got herself a job at Alec Kelly's shoe shop in Perth, and because there were only two bedrooms Mr Larsen had to move into the lounge.

I used to polish and scrub the house while Mrs Larsen was sitting in the loungeroom. She'd write letters while I was cleaning the house, and if she needed me she'd call for whatever she wanted.

Anyway, Miss Ryan wanted to wash her hair. She carted this water through the house and spilt it on the floor. Just after I had finished polishing it mind you. I heard her sing out to me, 'Alice, bring a cloth and wipe up this water.'

'What water?' I asked.

'In the passage.'

'But,' I said, 'I've just finished polishing in there.'

'Look, there's water there — wipe it up!'

'Well, how did it get there?'

'Oh,' she said, 'it just spilt. I want to wash my hair.'

'You wipe it up,' I said to her.

'No, that's your job. You wipe it up.'

I was that annoyed, I went into Mrs Larsen and told her what had just happened. Mrs Larsen called out, 'Kathleen,' and Miss Ryan came in. Mrs Larsen said to her that if she'd spilt the water on the floor then it was for her to wipe it up.

'No,' she said, 'she's the servant, she's got to do it.'

'Well, I'm not doing it,' I told her.

We were all in Mrs Larsen's bedroom and Miss Ryan grabbed the hair brush from the dressing table and started hitting me with it. Well, I lifted her, I dragged the brush off of her and I flogged her. She went flying out of the door and disappeared.

Later, she came back, and I heard her go into the bedroom and start talking to her Aunty. I was thinking to myself, I wonder what she's up to now? In that house we didn't have a telephone, so she'd gone out and got the lady police, Lady Dugdale, to come and give me a good thrashing. Lady Dugdale was going to take me out the backyard and flog me like a horse.

Mrs Larsen called me into her room and we all had a discussion. I'd smacked Miss Ryan in the face and she had a little bit of a bruise there. Lady Dugdale told me, 'You mustn't ever do this to your mistress.'

I was really upset. I said to her, 'What about me, look at me. She broke Mrs Larsen's brush on me.'

'You know, you people, you let your temper run away with you,' she said.

'Yeah, well I work hard here. I've got more jobs to do than one. I've got a right to get cross,' I told her.

'Yes, well, look, I'll take Alice out there and I'll give her a good thrashing,' she said.

I was really frightened then, and angry too. I said to her, 'Lady, you better not, you better not Miss, because if I get that whip off of you, you'll get it too. You touch me and I'll get Mr Larsen. You better talk to Mr Larsen first.' See, he was on duty in town at the time, he was working as a mounted policeman.

'Will you apologise to Miss Ryan?' she said.

'You make her apologise first. I didn't start the trouble.'

Miss Ryan was crying and she came over to me and said sorry. I apologised back to her, and I apologised to Mrs Larsen.

Lady Dugdale said, 'There's nothing I can do, because I can see Alice is in the right.'

Mrs Larsen said to her niece that she might as well go back to Sydney, as I had never done anything wrong all the time I'd been with her.

I think Miss Ryan thought that me being the servant made me just a bit of dirt she could push around. But I wasn't one of those kinds, I rebelled — I had to because I was so keyed up all the time. I thought to myself that if I was humble all the time then it would be worse for me in the long run. I think she should have been grateful that I had the place nice and clean for her. But she was someone who just pleased herself sort of thing, like she'd go to work one day, then stop home for the next couple of days.

So that was that. But the whole thing was sad, you know, I felt so sad about it all. Miss Ryan couldn't do enough for me after that. She bought me a nice pair of shoes and gave me a beautiful dressing gown. She took me to the pictures a couple of times, way up at the Rosemount in North Perth. She had a boyfriend who was a policeman and they'd take me with them. We used to have to walk about a mile or a bit more to get there, and Mr Larsen would say, 'I'll look after Mrs Larsen, you go to the movies.' She was trying to make it up to me but what happened was always there.

One morning Mrs Larsen woke me up at about ten to six. She used to have a bell she'd ring next to her bed to wake me if she needed anything. 'Alice,' she said, 'will you get up, please?'

'What can I do for you Mrs Larsen?'

'Would you get me some brandy?'

I went off and got it, and poured it into her little medicine glass. I was looking at her and she was looking at me and I thought she looked a bit funny. 'How much do you want of this Mrs Larsen?'

'Oh the usual amount,' she said.

So I lifted her head with one hand and she sipped at this brandy. She started to take funny little breaths and I said to her, 'You all right Mrs Larsen?'

'Yes, I'm all right,' she said, and had another couple of sips.

But her breathing wasn't getting any better so I asked her again if she was sure she was all right. Suddenly she called out to me, 'Get the robe, get the robe.'

Mrs Larsen was a Catholic and they have special robes made for when they die. She'd had this one made for her a few weeks

104

before and it was a beautiful light brown colour with burnt orange trim on the cuffs and hood. We used to rehearse with it so I knew exactly what to do. I ran to get it for her and she was calling out for more brandy.

I knew this was it so I yelled out to Mr Larsen to come, but he was fast asleep. I brought the robe over to the bed and held her while she sipped at the brandy. Then she took her last breath and I held her in my arms while she died.

I raced off down the passage shouting, 'Mr Larsen, quick, quick.' He jumped clean out of bed and ran towards me saying, 'Oh no, she's not gone is she?'

I went off to let Miss Ryan know and when I came back Mr Larsen was holding her. I carefully lifted her arms and slipped her into the robe. After I'd put the hood on her head I walked out into the kitchen, because Mr Larsen was crying and I couldn't bear to be in the room with him.

A little while later he came out to me, put his hands on my shoulders and said, 'Thank you, Alice. You've been wonderful to her.' I just stood there. I was that stunned she'd gone I couldn't speak.

Mr Larsen went out and got the priest and doctor to come. He wrote a note and told me to take it to a lady's house down on Scarborough Beach Road. I knew which house it was because Mrs Larsen had shown me.

I went there, gave her the note and she said, 'Yes, I'll be up.' She felt sorry for me and she took me inside and we talked for a few minutes. 'Big strain for a little girl like you,' she said, and I just said, 'I don't know what I'm going to do now.'

I went back home and the lady I'd taken the note to came up at around ten o'clock. Luckily I didn't have to do any of the laying out, she did it. People were coming and going and late in the afternoon I caught up with Mr Larsen and asked him, 'What's going to happen to me Mr Larsen?'

'Don't worry,' he said. 'I'll take you to wherever the girls go when they are waiting for another job because you've been very good here.'

It was New Year's Eve, the end of 1928, when Mrs Larsen died. Because it was the weekend the funeral wasn't until Tuesday, so we all had to take it in turns to sit in the room with her. Mrs Yates came up from Kojonup, and her, Mr Larsen and I took it in shifts to keep the candles alight.

I'll always be able to picture that room; it was dark, with white candles burning, and she lay there in her robe with pennies on her eyes. When it was my turn to be in with her I'd sit at the foot of her bed and embroider, never looking up, because I dreaded having to set eyes on her.

To the Farm

I didn't go to Mrs Larsen's funeral, and a couple of days after she was buried I was taken out to Mrs Mulvale's. Mr Larsen drove me there and I didn't really know where I was going, or what to expect when I got there.

When I first met Mrs Mulvale she had a home in West Perth. That was the time when we were kids and we'd come up from Pallinup to go to Moore River. She was still there when I went out to work, but since then she had moved to a house in Sixth Avenue Maylands, across from the blind school.

When I got there quite a few other girls were staying too. I remember Lucy Hester being there, she came from home, from Abydos Station. Mrs Mulvale's daughter lived there also but I can't remember her name. Anyway, Mrs Mulvale used to do all the cooking and we did chores around the place. We used to clean our tables, wash the dishes, make our own beds and keep our rooms clean. Mrs Mulvale used to keep in close contact with the department, so if any of the girls got snappy or something she'd report them, and they'd have to answer at the office.

She wasn't a very fussy sort of a person, Mrs Mulvale, and one of the things I distinctly remember was the tea she used to make. She had an old wood stove and the tea used to be stewed up in a teapot on top of it. Instead of emptying the tea leaves to make a fresh pot, she'd let it stew and stew. It was, errr, horrible — you just couldn't drink it. We used to take our cups and tip it down the sink in the laundry.

One time, while she was out, some of the girls grabbed the teapot and tipped all the leaves out, then rinsed it clean. When she came home and found it she wasn't too happy. 'Who's been in here cleaning the teapot out?' she demanded to know. One of the girls who'd emptied it said she'd just got it ready for her. 'Well, I could have done that,' she said. But she never did do it.

Mrs Mulvale's was mostly for girls, but I remember a boy named Willie Hunter was staying there for a few days. He had a job in Kalgoorlie to go to so he was just there until the time came for him to leave. I know he never, ever, slept in the house where the girls were, so I think he might have slept out in the laundry. We didn't see that much of him, only when he would come into the dining room to have his meals with us. Because he was the only man there he used to like to take his breakfast and sit out on the steps to eat. I guess he was a bit frightened because there were so many of us.

Anyway, as it turned out I only stayed for about two weeks. Although I really needed a break after being with Mrs Larsen for so long, I was only there long enough for them to make arrangements to send me out to another place to work.

They never gave you time, they just choofed you off when they decided you were ready to go.

So towards the end of January, I left Mrs Mulvale's and I was sent out to Wyalkatchem to work for Mr and Mrs Cashmore on their farm called Avon Park. I never got used to going to a new job, there was always a lot of adjusting to do. Working there was different to Mrs Larsen's because they had children, and because I had a lot of outdoor work to do.

I had my routine at the farm, which was the same every day. I'd get up at four o'clock in the morning, light the fire and put the kettle on. Then I'd go out to the yard and milk five cows. When I finished there I'd come back inside, make a pot of tea, two slices of toast, and take it into Mr and Mrs Cashmore. Then I'd go and separate the milk, go down and feed the calves and pig, and come back and make breakfast.

Mrs Cashmore used to get the kids off to school, but I'd make their lunches. After they'd gone to school I'd get stuck into the washing-up, and go outside to clean the separator. Mrs

Cashmore had said to me to do all the housework, the washing and cleaning of the house, and she'd do the cooking. So I'd go about scrubbing and polishing the kitchen and cleaning the dining room.

It was my job to wait on the table too. They had a servery, and when they were ready they'd ring a bell and I'd go and deliver. Then after I'd finished waiting on them, I'd go and eat my meal in the kitchen by myself. This wasn't a cap'n'apron job, they were plain country people, so I'd just wear my ordinary apron. Even though they were plain sort of people I wouldn't speak when I was serving, unless of course they wanted to know something, then they'd have to talk to me. It was a speak when you're spoken to sort of thing.

Mrs Cashmore was the one I always dealt with. She was brought up amongst Aborigines, because her father owned a station out of Derby many years ago. She was reared up there, and she told me how she used to go down to the creek and eat frogs and goannas. Mr Cashmore, I don't think, ever had anything to do with Aborigines, but he was all right. He hardly spoke to me really. He was a very quiet man, a World War One man.

I didn't only work in the house — I worked inside, outside and everywhere else. Sometimes when Mr Cashmore was fixing the old Trojan, or the tractor, he used to sing out, 'E-dith, can I borrow Alice for awhile?' and I'd have to go and help him fix it.

Then there was the farm work too. Mrs Cashmore and I used to finish up in the house at about ten or eleven, and if anything had to be done down at the paddock we'd head off there. Around harvesting time was the busiest. We'd go and help bag wheat or sew up the wheat bags. We'd take the youngest kids with us and carry down the morning tea for the working men.

There was a lot of work to do on the farm and I never got any days off. Once a fortnight, though, on a Thursday, I drove the sulky eleven miles into Wyalkatchem to pick up the mail and do the shopping. I'd do whatever was wanting, take a list in and go around to all the different places. I used to think of it as my day off, because it was a day on my own. But sometimes one of the kids would stop off home and come with me. Then, on the next Thursday, I'd have to go on the tractor or the team. If I went seeding with Mr Cashmore he would build up bags of wheat in bushel bags so I could handle it. But I could lift a bag of wheat, no problems. I was that strong, I used to just hump a bag of chaff down to the cowyard.

When I first got there Mr and Mrs Cashmore didn't have a garden, so I got one going. I had a vegie garden in one corner and a flower garden in the other. Because of all the sheep I just used to go right outside the back gate and get shovel loads of manure for my garden. I grew cucumbers, beetroots and carrots — just things that we could go and pull up. The flower garden was beautiful too, with phlox and delphiniums. The Cashmores were very happy about having a few radishes and things around. It was a lovely garden you know, because I was a bit of a tiller in my own way. Mrs Cashmore reckoned I had a lot more patience than she did, but I just loved to see beauty. To me you've got to have beauty as well as the plain.

After I'd been working there for about a month, Jeffrey, one of the kids, got sick, and Mrs Cashmore had to take him for medical treatment to Perth. So she went off and put the kids in Lady Lawley Cottage for the break. (I reckon Doris, Herbert and my shillings must have kept that place going!) Then she went down to Albany to see her dad. I was left at the farm to look after Mr Cashmore and to run the house.

One day while she was away, Mr Cashmore, and David, who was one of the working men, had to go into Benjaberring to get a new drill. I asked Mr Cashmore what time he'd be home and he said that he'd be back later that night, not to wait up for him, but just leave something for them to eat.

Well they went off in the morning but they never returned that night. I got up the following morning and went through the same chores as I always did, then went down to get the chaff for the cow. After I'd finished up there I went back up to the house but they still hadn't turned up. So I had my breakfast and did all that I had to do in the house. It was getting to lunchtime and I thought they'd probably be back for lunch, so I cooked something for them. I waited and waited but nobody turned up. So I set the food aside thinking it would do for tea and save me cooking again. But by tea time, still nobody.

I waited up for a little while and then I went off to bed. But I couldn't sleep, I was feeling scared being on my own in the house. The farm was eleven miles out of Wyalkatchem, with the nearest farm three miles away. So I picked up my pillow, two blankets, and off I went over to the wheatstack.

The wheat was all bagged and stacked up out in a paddock not far from the house. I had a lamp with me and I made my way there in the night. There was a generator for light in the house, but I hadn't been shown how to start it. Anyway, I got down there, got hold of the ladder and climbed up onto the wheatstack. When I was on top I pulled the ladder up and slept there out in the moonlight.

I ended up sleeping there for three nights running. Then on the fourth night I thought to myself, I'm sick of doing this, and I wasn't going to go. But when I went to bed I thought I heard noises, just like someone walking around the place. So I braved it, I picked up my pillow and rugs, ran down to the wheatstack and shot up the ladder.

On the fifth night someone came. A man rode up on a horse and he had a big white dog with him. He rode around the place, looking about, and I was laying up in the wheatstack listening to him. I said to myself, Alice Bassett, you're smart, you got away from that one. Then I heard him come right down to the paddock, get off his horse and start walking around. I watched him, hardly breathing, laying down flat, and his dog started to sniff around the bottom of my wheatstack. I was worried because the ladder was up with me, and if he'd seen it he would have known that someone was up there. Anyway, thankfully, he only stayed there for a little while, then he got on his horse and rode off. I don't know who he was, I'd never seen him before, and I don't know what it was that he wanted. I'm just glad that he turned around and left.

Well, the next morning I climbed down at around four o'clock and went off to milk the cows. Every night I'd cook a meal and leave it out for Mr Cashmore. And every morning I'd have to feed the pig with it. See, we never had fridges in those days, you couldn't keep things. Anyway this had been going on for a week now; doing my work, cooking a meal and sleeping up in the wheatstack. On the seventh night I decided to boil a leg of mutton with all the trimmings — potatoes, carrots, pumpkin, cabbage and gravy — and when I went off to bed I left some warming in the oven.

At about nine o'clock that night I woke to hear chains rattling; click click click. I sat up thinking, who could this be, when I saw this big, new drill coming along. I could see it was Mr Cashmore and David home, and I was glad. I didn't say anything though, I just stayed put until I heard them yoke the horses and put them in the stable.

I climbed down then and went up to the house. Mr Cashmore came in and said, 'What are you doing walking around in the dark?' I was close to tears. I told him he hadn't shown me how to turn the generator on. Then I asked him what had happened to him and David. He said that when they went to pick up the drill on that first day they'd dropped it taking it off the rail-truck, so they'd had to wait around for a new part to come up from Perth.

I never said anything, but I couldn't see why he or David couldn't have got on a horse and come over and told me. I told him about the man who'd come, but he didn't know anything about him either. He was full of apologies over leaving me there on my own, and after a few days everything was back to normal.

While Mrs Cashmore was still away, her father, Dr House, drove her back up to the farm to see how I was coping.

It was lunchtime and I had all the lunch ready when I looked out of the window and saw this car coming towards the house. I went into the servery and I told Mr Cashmore that a red car was coming down the drive. He said it sounded like the doctor, because he knew his father-in-law's car, and when he walked outside he said, 'Oh, and Mrs Cashmore's there too.'

So in they all came, and I was worried because there was really only enough lunch for Mr Cashmore and David. I'd cooked crumbed chops, vegies, bread'n'butter pudding — all the works. So I sacrificed mine to make it go around, and they all sat down and had their lunch.

After they'd finished eating, Mrs Cashmore came into the

kitchen and said to me, 'Well, I wondered how you were coping, but Mr Cashmore said you were doing really well. So from today, I've washed my hands clean.'

'What do you mean by that?' I asked her.

'You can have the kitchen,' she said. 'I'm not going to do the cooking any more. See, the boss here tells me you're putting me to shame!' That's what she said, and I felt terrible, but from then on I took over all the cooking and she helped with some of the cleaning.

After a while, Mrs Cashmore and the kids came back and things settled down to how they were before. But I was having a bit of trouble with this bloke that was working on the farm. He was cheeky, you know, trying to do a line with me. He was really bothering me, telling me I had nice little fingers and things like that.

I told him off. I said, 'No way.' But I used to have to serve him his meals, and one day I put his plate down and he grabbed me on the leg. Well I just went straight back and slapped him in the ear. It was that quick. Anyway, he saw red and gave me a real killing look.

He left off for a few days, then he sent little Mickey down to tell me, in no uncertain terms, you know, something you'd never tell a kid to say. I was that upset about it I told Mrs Cashmore and Mr Cashmore sacked him.

But that bloke didn't want to get the sack, so when Mr Cashmore was taking him into Wyalkatchem he pulled a spreader off the team and whanged Mr Cashmore over the head with it. We were all sitting at home waiting for him until eleven o'clock that night. Mrs Cashmore was worried so she sent me and Mickey out in the cart to look for him. We headed out towards Wyalkatchem and we met up with him making his way back to the farm. He'd had to go to the hospital and have all these stitches in his head. That's how bad that bloke was, see. I can tell you, I was glad Mr Cashmore got rid of him.

I'd been out on the farm for nearly four months and I was feeling really run down. See, I never really had enough of a holiday from being with Mrs Larsen before going there. I ended up getting very sick — I got mumps, measles and tonsillitis, all at the same time, I was run-down I suppose, and couldn't fight the sickness.

When I first went to Avon Park I used to sleep in the big room, but that was depriving the kids because then they all had to sleep in the one room. So they built me a room on the edge of the verandah. They had, like, a bungalow, and on one end of the verandah they made my room. It was a nice room, with high windows, which I was glad of. With low windows somebody might have come and peeped in.

Anyway, I was very sick, so they sent for Dr Beamish to come and see me. Dr Beamish was Mrs Cashmore's brother-in-law and when he came he found me laying in my room delirious. Dr Beamish held my hand and I heard him say, 'She's on fire.' He ordered me away to Perth to have medical treatment. I was in a terrible state, I had jaws out here with those mumps.

Girls Like Me

I came down from Wyalkatchem by train, and I went out to Mrs Mulvale's again. In those days there wasn't a choice about where you stayed, we all had to stay there. That was the department's orders, because they could be sure to keep an eye on us.

This time at Mulvale's there were about six girls, maybe more. Usually there were only three or four girls, so I shared a room with Jessie Argyle because she had a big room to herself.

Jessie and I became really good friends. We'd talk about things, and for me she was just like having a big sister. If you were around sixteen or seventeen, you were not allowed out on your own. You always had to have one of the senior girls to be an escort for you. All of the senior girls would get together and go out, and they'd always take one or two of us with them. Jessie was older than me, and we were both Nor'westers, so she took me under her wing.

I wasn't at Mrs Mulvale's for long, maybe only a month. At first I was very sick and Mrs Mulvale used to take me to outpatients at Royal Perth Hospital nearly every day. After a little while I was getting better, and I used to go out with Jessie during the day.

We used to go everywhere together, to all sorts of places. A couple of times we went to the zoo, and another place we went was Crawley Baths for a swim. At the baths we used to be able to hire bathers, one pair for a shilling. But usually they were wet or they were smelly. So I said to myself, I'm going to buy myself a pair of bathers, and I did. I paid two and six for my very first pair of bathers, and I really felt the part when I wore them to the baths or down to the beach.

Other days Jessie and I used to go to the pictures, like to the Luxor Theatre, or the Hoyts Theatre. I've got three bricks in the Hoyts Theatre. See, when it was being built everyone had to donate some bricks. Mr Larsen said to me, 'Would you like to donate some bricks?'

'Where from?' I asked.

'Out in the heap out there.'

So I went to clean my three bricks, and Mr Larsen got me to clean a dozen for him as well. He took them all in and when it opened he got a free pass to go and have a look around. I went along too and it was the most beautiful picture theatre. They had this fountain there; a lion with water dripping out of its mouth, painted stars all twinkling, and clouds rolling. There were all these palms in the foyer, and everything about it was just beautiful.

Some days, Jessie and I would just go into town together, and our first stop would be the railway station in Wellington Street. We'd be on the bus from Maylands and when we came to the corner near Barrack Street, Jessie would look down Wellington to see if Squeaker was there. Squeaker was Jessie's boyfriend, and he had a friend who was a Yellow Cab driver. One time he was over talking to his friend and Jessie said to me, 'Come on, I'll introduce you to him.'

This was when I met Squeaker for the first time. He was called Squeaker because he had something wrong with his throat. He joked to Jessie, 'What! Now you come along and introduce me to young ladies! You should have introduced me before.'

'Well,' she said laughing, 'I'm lucky I met you first then.'

I was only a shy young lady, but he used to tease me, the old fella. He was really lovely though. I said to her, 'Jessie, you naughty girl, don't go pushing me around with men.'

If any of the girls were going with a bloke they never used to let Mrs Mulvale know. Not far from her house was the

Maylands primary school and that's where all the girls would see their boyfriends off. They'd say their farewells there, and then go home as innocent as you could imagine.

Mrs Mulvale was very strict on us girls and she'd growl at us if we came home late. We'd go out at around five o'clock and we were supposed to come back by eleven. Eleven was the very latest. If you did get back late Mrs Mulvale wouldn't chastise you herself, she'd go and get in touch with Mr Neville. She'd just say to you in the morning, 'You're wanted at the office.' Even the older girls had to be in by eleven. They were expected to set an example for the younger ones. Some of those girls were fully grown women, like in their late twenties and early thirties, but the department still called them all girls. We were always girls no matter how old we were, and the men were called boys.

Sometimes a clan of us would get together, like the ones from Mulvale's would meet up with some of the others working around Perth. We'd go out in this big group and we all stuck together. People in the street would stare at us but we'd just ignore them.

We'd go out somewhere like the zoo, or we might go to the government gardens and just sit around and have a good old talk. There'd be Gladys Gilligan, Carrie Leyland, Bertha Isaacs, Jessie, Lucy Hester, Annie Cunningham and myself. We used to like to take photos of ourselves too, and some of the girls had those old box brownie cameras.

One time we were walking back from government gardens and there was a bunch of louts coming up the street on the opposite side. Carrie and Bertha, those two were dynamite, they were very, very, touchy, and if anyone passed a remark about them they'd get really uptight. Anyway, these fellas were walking down the street, and they always slung off at our colour you see. This one bloke, he looked over and he said, 'Pfoo, look at all the dark clouds. It sure is going to rain.' Well, we tried to stop those two girls, Bertha and Carrie, but they were off across the street and into those fellas, left, right and centre.

I could hear Carrie yelling, 'Don't you ever say that, don't you ever, because the only time it will rain is when you rain over china tonight.' She was talking about the chamber pot he'd have under his bed, see. We all went across then and had our tuppence worth. And I tell you what — they bolted, off they fled. Jessie shouted, 'Look you girls, pull yourselves together.' She was very strict on silly things like that. 'You know if the police come we'll be in big trouble. They'll get away with it, and we'll be the ones in hot water — all for the likes of them.' See Jess was a leader, she always kept us all in line. 'But ohh,' they'd say, 'they're not going to call me names, not going to insult me.' But that was it, she was right — it was just what we had to put up with.

That sort of thing used to happen quite a bit, we'd get called names like dark clouds or black velvet. Once we were sitting down, minding our own business in the government gardens, when some white blokes came along and kicked one of the blokes with us in the shins. Those white fellas ended up sorry they'd ever done it, because I tell you what, the Aboriginal boys chased them until they got them. When things like this happened us girls all used to say, 'Why can't we come here, sit down, and have nobody bother us? We don't bother you people, why can't you just leave us alone?' But ohh, we got plenty of it.

Another place we used to go was to our special tearooms down in Adelaide Terrace. We had our own special room that was curtained off. We could sit in there and talk, and we could hear everything that was going on outside. The other customers wouldn't know who was behind the curtain, you see. I can't think of the name of the bloke who ran it, I think it was Con. He was a Greek fella, and he looked after us — he was really good. But I think the curtain was put up because white people wouldn't come in and eat if they saw us in there. That's just how it was. But in Boans it was different, we could go in there anytime and have a meal.

We were all working girls and to get our money that the department held in the bank we had to go into the office and ask for it. You had to tell them what you wanted your money for, and they would fill out a request form. Then the lady at the office would have to go and ask Mr Neville if she could give us our money. Then he'd send her back to ask what we wanted it for. If he said yes, she'd say to us, 'Now don't you squander it. You make it last.' Always she'd say that — even though it was our money!

Us girls used to be scared going in there to ask for our money. Going up the stairs we used to whisper, 'Who's going to get knocked back this time?' Then someone would say, 'Well if I get knocked back, you could share your money with me, and I'll share mine with you next time.' See, that's how we'd get around it.

We used to do a lot of our shopping in Boans. One time there I had my eye on a dress, so I went and asked for some money.

'How much?'

'Seven and six,' I said.

'Anything else?' You had to tell them everything you wanted it for. Then they'd give you a little form like a coupon. They never gave you money, only a coupon. Then you'd take that along to the shop and buy what you wanted. We used to be cunning too, we'd buy something as cheap as we could because then they'd give you change and you could pocket that.

Clothes were really cheap then, dresses were only two and six each, or five shillings for something really nice. Underclothes were only one and threepence then, and singlets or petticoats a shilling each, see everything was so cheap. But still, for us girls, five shillings would be a whole two weeks pocket money.

Anyway, on this day I went along to Boans to buy this dress. When I got there I ran into old Mr Harry Boan, the man my father had introduced me to when I was a kid. Mr Boan said he recognised me and was surprised to see me grown up. He also said that it was his birthday that day so I could choose another dress and have it for free. I was really thrilled. I only had the one frock when I came down from the farm because I was too sick to pack. I'll always remember that old gentleman for that.

One evening Jessie and I went out to the Luxor Theatre in Beaufort Street. On the way home we came to this fish shop. I saw this beautiful crayfish in the window, only I didn't know it was a crayfish. I said, 'What's that!' She said, 'That's a crayfish — I'll buy it for you.' So she bought it and we took it home to Maylands.

We didn't have anything to eat it with, like salad, we just ripped into it. 'Mmmmm, that's beautiful,' I said, and I ate and ate until I made myself sick. Ooooooh, horrible I felt! But in the meantime, while we were eating, we were talking about up North. We were Nor'westers, see, we all stuck together. We loved one another, all the Northies always loved one another. We all belonged to the one country, never mind if you're not related by blood, it's the North and that's our country.

So anyway, we were talking about everything, about her mother and that, and I said to her, 'Jessie, would you ever go back?'

'Nuh, I wouldn't want to go back,' she said, 'but what about you Alice? You ever going back?'

'Well, I'd like to...but I don't know how.' See, if I only knew then what I know today, I would have been back on my first holidays from work. But I never knew, and you become...sort of lost. Besides, the department had a rule — North girls were sent South to jobs and Sou'westers were always sent North. They were very strict about that because they meant for us to never find our way back home.

'Well,' I said to Jessie, 'what about your father? You got a father?'

'No,' she said, 'what about you?'

'Ohhh, I had a mother and a father, but he was good to me, loved me.'

'My father never claimed me,' Jessie said, 'but I don't care. I remember my mother and I've got a life.'

'Yeah, that's good,' I said to her. 'We've always got to think like that.'

Jessie was from Argyle Station and she was taken away when she was only young. There were lots of girls who never knew their fathers or never saw their family again. And if they had a white father, chances were it was never owned up to. So what we all had to do was just cut off from the life we had before, just try not to think about it, and get on with the life we were living at the time.

When I had been down in Perth for about a month they decided I was well enough to go back to the farm. Then, one morning, Mrs Mulvale said to me, 'You better get up to the office, Mr Neville wants to see you.' I thought to myself, for goodness sake, what have I done now!

When I got there he said, 'The girl I had helping Mrs Neville has left. How would you like to come and relieve in her place until we can get someone else?'

'But I've got to get back to the farm,' I said.

'That's all right,' he said. 'You can go back to the farm after.'

The girl who'd been working for the Nevilles was named Maggie. She'd left all right — she'd run away. So they borrowed me as a replacement for about a month. They had a house up in Darlington, and two nice little girls and one boy. I was paid twelve and six a week from him, which was generous compared to what I'd been getting. I'd get five shillings pocket money for me, and seven and six would be put into the bank by Mr Neville. I also used to get one day off a week, on a Thursday, and I'd go into Perth and meet up with the girls.

I used to call Mr Neville Sir, and his son I called Master John. But I called his wife Mrs Neville and the girls by their names, Anne and Cynthia. This was a cap'n'apron job, you know, you've got to wear a uniform. Mrs Neville used to buy material and I'd make them up for myself.

I'd wait on them at the table and after they'd finished eating I was allowed to have my meal in the kitchen. If it was in the mornings I'd have my breakfast, do the washing-up, then prepare for the day — like make cakes, biscuits or whatever.

I did all the preparing and cooking of the meals, just plain, ordinary cooking, and they were very big bridge goers. I used to have to take notes way down to different houses, all the invitations for bridge. On those nights I'd sit up until eleven o'clock waiting for their game to finish. I'd serve their supper, and when everyone had left I had to wash up the dishes before I went to bed.

It was while I was at Mr Neville's that I started to really learn to write. See, when they took me and brought me down they promised to educate me, but they never did. As I said before,

121

as far as Mr Neville was concerned, 'All they need to do is write their name and count money, that's all the education they need.'

Because of that, I only ever got up to grade three in school. When I was at Mrs Cashmore's I never had the chance to learn to write because I'd be up at four in the morning, and to bed at eleven at night. I had no chance to do anything else as I'd be hard on my feet all day. When I was with Mr and Mrs Larsen I did have a bit of a chance writing out all the messages. But now I was at the Neville's I really got a good chance, and I really got my hand going quickly.

On bridge nights I used to sit out in the kitchen to hear if they rang for me, and I'd practise my writing. I'd get jam tins and milk tins and copy all the words out. Some people say to me today, 'Where did you get your education?' And I always say, 'I learnt it off jam tins.' They laugh at me but that's the truth. I'd get the golden syrup and write, G O L D E N S Y R U P. I'd wear one page out writing Alice Isobel Bassett, Alice Isobel Bassett, to get it right. And it was only through doing that I learnt to write.

After I finished up at Mrs Neville's I went back to Mrs Mulvale's place to get ready to go to the farm. The Neville girls, Anne and Cynthia, really liked me and didn't want me to go. But Mr Neville got Ruby to come and work there, and sent me back to Wyalkatchem.

When I got to Mrs Mulvale's Jessie had been sent to work at Yundamindra Station, out near Kalgoorlie. She wrote me a letter and said she wanted me to come up and work with her. So I went up to see Mr Neville to ask him if I could go to work there.

I explained to him that Jessie wanted me, even the Yundamindra people wanted me. He said, 'No, you go back to the farm.' It was just to be, you know, opposite. You never got away with anything with him. If you were sent to a place you had to go there, and once you were there you were tied down until it suited them.

So I had to go back to the farm. I wasn't very long at Mrs Mulvale's before I left, but I still had a bit of a chance to meet up with my Aunty Daisy Corunna, Aunty Nellie Bark and Aunty Helen Bunda. We had all accidently met once through being introduced by someone else. They'd all been taken from the North too, and we found out that I was their people and they were mine. So we used to make it a day. I'd come down from Maylands and wait outside Boans and they'd come from Claremont and meet me. They were all working in Claremont then, and we'd try pot luck to all get together and have a day out in town.

While I was staying at Mulvale's, Dorothy — who I used to work with in the sewing room at Moore River — and a girl named Lilah, came out visiting. They were both working for the Woodmans in Swanbourne, and they asked me to come and spend the day with them. Dorothy and I had always got along well so I went down to Swanbourne a couple of times to visit her.

I spent the night there once, and I really got into hot water over that. I'd gone down to visit Dorothy and Mrs Woodman had said, 'How would you like to spend the night with us?' Well, Dorothy didn't want me to leave, and we were good friends, so I stayed the night. When I went back the next morning Mrs Mulvale said, 'You're in big trouble. You go up to the office.'

I had a shower and changed, then I went up to face the music. I had to explain every little thing. See, they thought I must have been out with a boy, that's just the way they thought. I had a terrible time trying to explain. They twisted everything I said around. I kept saying to them to get in touch with Mrs Woodman to straighten it all out but they took their time about it. Finally they did, then they had to believe me.

I remember one time I was staying at Mrs Mulvale's, there were about nine girls staying and the place was overcrowded. Mary Benjamin and me were the last two to come so we had to sleep out on the verandah. I didn't know Mary from a bar of soap, and she didn't know me, but we had to share the one bed.

'All right mate,' we said to each other, and we hopped into bed. When we were laying there the next morning two old blind fellas were walking across the road. These old fellas had their canes and everything. One said, 'You know that house across the road there, that's where all the sun-kissed maids live.'

I said to Mary, 'Did you hear that?'

'Yeah,' she said, 'they're supposed to be blind, so how do they know we're sun-kissed,' and we just fell about laughing.

Anyway, all too quickly the time came for me to go back to the Cashmore's, so I got my things together, said goodbye to the girls, and caught a taxi down to the train station.

No Aborigines Allowed

I caught the train to Wyalkatchem, and when I got there I walked out and looked around, but there was nobody to meet me. I stood around and waited and waited. It was a bit cool that day so I put on my coat and walked around a bit, looking to see if Mr Cashmore was parked somewhere. I stood outside the station straining my ears for the sound of the old Trojan. Suddenly I thought I'd heard Mr Cashmore coming, but when I went towards the road I was just in time to see him disappearing over the railway line, out of town. I was really upset, I didn't know what to do. I walked into the waiting room and sat down to think.

There was a gang of workmen nearby and they had just knocked off. They came along and one of the blokes saw me there in the waiting room. He was a new Australian, and he said to me in broken English, 'What you doing here?'

I was a bit scared of him and I said, 'I've just come back from Perth. My boss was supposed to meet me but he went without me.'

'Who your boss?' he said.

'Mr Cashmore.'

'Well,' he said. 'You no stop here. You get from here, cos if you don't...I'll kill you!'

When this bloke threatened me I got the shakes, I was really frightened. I just looked up at him and I said, 'But where am I going to go?' He got a bit closer to me and he said, 'That your problem, just get, go on, get out of here!'

There were other men with him as well. They were all Aussies, you know, but they never said anything. Thinking about it now I think they could have said something, could have stood up for me somehow. But I just had to pick up my case and walk off.

The Greaves had the bakery in town, and I knew them from when I worked at Mrs Cashmore's before. I walked over to their place and Mrs Greaves was surprised to see me. I explained to her that Mr Cashmore hadn't picked me up. She said, 'You look upset.' I told her it was just about not being picked up. I didn't want to say anything about what had just happened. I asked her for directions to the police station because I thought that was the best place for me to go. She told me how to get there and I walked off.

As I was walking along the road I put my case down to have a spell, and I just burst into tears. I had travelled up on the same train as Mrs Spencer — she was the engine driver's wife — and she lived in the street where I was standing crying. She must have seen me because she came running across the road and took me into her place.

By this time I was howling. I was that broken-hearted about the way that man had treated me, and I was worried too that he might be going to come after me. Mrs Spencer kept saying to me, 'Come on Alice, there's something hurting you. What's hurting you?' I told her that this man had threatened to kill me if I didn't get off the railway siding. She was really shocked. 'Come on,' she said. 'We'll go up to the police station.'

Lou Pollock was the policeman at that time and I told him what had happened. He said it was too late to run me out to the Cashmore's farm that night but he'd take me out the following morning. I said to Mrs Spencer that I was going to ask him if I could stay there for the night. I was thinking that if I was locked up in a cell that man wouldn't be able to get to me. She said I wasn't to do any such thing and she took me back to her house.

The next morning at about nine o'clock, Mrs Spencer took me down to the police station. She really was a lovely lady to have helped me out like that in such a prejudiced town.

126

Anyway, Seargeant Pollock and his two little boys drove me out to the farm.

We got there at about eleven o'clock and Mrs Cashmore came running out. She was dancing around and saying, 'I knew, I knew Alice would be there. I told Bob, make sure, make sure you look around properly.' She said she had been worried about me, and I said to her, 'You nearly didn't have me either.' I told her the story about that man and she explained to me how Aborigines weren't allowed in town after dark.

Wyalkatchem was a very prejudiced town. It was a real colour bar place, no Aborigines were allowed there. All the people who were working on farms out there — like Muriel Ugle, Minnie Darby, Alma Bell, Charlie Sandstone — all of them would just go into town to do their bit of shopping, then they had to go straight out again. That's what it was like, not a soul allowed after dark.

Anyway, I settled back into my old routine of working inside the house and helping down at the paddocks. Mrs Cashmore and I used to have to go down and help the ewes have their lambs. The poor things used to have trouble and we'd get in and help deliver them.

For a bit of a break I used to take the kids on picnics some Sunday afternoons. I'd make pastry for an apple pie or whatever for tea, and I used to keep some pastry back. I'd use it to make little snakes and goannas, and I'd put currants and things in for faces. Then when I took the kids out we'd have these to enjoy.

There was a government well where the kids liked to go for their picnics. One day I took them up there in the horse and cart for the day. At the well there was a whipple tree that you use for drawing water. It works like this: there's a bucket there and you pull the bucket down and the whipple tree goes down, then you pull the whipple tree and the bucket comes up. So anyway, we got some water, made a fire, and let the billy boil. We got out our lunch, and the pastry animals, and settled in for the afternoon.

The kids were running around and playing, picking flowers and things, and we had a real nice time. But Mickey, he was mischievious. On the way home, when we were all in the cart, he said to me, 'I saw something back there Alice, would you pick it up for me.' So muggins got out and went to look for it for him, when he suddenly hit the horse and left me behind. He was a real little monkey, Mickey was. I had to walk back towards the farm, and everytime I got close he'd hit the horse and move it further.

I never lost my temper, but I just thought, right, I'll give you something too Mickey Cashmore. I managed to catch up with them, and he sat there while I took the reins off of him. I said, 'Oh that was a lovely walk, thank you, Mickey,' and I got the horse going. I was thinking, just keep your cool and he'll be off guard.

We came to this government road, where we turned to go into our gate. 'Mickey,' I said, 'I think it's your turn to open the gate.'

'No it's not, it's Jimmy's,' he said.

'Mickey,' I said, 'Jimmy opened it when we were going.'

'Oh, that's right,' he said, and he jumped out to open the gate.

I drove through and pulled up waiting for him to shut it. Then as he got close I shouted, 'Come on Let,' and I just took off. Lettie was the horse's name and she bolted away. Micky was running along behind crying, 'I'm going to tell Mum on you.'

I let it go for about half a mile, then I pulled up and waited for him. He came and got in and he was fuming. 'No way are you going to get away with this,' he said.

I turned to him and said, 'Just think what you did to me, Mickey. You'd better remember that you wouldn't go on picnics if it wasn't for me, you'd just be sitting at home.'

When we got back Mrs Cashmore came out to ask us if we enjoyed ourselves. I said we did, but she said it didn't look like it. I explained what had happened, and when Mickey came back from the stable she said, 'And what sort of a picnic did Mickey have?'

'No good,' he said. 'Alice ran away and left me.'

'Oh,' she said, 'and what did Mickey do to Alice?'

But he wouldn't be drawn, he was a right little monkey that one. See, although it was my job to look after the kids, and there were five of them at that time, I was never allowed to discipline them myself. That was out — if there was any trouble I had to take it to Mrs Cashmore for her to decide what to do.

That year the Cashmores decided to go to Perth for a holiday, and take me with them. It was the end of the harvest and it was raining. We were still sewing up bags on the day that we were leaving. There was a storm on that day, thunder and lightning all around us. I was scared stiff, I don't like electrical storms. I finished sewing up the bags, then Mrs Cashmore and I started packing for the trip. We were going all day until three o'clock in the afternoon when Mr Cashmore came in.

I'd been that busy I hadn't eaten anything, so I sat down to have some lunch. While I was sitting there Jimmy came along. He wanted me to make him a gun out of this piece of fruit case. I used to make guns and things for them all the time but I just didn't feel like it right then. I said, 'Look, I'm too busy. You'll have to leave me alone. I'm going to eat my lunch and then I've got work to do.'

Well he got really upset, 'You don't like doing anything for me,' he said, and he hit me on the hand with a butcher's knife. Actually you can see a white mark there today, that's Jimmy's mark on me. The blood spurted out all over my lunch. I jumped up and I yelled at him about how bad he was, and that I was going to tell his father.

Just as I was saying this Mr Cashmore came in and wanted to know what was going on. I was that tired, I was worked up over the thunder and lightning, and I just felt awful. Of course Mr Cashmore, when he saw what his son had done, got his belt and he ripped into this poor little Jimmy.

I felt terrible. I said, 'Mr Cashmore, please, don't, it's all right.' I was so depressed. I went into my room and I had a big cry. I still had to scrub my room out and to pack, and to do this and that. I just went about silently and finished what I had to do. Then it was five o'clock and we had to leave for Wyalkatchem. I can remember I was that down, and I was never like that, but I couldn't even talk to them. I felt like I wanted to say, 'I'm not coming back.'

Anyway, we got into town and Mr Cashmore went and did a few things. Then when the train came we all hopped aboard.

Alice with young charge, Wyalkatchem, early 1930s.

Mr and Mrs Cashmore were in one carriage with Margaret and the baby, and I was in another carriage with the three boys.

When we got to Perth they went and stayed at the Savoy Hotel in town, and I went out to Mrs Mulvale's. It never ended up being a holiday for me — every morning at nine o'clock I had to go to the Savoy and babysit. They stayed for a week, and I'd sit with the baby while they'd come and take the other kids out. At dinnertime they'd go to have their lunch somewhere, and I'd have to go somewhere else to have mine. I used to go down to Boans tearooms a lot and back to Mrs Mulvale's in the evenings. That was what it was like every day until we went back to Wyalkatchem.

We all went back to the farm but I didn't stay long. Things didn't end up going too well between Mrs Cashmore and myself. I hadn't been too happy there lately, and I'd been getting letters from the Neville girls. Anne used to write and ask me if I'd come back. The girls were missing me — I was only relieving that time, but they hadn't wanted me to leave.

Then Margaret had a nice little girl from another farm come to have a holiday with her. She got a bit cheeky with her little friend and I told her, 'This is your guest. You ought to treat her like a guest.'

As I was saying it Mrs Cashmore just happened to walk in the door. 'What's going on here?' she said.

'I'm just telling Margaret, as she's picking on Roma, that if you have a guest you have to treat her as a guest.'

Well, Mrs Cashmore flew at me for telling her daughter off. I flew back at her and ended up shouting, 'Well, if that's the way you feel — you can keep your job. I'm off.'

I guess it wasn't only one thing, but everything just came to a head. I knew I wasn't allowed to leave Mrs Cashmore's without permission from Mr Neville, but I just decided to go.

I thought I'd go back to Mrs Mulvale's and see what happened. I had a feeling from the letters that Anne and Cynthia wrote that I would at least be able to go back there for a job.

131

Back to Darlington

I came down from Wyalkatchem to find that Mrs Mulvale's had moved to Bennett House. It wasn't Mrs Mulvale running it any more, Mrs Campbell from Moore River was, and it was where all of us had to stay now. It was in East Perth on the corner of Royal Street and Bennett Street. There was a school there and Wellington Square was just behind it. The house was big and it had a passage up the middle. At that time it was for both boys and girls, and all the girls lived on one side of the passage and the boys were on the other. We were always kept separate from the boys, except for meals when we all ate in the dining room together.

I stayed there for a few days before I went out to Mrs Neville's. The rules were the same as Mulvale's, and we never went out with any of the boys staying there — that was strictly forbidden. During the day the boys went their own way and we went ours, but we all had to be in at the same time. The only difference was the boys didn't have to have an older escort like we did.

I remember while I was staying there a group of us girls used to go for a swim in the Swan River, behind the East Perth Gas Works. The water used to be beautiful in those days, fresh and clear, not polluted and murky like it is today.

When I first got there I asked the new lady to let Mr Neville know I was staying, and that I wanted my old job back. I heard that Ruby had left, and Mr Neville said they would gladly have me back. So I stayed at Bennett House for a few days before going up to Mrs Neville's.

When I got the word I got all my things together and caught the train up to Darlington. Ruby had left because a bottle burst and cut her hand. See, Mr Neville wouldn't have a flask, he liked a bottle to carry his tea in. Ruby made up the tea but she put it in too hot. So when she had to leave, the Neville girls had been asking to have me back.

There were four of us girls working in Darlington, and we used to meet and go to church on a Sunday night. Doris, who came down from the North with me, was now working about two streets away. She was one of the girls I used to meet up with and the others were Suzy Smith and Annie Wheeler.

Sometimes, when we were allowed, we would all go on a picnic together. They were really good times and the girls who had boyfriends used to invite them along. But Mr Neville never saw them, they made sure of that. We'd all get together and take some cool drinks with us, and cakes or whatever we'd made, and have a little party in the bush.

I used to get a day off every Thursday and usually I'd go into town. Sometimes I'd meet up with the other working girls, and sometimes I'd meet Dorothy's brother, William.

I first met Will when I was staying at Mrs Mulvale's and I'd gone down to visit Dorothy in Swanbourne. She'd said to me, 'I'm going to meet my brother today Alice, and I'd like you to meet him too.'

Dorothy and her brothers, Thomas and William, were all Swan Mission children. When their mother died they were all put in there, but they ended up at Moore River. I'd seen Will when I was in the settlement but I had never spoken to him.

Dorothy was really keen for us to get together, but when I first met him I just thought of him as a friend. Then, when I went back to Wyalkatchem we wrote to each other a couple of times, and I suppose we sort of got together from there.

Anyway, I'd meet him somewhere in town and we'd go to his cousin Ted Nannup's place in Tuart Hill. It was all bush out that way then, and we'd walk about a quarter of a mile to Ted's house, have lunch there, and then I'd catch the train back to Mrs Neville's.

There was only the one train to Darlington in the afternoon, and that was the workers' train. Every Thursday Jackie Leyland knew I'd come down to Perth, and he'd come to the railway station and wait with me until it was time for the train to leave.

Jackie was Carrie Leyland's brother — he used to watch out for us girls when we were in town, or escort us back to Mulvale's. I can remember on warm evenings when I was staying at Maylands, Jackie would walk a group of us girls all the way home. We'd walk along, play the mouth organ, and just skylark around. We used to dance all the way along Beaufort Street and nearly wear our shoes out. When we got home he would walk off to catch the train and we used to tease him, like follow along behind him waving and carrying on. We'd pretend we weren't going inside, that we were going back into town, and he'd be yelling at us, 'Go on, off you go...now get.'

Anyway, come Thursday afternoon he'd be there waiting for me. One evening I was sitting in the train and he was out on the platform talking to me when Mr Neville came along. Jackie saw him first and he quickly shoved his head in the window so Mr Neville wouldn't see him. I was going, 'What's the matter, what's the matter!' He was standing there with his back to Mr Neville and trying to motion to me with his eyes.

I saw Mr Neville stroll past and I said to Jackie not to worry about it.

'Oh I don't like him,' he said. 'He'll chip me.'

'He won't chip you,' I said. 'You're only standing there.'

'Yeah, he'll chip me all right. He don't like me,' Jackie said, and he waited poked through the window until Mr Neville had gone.

Although Mr Neville would be on the same train as me he'd be in the workers' carriage, so I wouldn't see him until we got off at Darlington. We used to walk home together and he'd say, 'What sort of a day did you have?'

'Oh fine, good,' I'd say, and I'd leave it at that. I couldn't tell him what I'd done with my day off because I knew he wouldn't have liked it.

While I was working there, Mrs Neville and her mother, Mrs Lowe, went on a holiday and took the girls with them. That left only Mr Neville, John, and I there. John had all these toy steam trains outside in the garden and he used to come and ask me for boiling water to put in his engines to make them go.

During this time I never went anywhere, I never even went to Perth. The furtherest I got was down to where Doris was working for an afternoon. We used to enjoy one another's company and talk about home up North. I think that's the only thing that kept me sane at that time.

After Mrs Neville and the girls came back things went back to normal.

One day Will decided to come up and see me, but I didn't know he was coming. He was working at Wanneroo at this time, clearing all that country with his cousin Ted. He caught the train up and was at the Darlington hall when Mr Neville went past and saw him. Mr Neville wasn't very pleased and he went and told him off.

When Mr Neville came home and told me, he asked me if I knew Will was coming up.

'No, Sir,' I said, 'but could I go —'

'— No, you can't go anywhere.'

Mr Neville said to Will, 'Nobody comes and visits the girls when they are at their jobs,' and he told him to get going. Will told me later that he walked all the way back home. I tell you, we didn't get it smooth in those days. I wasn't allowed out for two Sundays over that, and I was ropeable!

I never had any problems working for Mr Neville, but Mrs Neville was very fussy. She had a habit of following along behind me and watching everything I did. Like I'd be doing cooking or something, and she'd be there, over my shoulder.

When I used to make porridge for breakfast I always put the dirty pot outside on the tank where I could get to it later. I did that to give myself time for all the other work I had to do, while the pot soaked.

But one day Mrs Neville happened to walk past and she saw it. I was inside polishing in the house when she came in.

'What's the porridge pot doing outside?'

'Well, I'm going to wash it up in a minute,' I said. 'It's a bit hard to do and I want to get what I'm doing now done first.'

'Oh,' she said, 'but I don't like to see the porridge pot on the tank.'

I felt myself getting cross — she always was one step behind me. She started to say something to me and I said, 'Well if you don't like it, you know what you can do about it.'

'Oh,' she said, 'you don't need to get upset about it.'

'No,' I said, 'I'm doing my work and there's no need to walk behind me. That pot doesn't stand out there all day, and it's not the first time I've put it out there.'

Well, she went and spoke to Mr Neville about it, and then Mr Neville spoke to me. He said he wasn't very happy with me, and I was not to speak to my mistress like that. I was very upset because I was on good terms with Mr Neville and I always did my work well while I was there.

See, when I worked for Mr Neville he was different towards me than he was when I worked for someone else. If he came home in a good mood he'd say, 'How's my girl today?' He used to ask me if I was happy and I'd always say I was — even if sometimes I wasn't happy at all.

There were a few things that happened around this time, but mainly I wasn't happy there, so it was decided I would go back to Moore River until another job came up for me.

I was taken over to the East Perth Girls' Home and Mr Neal from the settlement came to Perth and whisked me back to Mogumber.

I was a bit hurt about how it had turned out, but I didn't rebel. I just took it quietly. I went straight to the Big House to work, but I didn't end up staying for very long before I was sent to my next job.

But honestly speaking, I wish I'd never gone to the Neville's that first time when Maggie cleared off. I'd only known the two jobs, like Mrs Cashmore's and Mrs Larsen's, and then going to Mrs Neville's was too different. They were a different sort of people, you know. I think if I'd gone back to Wyalkatchem after being sick that time that I would have been happier. That's a real regret in my life, that I didn't get to go back, and ended up restless and sent from place to place.

Out of the Frypan

When I left Moore River I went to Leonora to work on a station called Ida Valley. I jumped out of the frypan and into the fire when I got there!

Mr and Mrs Male, who owned Ida Valley, had pearling luggers, and a big house in Mounts Bay Road, Perth. They were the Males of Streeter & Male, the big pearling company in Broome. Most probably they had white servants for their house in Perth and Aboriginal girls for up there.

Although they were pretty well off, it wasn't only rich people that had us working for them. See, we were cheap labour, you know — well, that's my impression. It's just like with the squatters of yesteryear, that's how they made their money — a stick of tobacco and a bag of flour to pay the Aborigines that did all the work for them.

Anyway, Miss Manford, one of the Male's friends, took me up to Leonora on the train. We left Perth at half past seven in the morning and we didn't get to Leonora until eleven o'clock at night. That's how slow those trains were; you could just about run along beside them picking flowers as you went.

Ida Valley looked something like Mallina Station, except it had brush fences around it to try and keep the wind and dust out. When I first got there they only had myself and Mary Stack. Mary was the cook in the kitchen, and I was in the laundry and the house at the same time. There was a white woman working there too. She was a cap'n'apron woman, and

137

I think she was earning close to twenty-five shillings a week. White servants were paid a lot more than us. She didn't stay there long after I arrived though, because her father was the carpenter working on a spare room, and when he finished they left.

After a short while Mrs Male decided to get another girl for the laundress, so Jess Parfitt was sent up. I'd met Jess before in Mogumber when she came for a couple of days between jobs. I knew Mary from there too. That made three of us girls working on Ida Valley, and I tell you what, we worked. We didn't sit around twiddling our thumbs all day, there was no time for that.

When Jess arrived she didn't want to work outside in the laundry, so Mrs Male said to me, 'Oh well, you'll have to go into the laundry.' So I went there, washing and cleaning, and waiting on the outside table for the working men.

Mrs Male was a quiet, docile old lady, and it was her daughters who were really the bosses. Especially Miss Dolly. But if there was anything to be said, Miss Dolly would take us to her mum to be told what was what.

Jess went into the house but for some reason they didn't like her. She was there for about a month when Mrs Male came out to me and said, 'Alice, you're coming back into the house.'

'Why?' I asked.

'Oh,' she said, 'Jess is not satisfactory.'

I won't be in Jess's good books now I thought, and I went up to the house again. This was a cap'n'apron job too. I used to make my own aprons out of white material and they looked like a nurse's apron, only more dainty and with lace. Those were my own property, but the cap and apron that belonged to Mrs Male belonged to the house.

The station house was a bungalow type, with a verandah running all the way around. The three of us shared a sleepout, just a bit of the verandah enclosed off. There were three beds in there and just enough room for a couple of cupboards. While I was there they built a bathroom for us which was way down the back, away from the house.

One day I was out stitching up the tennis net when I heard Jess talking about me. We had fallen out over me getting the job in the house. I heard her say, 'Huh, she got that job in the house, I'm not good enough. Well, I'll fix her.' I thought, Ooooh, and the adrenalin went all through me. It wasn't my fault about what had happened. I'd have much rather worked on my own because, with too many of us, you never knew when you were doing the right thing or what.

I walked into the kitchen and I said to Jess, 'If you want to talk about me, talk to me.'

She jumped. 'I wasn't talking about you,' she said.

'I've got ears girl,' I told her.

Mary the cook tried to stop anything from happening. 'Don't start any arguments in here', she said. We didn't, and Jess calmed down a bit after that.

I started waiting on the two tables, the inside one and the outside one. Jess was supposed to do hers, but she reckoned if she wasn't good enough to do the inside one, then she wasn't doing the outside one. I felt sorry for her but it wasn't my fault — it was all up to the mistress and what she wanted. Things didn't really get much better between Jess and I, and with all three of us having to share the same room it didn't help matters either.

After tea one night the three of us were in the kitchen washing up when Miss Dolly sang out, 'Could you come down to the dining room please Alice.' I thought, goodness me, what have I done? At night it was my job to clean the table down, then set it up ready for breakfast, and I thought I must have left something undone.

I went off down there and she came in and stood at the head of the table. 'I'm going into Leonora tomorrow, would you like to come with me?' she asked. She was going to do some shopping and she needed someone to come along and help out, so Mrs Male said to ask me.

'Oh I'd love that,' I said.

'All right, we're leaving at four o'clock in the morning. I'll give you a call,' she said.

I went back into the kitchen dancing around and singing, 'I'm going to Leonora in the morn-ing.' Jess looked around and said, 'You're what!'

I told them both what had happened, and Jess was really

cross that they hadn't asked her to go. Mary was probably a bit hurt too, but she was the cook, so she couldn't have gone. She said to Jess that there was no point growling about it, it was just a matter of who was asked.

I said to them, 'If you've got any money and you want anything I'll bring it home for you.' See, none of us had been paid yet. Mary had some money from when she came up from Perth, and Jess had a bit left from her last job, so out of that they gave me some for the things they wanted me to buy.

In the morning Miss Dolly woke me up, and I ran out the back to the bathroom and had a quick shower and got dressed. I was so pleased to be going out for the day because we never got days off there, and we were always so busy.

We headed off to Leonora in the car and stopped to have morning tea at Sturt Meadow Station. Then, when Miss Dolly had finished, we left there and got to Leonora at about eleven o'clock. We stayed there all that day, and that night we went and stayed at the White House Hotel.

The next morning we did a bit more shopping and I got the things for the girls; lollies and fruit and things like that. Miss Dolly gave me ten shillings to spend on myself and that could buy a bit in those days. Leonora was a lovely town, just a one-horse town, but very peaceful looking. I helped Miss Dolly carry her shopping around, and we left at about ten o'clock to get home by five.

That was the only time I had a day off because usually we just worked and worked. They used to have all these tennis tournaments. More tennis tournaments than anything. People would come from stations all around there, and the Bunning girls and Nellie Manford used to come up from Perth to have these big parties and play tennis.

They were a real high society crowd — they'd arrive about eleven o'clock in the morning to play tennis until three or four in the afternoon. They'd all be dressed to the nines with the men wearing striped sports jackets, nice pants and Bing Crosby hats — you know, those straw hats with the flat roof.

For these parties we'd set up big long tables out on the verandah with sandwiches, cakes and refreshments. Poor old Mary would be going flat out cooking for these parties, though

Miss Dolly and Miss Barbara would do a bit too.

It was my job to wait on the table, serving sandwiches and pouring cups of tea from long silver teapots. The table was loaded with the best china, silver cutlery, silver cream jugs and cake platters. Then after they'd finished playing and had something to eat, they'd retire into the drawing room for coffee in those tiny little cups. I knew how to handle all this because I'd done it at Mrs Neville's.

I remember one time, for one of these parties, Mr Lockett, the manager, wanted to get his sports jacket dry-cleaned. There wasn't anybody going into Leonora to take it in for him, and I don't know why I did these things, but I said to Miss Dolly, 'Oh I can do that for you if you want.' So I went off to the laundry and spent ages washing this thing properly. I hung it out to dry, took it in and ironed it, and made it look like it had just come out of the shop. When Miss Dolly saw it she was that thrilled she ran off with it to show her mum and dad. Mr Lockett came home and when he saw it he came down to thank me. He said to me, 'My jacket never goes to the dry-cleaner's again.' I stood there and I thought to myself, oh no, I've hung myself yet again. I just did that sort of thing too many times.

Thinking back, I'd say Beeginup and Ida Valley were the two places where I was the most flat out. It was really terrible. All of us — Jess, Mary and myself — were just worked and worked. I was supposed to get five shillings a week there but they never paid me. They never paid any of us.

We used to do our ordinary chores at the house, and then we had to go down and do the gardening. We'd have to do that gardening even though it was heavy man's work. And the dust there, it was terrible! They had flywire netting on the verandah right up to the roof. When a big wind used to come it was like sweeping up cocoa, and we'd be sweeping it up all through the day.

It wasn't as bad for the other two girls because they didn't work in the house. In the afternoons I'd only have about ten minutes to rush off and have a shower and then hurry back to prepare and serve afternoon tea. It was all too much.

Mary and I talked about how much we didn't like it. We'd

been there for four months, but you had to stay twelve months before you were allowed to leave. But I decided to make a dive for it, and Mary wanted to come too. We were pretty nervous about doing it but we were both that determined to go. When Jess found out we were going to run away she didn't want to come because she didn't want to walk. But when she saw us getting ready she said, 'Oooh, I'm not going to stop here by myself,' and she started to pack her bag.

We packed up our cases and hid them until we were ready to go. The toilet we used was a good two hundred yards away from the house, so we hid our cases there. I waited until it was time for me to go and serve afternoon tea, and then I said to them, 'Pack a few things for us to eat and drink along the way. While I'm serving, you girls take those things and go up to the toilet and wait for me.' So that was the plan, and we made our run for it.

On the first day we just walked and walked. We came to a mill where there was a corner paddock on one side. These two big bullocks, about fourteen hands high, chased us. Luckily they were on the other side of the fence, but they followed us for miles. My heart was in my throat — if they'd got through that fence they would have ripped us to pieces. Finally the road branched off and we left them behind.

We walked and walked until the sun set, and being so tired we laid down and had a sleep. We got up early the next morning, and walked and walked and walked again. At about seven o'clock in the morning we heard this droning noise.

I said, 'You girls, there's a motor car coming — can you hear it?' We all quickly ducked behind the bushes, and sure enough, it was the Ida Valley mob out looking for us. They passed us and went into Leonora to report us to the police.

When it was safe we headed off again and came to a mill. We stopped there and made a billy of tea and had some bread. Half a loaf of bread they'd got mind you! And a bit of tea and a tin of jam to sweeten it. That wasn't going to feed three people so we had to ration ourselves.

We were walking along and it was about half past three, or it could have been later as the sun was starting to sink. We came across this pool, and as it was hot, so very hot, we went

142

for a paddle. We splashed around and stood knee deep in this beautiful pool, and had a wash. The road was shaped like a snake, see, and we didn't notice a car driving up. So that car was right on us before we could do anything about it.

Mr Lockett was in the car, and with him was Nellie Manford, Dolly Male and one of the Bunning girls. I said to Jess and Mary, 'Let me do all the talking.' Those two were older than me but I said, 'Let me do all the talking and you just back me up. If Mr Lockett lays a hand on any of us, we'll deal with him.'

Mr Lockett started with, 'What's the big idea?' and 'What are you trying to prove?' Blah blah blah.

'Well,' I said. 'We are just slaves there and we want to go.'

'You're coming straight back with us, because we've been to town and seen the police, and rung Mr Neville. Mr Neville said you've got to come back because you haven't been there six months yet, and you can't leave until you've done your time. You've got to stay twelve months before you can even think of going anywhere else.'

'Well, Mr Neville's got another thing coming,' I came out with, and these two girls just looked at me. I looked back at them and said, 'Do you want to go back to Ida Valley?'

'No,' Jess said.

'What about you Mary?'

'No,' she said.

Then Mr Lockett said, 'Well, how are you going to get to Leonora?'

'We're walking now aren't we? We'll get there,' I said.

'Get into the car!' He was trying to be rough.

I was looking around for a stick, and he saw me looking.

'Right,' he said, 'perish if you want to perish. But you won't get far because the police are on to you.'

'That's all right,' I said. 'We'll go to jail — we are in jail here so we might as well go to jail over there!' and off we all went walking again.

After a while we came to this well, so we got a drink of water and had a wash to freshen ourselves up. We decided we couldn't carry our cases any further, because they were so heavy that our hands were starting to swell up. I had a bedspread with me, so I put all that I wanted in there, and stuck the bundle under my arm. The girls picked out all their little bits and pieces that they wanted and off we set again.

As we walked it started to thunder and there was lightning all around us. Ooooh, you've never seen anything like it! We didn't want to stop, we wanted to keep on walking because we had no tucker left. So we kept on walking and the lightning was lighting up the ground around us.

We came to this clear patch in the land and Jess said, 'I can't walk any longer.'

'All right,' we agreed, 'we'll sleep here.' We lit a fire and cleared all the stones away to make a bit of a bed. I had the bible with me and we all had to read a chapter. Mary was a Catholic and she said her prayers on her rosary.

When it came time for us to get some sleep we had to talk about who was going to get in the middle. To avoid a fight about it we let Jess, with Mary and I on the sides. Then we put the fire out because we could hear Aborigines a long way off and we were afraid. See, these were tribal people, and we didn't know what they'd do if they found us in their country. Anyway, once the fire was out, we went to sleep.

We woke up early again the next morning, and I said, 'Come on, we'd better move. There's a mill not far from here and we can get a drink of water.' I knew that from when I'd been to town with Miss Dolly that time.

At about ten o'clock that morning we were going through a swamp when we could hear chains going: click, click, click, click. It was the sound of the station owners going mustering you see, and of course their dogs spotted us. They came towards us and we ran for our lives.

We ducked for cover behind a group of tea-trees when we heard this voice, 'Come on girls, come out of there. We know you're in there, and if you don't come out, we'll send the dogs in for you.'

So we surrendered and we walked out like little lambs.

They had with them a big baked leg of mutton, a loaf of bread and some tea and sugar. The cook had sent it with these boys for us. The Ida Valley mob must have warned them we were heading that way.

Anyway, we talked to these boys, and they were joking

144

around with us. They said, 'We're going into Leonora next week, so now we've brought you all this food, you've got to come to the pictures with us.'

'Yeah, yeah, yeah,' we said, but we never ever saw them again.

The mill was only about a hundred yards away, so they said for us to go and boil a billy and have a feed. They told us to head for the station house because Marie, the housekeeper, was waiting for us. So we went and had a feed, and when we felt satisfied we headed for the station which was about three miles away.

As we were making our way with our bundles slung over our backs the girls shouted, 'The bullocks, the bullocks are coming.' We were about half a mile from the station and they were running towards us. This was Sturt Meadow Station I mentioned earlier, and it was called that because of all the sturt peas growing out in the paddocks. Yards and yards of it, trailing this way and that, really beautiful it was.

I looked down at these flowers and I said, 'Look, get them, pull them up by the roots, and we'll all go straight towards the bullocks and shout and shout and wave our arms.'

'They'll bloomin' well kill us!' they said.

'No,' I said, 'we've got to do something, or they WILL kill us.'

I tied my bedspread tightly to my back and I ran and pulled up two plants with really long runners. The girls did the same, and with me in the front and those two behind, we ran, waving our arms and shouting. Well, those bullocks just took one look at us and they stampeded off the other way. Quickly we headed straight for the fence and we ducked through.

We made our way up to the main house, and the yardman told us that Marie was waiting for us inside. So we went up there and had a nice cuppa. Then she sent us down to the quarters where she'd made up beds for us, and we had a shower. We put on clean clothes and took what we had on and washed them out and hung them on the line to dry.

We were all so flagged, we had a sleep until the yardman woke us up at about six o'clock. He brought all our clothing down, all folded up, and we went up to the house.

While we were up there having tea, a policeman came. He told us that Mr Neville had said we should go back to the station, and we should never have run away because it was dangerous.

So we told the policeman how we were treated and that, and he said, 'Well, I can't force you, so you'll have to come into Leonora.' Then he asked, 'What do you plan to do?'

'We'll get a job,' I said.

We went off and thanked Marie, got our things and went to the car. 'You sit in the front,' the girls said. So they got in the back and I climbed in the front.

Just as we were taking off the policeman turned the car around towards the direction of Ida Valley.

'Where are you going?' I cried.

'I'm taking you back to Ida Valley,' he said.

I just swung the door open and I was about to jump out, when he grabbed me by the arm and held me there. 'I didn't think you were that serious,' he said. 'Get in here, I'll take you to Leonora.' So off we went.

When we got to Leonora he took us down to the Bonny's place. They were Aboriginal people, and we stayed there with them. The policeman had said to us to come up in the morning and get some rations. We did that, and then we started looking for work.

The two girls both got jobs, Mary got one at the boarding house for Mrs Brennan, and Jess worked for the Hatfields down at the dairy. It was only me left to get a job so I asked Rosie, the lady we were staying with, if she knew of anything. She was working over at the White House Hotel where she was a jack-of-all-trades. They needed a pantry maid, and although I wasn't yet twenty, Mrs Blair said it would be quite all right. So I went up there and worked for her for ten shillings a week.

While I was at Leonora I wrote a letter to Mrs Cashmore. I had written to her from Ida Valley and we'd straightened things out between us. She wrote back and told me she was having another baby and she wanted me to come back home to help her.

Mary had itchy feet and wanted to leave Leonora. Her and I had always got on well together, so I told her I'd travel back to Perth with her. I sent off a letter to Mrs Cashmore and told her I was coming back to Perth, and if she wanted me she'd have to get in touch with Mr Neville. The other girl, Jess, ended up staying in Leonora and that's where she met her husband.

When we got back to Perth I went up to see Mr Neville and told him that Mrs Cashmore wanted me back. So he just wrote me out a train pass to Wyalkatchem.

Getting back to the farm felt good. I had lots of fond memories for the times I'd worked there. The Cashmore kids and I had a lot of fun together, because when I first went there I was really only a kid myself. I can remember little John wouldn't go to sleep unless he went to sleep in my bed. He used to call me Kay, because he couldn't say Alice. He'd say to his mother, 'Mummy, me go Kay fur.' See, I had a big fur collar on my winter coat, and he used to get the fur, rub it on his face, and he'd put himself to sleep. He was only a little fella then, about a year old, and we used to call him Bing. He had this toy wagon he'd pull along when I went to collect the eggs. He'd go and get that wagon and say, 'Me go egg-egg with Kay.'

Anyway, as it turned out I was only at Mrs Cashmore's for a couple of months when I got a letter from Mr Neville to say Will was at Moore River and we were to get married. He said there was a job going out at Meekatharra for a married couple and that they wanted Will. So I said to Mrs Cashmore, 'I'm off to get married.'

Getting married wasn't that easy in those days. I think housemaids were very scarce and they didn't want us to get married out, because they never had enough working girls. There were lots of girls in service but just as many people wanting them.

And if I had wanted to marry white, well, that was a no no. They wanted to keep all Aborigines together and let them die out. That was their plan. If we inter-married we would still be going on you see but they wanted to brush us all out. I heard that too, you know, just through white people talking, saying they wanted a white Australia.

So, in Febuary of 1932, I travelled back to the settlement. Will was living down at the camps with his relatives, and I stayed up in the compound dormitory. Aunty Jean and Uncle Jack were living in the camps again so I used to go down and see them. Sometimes we'd go up the river for a picnic and Will would come along too.

The place had really changed, it was horrible, even more run down than it had been when I was a kid. The atmosphere about the place was awful too. Girls were still coming in, and being sent out. In my time I reckon there would have been hundreds, easy, of girls sent out to work. The whole place was crowded with strangers, and if Aunty Jean hadn't been there I think I would have gone mad.

It was strange too, strange to think back to Doris, Herbert and I all coming down on that boat and ending up there. Doris and I had kept in touch over the years, but the last time I saw Herbert was when I left Moore River, and went out to Mrs Larsen. Doris went out to work not long after me, and in later years she came back to the settlement and got married. But Herbert, he was the luckiest of us all. After Moore River he was allowed to go back to Roebourne, and he got to go straight back home. He got a job as a lumper, unloading and loading up the boats, then he got married up there and had a family.

They put me to work in the sewing room again, so there's something that hadn't changed. Also the food was still putrid. I hardly ate the whole time I was there. I was ten stone when I got there and around seven stone when I was married.

It was nearly three months after I arrived that Will and I finally got married. We got along all right, but we didn't really know each other that well because we'd never got the chance. In one way I got married to get away from the government, and I think a lot of women did that.

We were married in the church at the settlement. It was a double wedding, with Will and I, and Dorothy and her husband. I was nearly twenty years old, and I wore a beautiful wedding dress from Russia.

This dress belonged to Mrs Sesskas who was working with her husband on the farm at Wyalkatchem. When she heard I was getting married she gave me this dress. She said, 'I got married in this dress Alice, now you get married in it.'

It was really beautiful, it was voile and lace. I kept it and

*Alice's wedding, Moore River, 1932, Alice and her husband
Will Nannup are on the priest's left.*

later dyed it green when I was short of a dress. Will didn't have
any good clothes to get married in, so I wrote to the department to ask for my money in the trust account, and had the
whole outfit sent up for him. They used to have veils there for
the weddings that the girls made in the sewing room, and if
you didn't have a ring Matron might lend you hers.

We were married by the Reverend Webb from Midland, and
the church was full of people. Everyone came, from the camp,
the compound, and the superintendent and matron.

Dorothy met her husband Frank outside of the settlement,
when they both worked on the same station. However the rules
were that none of us girls were allowed to get married outside,
so if Frank wanted to marry her, he had to come into
Mogumber.

Frank had an Aboriginal mother, and his father was related
to old Mr Latham, the member of parliament. Because he
wasn't brought up with Aborigines, they treated him differently
when he came to the settlement. He didn't stay down at the

camps where the other blokes had to go, he stayed up at the Big House with the superintendent.

After the ceremony, we had a lovely wedding breakfast up at the Big House that the matron put on for us. That wasn't usual though, and I think it must have been because of Frank.

When the breakfast was finished, Dorothy and Frank left to start their new life together, and we went to stay at the camps until the job in Meekatharra came up. And I tell you what, when the time came, Will and I gladly left that place behind.

PART THREE

ALICE NANNUP, Ngangka

1933–1965

The Three Pebbles

When we left the settlement we travelled to Yarlarweelor Station in Meekatharra. Will worked out in the yards and I worked up at the station house cooking and doing housework. We were supposed to get thirty shillings a week pay between us; ten shillings for me, and twenty for Will. We were told by the department that we had to stay for twelve months, but when the station owner and Will had a falling out we had to move on and were never paid our wages.

From Yarlarweelor we moved on to Mount Seabrook Station, and again Will worked outside while I worked up at the house. But we weren't there for very long before we moved to an outcamp on the station. It was called White Well, and Will was looking after the flock out there.

I started up a lovely garden while we were at that place. I had flowers on one side of the mill, and vegetables on the other side. I grew everything; apple cucumbers, long cucumbers, radishes, tomatoes and iron-bark pumpkins. We used to have a water trough out the back that I used to clean everyday to make sure there'd be clean water for the animals. So to water my garden I made all these little lanes in the sand leading down from the trough. Then, when I pulled the plug, everything would get a good watering.

While we were living out there I had my first baby. In the middle of Febuary the manager, Mr Campbell, came out and brought some food. He said, 'This is for Will. You're not having any of this food Alice, you're coming back with me. We don't want you to have the baby out here, we'll take you into Meekatharra a good fortnight before.'

So I packed up a few things and took off with Mr Campbell. Will wasn't too happy about me going — he thought there was still plenty of time — but Mr Campbell just said I was going.

On the following weekend Miss Arnott, who was Mrs Campbell's sister, and Marjie Campbell, who was the boss's daughter, and myself, all took off in a Chev ute. It had been raining and we travelled along with Marjie driving, Miss Arnott in the middle, and me near the door.

Anyway, we got to this slippery part of the road and, being wet, the ute got out of control. I remember that very clearly. Marjie couldn't hold it and we sort of spun straight around and were facing back to Mount Seabrook. We all got such a fright. Marjie got out and checked everything was okay with the ute, and Miss Arnott was saying, 'We better go back and get Mick to drive us in.' But Marjie was going, 'Oh no, we'll be all right Aunty.'

So she got back in the ute and started it up, and we slid around for a while getting back on to the road. When she hit the road she took off again, and every time she'd put her foot down Miss Arnott would say, 'Please Marjory...we'll go for another spin and we might roll over.' But Marjie reckoned we were all right, and that was how I got into Meekatharra.

I knew nobody in Meeka, so they took me to a boarding house in town. This was a boarding house for railway workers, and it was run by Mrs Williams and her daughter Annie. Miss Arnott and Miss Campbell went and saw Mrs Williams and she said she had a room, so they left me there to wait to have the baby.

Well I was a boarder there, the boss was paying for my board, but I wasn't treated like a paying boarder. I had a little room and I just sat in there all day with nothing to do, and no one to talk to. At meal times I ate in the kitchen while all the other boarders were served in the dining room. It wasn't that I wanted to eat with them, because they were all men, but I should have had the same treatment as the other boarders. I thought Annie and Mrs Williams would sit and eat with me, but as soon as the men were finished they'd go and have their meal in the dining room, and never invite me.

Then, when I was in my room, Mrs Williams started to call out to me and say, 'Could you come and peel some potatoes?' or, 'Could you wash these dishes?' and anything else that needed doing. She'd put a meal on and she'd say, 'Would you like to just keep an eye on this while Annie and I go down the street?' Well, that wasn't my job! But I'd say I would because I didn't have anywhere else to go.

I'd been there for about a week I suppose when I decided I'd go out for a walk down the street to Garrick's. I wanted to buy a couple of little pieces of material so I could sit down and make something for the baby. While I was in town I went into another shop and I met an Aboriginal lady named Mrs Ingram. She saw me there, walking around, and she came and introduced herself. She asked me where I was staying and I told her I was up at the boarding house. I asked her where she lived and she said, 'Behind the hotel, just near the creek.' Anyway, we talked for a bit longer and as we were parting she said, 'Come back tomorrow Alice, and we'll talk some more.'

I went back to the boarding house feeling very pleased I'd met her, because she was a lovely person. As soon as I got back Mrs Williams started up, wanting me to do this and wanting me to do that. I was getting cross about all this, because I wasn't getting paid for all this work and the boss was paying them to have me there. Aside from that, they wouldn't talk to me other than asking me to peel vegetables or do some other work. I mean, if they wanted to befriend me they could have come and got me and asked me down to the kitchen to have a cuppa with them or something.

The next day I went and met up with Mrs Ingram and she asked me if I was happy staying at the boarding house.

'No,' I said, 'they don't talk to me, unless they want me to do something for them.' I told her how my board was being paid but I had to do work for them.

'Well,' she said, 'if you're not happy there you can come and stay with us.'

I jumped at this invitation, and I went back and told Mrs Williams I was off.

'But you can't,' she said. 'You can't go without letting the Campbells know.'

'I don't have to let them know,' I said, 'and I'd rather go and stay with these people because it's a bit lonely here.' So I got my things together and moved down to stay with the Ingrams.

Mrs Ingram had two daughters, and I shared a room with them. Not long after I moved in there was a big electrical storm. I got so upset with all the thunder and lightning that I went into labour. One of the men from where I was staying went out to try and get a taxi. But what had happened with the storm was the creek had flooded and I couldn't get across.

It was a very frightening experience for me having that first baby, and I wouldn't wish it on anyone. Luckily Mrs Ingram was experienced at delivering babies and she helped me through it. I had a little boy who we named Ronald George; Ronald after a relative of Will's, and George after Uncle George Ring. Then, the next day, as soon as the water went down, the doctor came across to see me.

I had milk fever and was very sick, so I ended up in hospital. This was Meekatharra Hospital and it was very different for Aboriginal women in those days. We weren't allowed in the main ward where all the other women would be, we had to be kept separate in a little place that was just like a meat-house. It was very small and hot, and because my baby wouldn't drink, they used to express the milk from me and give it to him on a spoon. I had little Ron in the room with me but they'd take him away to feed him.

Will was out on the station and I didn't have any visitors or anything. The nurse came over a few times during the day, and that's the only person I ever saw. It was just me and my baby in this little meat-house, and I used to bawl all the time. After about six days it was time for me to leave, so Will came and got us and took us back to the outcamp at Mount Seabrook.

We stayed at the outcamp until shearing time, then we went back to the main station to work. Then, when Ron was about five months old, we moved in to Meekatharra. Will got a job working for the butcher, tailing cattle, and taking them to the slaughter yard, and I got a job in a cafe. One day I had been walking along the street when I saw on the door of a cafe that they needed some assistance. I applied for the job and got it. I worked out the back in the kitchen and laundry, and I'd go there everyday and take Ron with me. I really enjoyed this job, and Ron was such a good little baby, he'd just sit up in the laundry and watch while I worked.

One afternoon Will came home from work and said to me, 'Your Uncle Lou Bassett's up at the sale yard.' I was that surprised. 'Really?' I said. 'What's he doing here?'

'He's brought some cattle down to sell and he wants to see you.' Lou and Will had got talking and Will told him he was married to Alice Bassett from Roebourne.

'Does he want to see me in town or do I have to go up to the sale yard?'

'No, he said he'll meet you in town,' Will said.

I was that excited to see him. We met in town and he asked me to have lunch with him. I had little Ron with me and Uncle Lou thought he was just great.

During lunch we talked about home and I asked him for news about my family. He said he hadn't seen my father for a while, but as far as he knew they were all doing well. He told me a few stories about what had been happening around the place. I was so relieved to hear everyone was well, because I was always thinking about them and wondering how they all were.

When it was time for Uncle Lou to go he said he wanted to buy me something, so I asked him if he'd buy me some material. I didn't want him spending a lot of money on me, just some material to make Ron some new rompers and a few things suited me fine. So we went off to the store and I chose what I wanted, then we said our goodbyes and he went back to where he was staying.

It wouldn't have been long after I'd seen Uncle Lou that a strange thing happened. One night I was sitting up feeding Ron, when a pebble came in under the tent door. Will saw me staring at it and he said, 'What are you looking at?'

'I don't know for sure, it's a sign.'

'What sort of a sign?' he asked, because he didn't believe in signs.

'A little stone just rolled in,' I told him.

Only a few seconds later another little stone rolled in. 'Did you see that one?' I asked.

'Nuh, you're imagining things,' he said.

'Well, just keep your eyes open,' I told him. 'Might be another one coming.'

Then, sure enough, a third one rolled in. 'You saw that one didn't you?' I said.

'Yes, and I'm going out there to see who's hanging around.' Will ran outside, and he shouted and carried on for whoever was out there playing tricks to show themselves. But no one was out there, see.

I said to him when he came back inside, 'No, Will, it's a sign.' I didn't know what it meant, or who it was from, but I knew it was meant for me.

We left Meekatharra soon after this, because the butcher Will was working for wanted a couple up at Wiluna. We had a camp way out in the bush, about nine miles out, at a place called Cockyarra Creek. I didn't really like living there much, and at one time we moved even further out in the bush.

While we were out there, once a fortnight I used to come into town with Will and some friends. While they went off together, I'd take Ron and we'd go to the pictures. I was walking down the street one afternoon when I saw this lady across the road. I was really looking at her, because she looked like an old friend of my father's, a German lady, Mrs Buggenthia. Anyway she stared at me too, then came rushing across the street and threw her arms around me.

'I've been looking for you,' she said.

'Why?' I said. 'What's the matter?'

'I've got news for you, but I can't tell you here. Come with me.' Mrs Buggenthia took me into a cafe and we sat down. She took Ron off me and hugged him a bit, then she ordered two cups of tea. 'Not good message, not good news,' she said.

I looked at her and waited for her to go on. 'Your sister Ella, and the baby...finished. Your mother so broken hearted she throw herself around and kill herself. And then your father, foul-play. Somebody come there and find your father dead.'

After a bit more talking I found out what had happened. Mr

Ben Hewitt had been in contact with Mrs Buggenthia and asked her to try and find me to give me this terrible news. Ella had been having her first baby and she had a very cruel husband. He kicked her in the tummy and burst her bladder killing both her and the little baby she was carrying. When my mother found out she was so heart broken with grief, she had thrown herself around and around, damaging herself until she died.

Then someone had been sent to tell my father about what had happened and found him laying dead in his little shack. From what I've been able to piece together, Tommy had gone back to Roebourne to live after he'd come down to Perth that time and been barred from seeing me.

When Mrs Buggenthia told me all of this it hit me like a ton of bricks. I didn't know how everyone was going, but I never dreamt of anything like this. It hadn't been long since I'd seen Uncle Lou and he'd told me everyone was doing fine back home, so I suppose he hadn't got the news yet himself. I just sat there, not knowing what to do. It was such a shock, I was in a complete daze.

After a while Mrs Buggenthia asked me what I was going to do. 'I'm going back home,' I said, and I picked up Ron and walked outside. This was the saddest day of my life, but I was too shocked to even cry.

A chap walked past me in the street and I heard myself ask him if he'd go and find my husband. He must have done that because Will came to me and said, 'What's wrong?'

'I want to go home,' I said.

'But we've only just come in!' Will said.

'Yes I know, but I want to go home because I just got very bad news. My sister, my mother and my father, are all dead.'

I suppose it spoilt the evening for the other chaps who'd come in with us, but I didn't know what else I could do, where else I could go. Anyway, Will was agreeable, so we bought a few stores and headed back to our camp. All the way home my heart was heavy with grief, and all I could think about was the three pebbles that had been sent to warn me.

To Geraldton

We decided to leave Wiluna in January of 1934, and travel down to Mullewa where we heard the Ingrams were. But when we got there and asked around to different people, they said that Paddy and his family had all gone to Geraldton.

When we'd caught the train from Mogumber to go out to Meekatharra we'd passed through Geraldton. It was a lovely looking little town on the coast. My husband had run right out onto the jetty and back and we'd walked around taking a look at the place.

Will's Uncle George and Aunty Minnie were living there, but we didn't have any time to try and catch up with them. We both said to each other that we liked it, and if we ever needed somewhere to live we'd come back. So when we found out the Ingrams were there I said to Will, 'Come on then, let's go to Geraldton.'

When we arrived in town we caught a taxi out to Will's uncle and aunty's place. They had a house up on the hill in Quarry Street, and we went and stayed with them for a couple of weeks. Then, after we got some money together, we set up a place of our own down the bottom end of the street near the Ingrams.

Quarry Street was at the back of town and there were both Aboriginal and white families living there. Most of the white people in the town pretty much kept their distance from Aborigines. In Quarry Street the two didn't mix much, but there where some very nice white families living there who were friendly. So I suppose it's just the same as it is today — you get the good and the bad everywhere.

There were only a small mob of Aboriginal people in Geraldton then, and nearly all of us lived in Quarry Street. In the street lived the Whitbys, the Rings, the Bairds, the Underwoods, the Dodds, the Camerons and us. Uncle George Ring and old Mr Ingram used to work on the Main Roads. During the Depression time it was hard going for them because they had to work six weeks on and then six weeks off. Ernie Underwood and old Mr Baird were drovers and they'd go away from time to time leaving their wives at home. The rest used to work around the place wherever they could, chopping wood, picking peas, farm work, or else on the tomato gardens.

Will was working on the tomatoes and we settled in for a while. It was summertime and in the evenings Will and I used to go down and sit on the esplanade. In years to come we used to go down there often, take all our kids with us, and sit out on the lawn cooling off by the water.

But getting back to when we first got to Geraldton, we were down there one Saturday night and a dance was being held in the hall. I could hear the music, and there was this beautiful dance that I always liked called the Canadian Barn Dance. Anyway I heard the music start up for this so I said to Will that I was going off to watch it.

Because this was a dance for white people only I wasn't allowed into the hall, so I just stayed out on the ramp and looked in. I stood there watching everyone dancing around enjoying themselves and my feet were just itching to get on that floor.

After this particular dance was over the MC came out to me and said, 'Can I help you?'

'Oh no, I'm just watching the dancing,' I said.

'Well, now that it's finished,' he said, 'I want you to leave, because you're not allowed to be here you know.'

I felt very hurt — I'd been quiet so as not to disturb anyone. 'But I'm only just watching, I'm not doing any harm,' I said.

'Yes I know that, but still, you're not allowed.'

I went back to my husband and I felt it was really wrong.

When I told Will he said I should have known that would happen. But goodness me, I thought, it's supposed to be a free country.

These dances that were held — it wasn't that they had signs nailed up on the door saying No Aborigines, but you just knew you weren't welcome to be there. Besides, if they had alcohol there then that cancelled us out because we weren't allowed to be on a licensed premises, or anywhere where alcohol was being served.

After we'd been living at Quarry Street for a while, Will got a job out at Bellvedere working for Mr Rowan. Bellvedere was only a couple of miles out of Geraldton and we moved into an old farmhouse on the property. It was a big beautiful old place but it had been left to ruin. There was a long kitchen we could use, and room for sleeping, but all the rest was full of chaff so we had to share the house with the rats.

Will's main job was fumigating for rabbits and looking after this big bull on Mr Rowan's farm. This bull was a docile old fella really, but Will reckoned he always kept one eye on him when he groomed him just in case. One day the bull did charge after him, he must of been having one of those off days, but Will was ready for him and got out of the way.

We ended up staying here for a fair while, and every weekend we used to walk two and a half miles into Geraldton and back to have lunch with the Ingrams.

My little bloke started walking while we were out there and I used to be run off my feet trying to keep up with him. Then when I was pregnant with Margaret we moved back to Quarry Street into our old camp, and Will and Jack both got jobs on the tomato gardens again. When the season was finished there was still work pulling up the stakes and ploughing and planting for the next year.

In August my daughter Margaret was born and old Sister Jones, the midwife, came out to tend to me. In those days Aboriginal women never went to hospital, we all had our babies at home. The majority of white women did too.

When you knew you were pregnant you'd contact the midwife and make all the arrangements with her. Then when I

161

went into labour someone would go and get her for me. The nurse would come, and Will would either give the kids to somebody to look after, or have them with him. They'd all clear out, and they'd go about a hundred yards or more away and make a big fire. Lots of people would get together down there and wait until the baby was born. Some of my labours were really terrible, and they'd go on for ages, but some weren't too bad. Then when everything was over and Nurse was ready to go, she'd go down and tell Will to come back home.

For a little while after having the baby I'd get some help until I was back on my feet. When we were living close by, Mrs Ingram used to do all the washing for me, feed the kids and give a hand with the baby. She was a lovely person, and very special to me, because she brought my son Ron into the world. Then later, when I had a couple of older girls myself, they used to pitch in and help look after the younger ones while I tended the baby.

Cathy Clarkson, Muriel Major and Madge Pass were these three girls who used to come and visit and take Ron out for the afternoon to give me a break. Those girls used to just love him, and they'd take it in turns to have him at each other's home. Today the younger Clarkson kids are still friends with the younger generation of my family.

Anyway, Muriel had a sister Florrie, and when I was expecting Margaret she sent word, 'If Alice needs to do any sewing for the baby tell her I've got a machine and she's welcome to use it.' So I used to go up there and spend hours at Flo's making baby clothes and rompers for Ron.

I always made my kids' clothes. I'd go to the Salvation Army and get these second-hand clothes for the material. Then I'd take them home, pull them to bits, wash them up, and cut them out to make pants for my boy or dresses for my little girl.

When Margaret was about six months old, my husband and Jack Ingram got a woodcutting job with two other men out at Oakajee, just the other side of White Peak. They were cutting posts and wood for fencing and we stayed there for about five months before moving on to Northern Gully.

At Northern Gully a bloke named Martin had a contract chopping wood for the condenser. He was a foreign chap and he had a team of men both white and foreign under him. Will and Jack both got jobs with him, and the deal was they'd chop the wood and this chap would come and collect it and pay them depending on how much they'd cut. There was a workers' camp set up there, but Jack, Will, me and the kids had to keep separate from the other workers.

Well, this was all going okay — Jack and Will were working hard and this chap used to come to pick up the wood and bring us some stores. Then one day he came and took the first load, came back for the second, but never showed up for the third.

By this time two of Martin's team had left, and only Mick Rooney, the Irishman, was still at the camp. After a few days of waiting for Martin to show he sang out to Will one morning, 'What's wrong with that bloke? He hasn't been back.'

Will called back to him, 'Yeah, I'm wondering about the same thing. Wonder if he's broken down?'

Anyway, they just decided to keep on working and give it a bit longer to see if he turned up.

This Martin hadn't paid us yet and our food was getting low. But there wasn't much we could do about it, so we just had to put up with what little tucker we had left. Then one day we ran out — no flour, no tea, no sugar. I was very worried about feeding the kids so I said to Will, 'What about going up to that farm nearby and see if the lady of the house will barter some food for this honey?'

See, where we were there were quite a few hives around. My husband was great on cutting beehives and I'd saved lots of tins and jars to put it all in. I always used to keep the mesh bag from the bacon and I'd wash and boil it up so I could use it to strain the honey. So I got together a galvanised bucket full of this lovely honey, with combs and all, and gave it to Will to take up.

Will went up to the farmhouse and spoke to the farmer and his wife. 'The boss hasn't been back for nearly a week now, and we've run out of food,' he said.

'Yes,' the farmer said, 'I noticed he hadn't been coming because we used to hear the truck grinding over the creek, and I was wondering what was going on. I think we can help you out.'

163

Will handed over the bucket, and when the lady opened it up and saw all this beautiful fresh honey and all the clean white combs she was really thrilled. It was a bit of a shame we were taking them their own honey, like honey collected from the trees on their farm, but we had to do something.

I was waiting at the camp and Will came back with some tea, sugar, porridge, flour, eggs, butter and even a forequarter of mutton and some vegetables. We thought we were made. I said to Will, 'Fancy us giving them their own honey,' but it was handy for them too because they didn't know how to rob a beehive.

The farmer had asked Will how long we'd be there and if we would go and rob another hive for them because they wanted all the honey they could get. Will told him we'd only just been looking at a tree the other day and soon as we got a chance we'd bring him some more.

So Jack and Will went back to work and a couple of days later this farmer came up on a horse. He had a white calico bag with him and in it were scones and cakes for the kids. I thanked him and took some cakes up to Will and Jack. I used to take them morning and afternoon tea and, if I could, I'd make jam tarts or something.

Well, when I took these up Will was laughing to kill himself. He said, 'Gee, this is a treat.'

I said to Will, 'Well, this is all good and fine, but we can't go on living like this. We'll have to do something.'

So Mick Rooney came over to us and said he was going to walk up the road, get a ride into Geraldton, and see what was going on. 'I might be a couple of days,' he said, 'but don't worry, I'll be back.'

About two days later he showed up and he had another chap, Mick Ahearn, with him. Mick used to help Martin cart the wood in and he told us Martin had taken all the money and shot through back to his own country. I couldn't believe it at first, that a bloke would do such a thing, leave us and the kids stranded out in the bush with no food or money. But that's what he'd done all right.

Anyway, we had quite a load of wood, and the condenser was getting short, so Mick Ahearn took over the contract and started carting it all in.

Then one day I said to Will, 'Well, we better go and get this honey.' So after they'd knocked off work for the day we went to where this tree was. I knew this tree was really loaded because I used to go and listen, and I could hear the humming of the bees fanning the honey with their wings to keep the hive cool.

We got a fire going and I made the kids wait a good few yards away, with the wind blowing in the direction that the bees couldn't smell them. Will started to chop the tree halfway and as it split the beehive just flopped open. Poor Mick Rooney was coming towards it and the bees started to chase him. You should have seen him go. He pulled his coat up over his head and he ran and hid in the trees.

Meanwhile Jack, Will and I were putting all the honey into this big galvanised tub we had, and then we carried it home. I'd saved these big three-pound coffee jars and we filled them all up and put honeycombs in too. We had a kerosene tin that I'd cleaned out and used to cart water, and we filled that up full to the top. Later Will took it up to the farmer and he was very happy with it.

The next day came and all the wood had been carted, so we borrowed a horse and cart from the farmer to take all our things up to the railway siding. Will left me and the kids there while he took the cart back, and at about five or six o'clock in the evening the train came from Mullewa. Mick paid us our money and we put all our things on the train and went back to Geraldton.

We moved back to our old camp in Quarry Street and I was expecting another baby. This camp we were in was like a tent, and it wasn't very waterproof or comfortable for us.

It wasn't very long after we moved back that Taff Evans said to Will, 'If you like, you can live in my place while I go away because it's going to be empty.' Taff was a wharfie and he had a nice place up the top of Quarry street opposite Aunty Minnie and Uncle George. He was going down to Fremantle to work for a while so we leapt at the chance to live in his place, and this was where Gloria was born. My husband was one for film stars and he wanted her named Gloria, after Gloria Swanson, so she was called Gloria Dawn because she was born at daybreak.

While we were living at Taff's a couple of tramps moved into our old place. We didn't mind because they needed somewhere to stay. Quarry Street is by the sea and one day these chaps went down to the beach and they found all these canvas tarpaulins. They were off the railway trucks. When the railways had finished with them they used to dig big holes by the edge of the shore and bury them. Well, when these blokes saw all these black tarpaulins, they thought they'd do just nicely to make the camp more comfortable and they dragged them home.

After Taff came back from Fremantle, we moved down to our old place. This was only a two-room place but these blokes had built it up a bit more with this tarp and sheets of iron along the bottom to keep the wind out.

One day, not long after we'd moved back, the police came along and we were nearly put in gaol over this. They said the tarps were government property and we'd gone out and pinched them. We had such a terrible lot of talking to do to get ourselves out of it. I told them it was our camp in the first place but we were given a house to live in when this gentleman went to Perth. I explained to them that, while we lived there, two white blokes moved in and they'd come by the canvas. Eventually, after a lot of explaining, they took some notice of me and did nothing more about it.

I had my next baby when we were living there, a little girl I named Pearl June. When she was born I didn't have a name picked out and I was wondering what to call her. I'd just had her that morning and I was in bed when this big lady came around looking for her brother. She'd come from Shark Bay and didn't know where he was living. Anyway, she had her daughter with her and her name was Pearl. When I heard that name I thought it was really lovely, so I named my own daughter after her, and June as a middle name because she was born on the eighteenth of June.

It was when Pearl was only little that I saw Mr Neville for the last time. I was at home with my four children and the three little girls were laying down having a sleep. Only Ron was awake, and he was running around amusing himself when I heard voices outside.

I walked out the door and I slammed bang into Mr Neville!

'Alice!' he said.

'Sir!' I said.

He looked at me and went, 'What are you doing here, tutt tutt tutt.' He was really shocked and I felt so ashamed I couldn't talk. 'Do you live here?' he asked, and I suppose he thought, cap'n'apron girl living in the slums. All I could do was just nod my head.

'Well,' he said, 'how many children have you got?'

'Four,' I said, and little Ron came running out the door.

'Who's this little fellow?' he asked.

'He's my son, Ron,' I said.

Mr Neville got hold of him and shook his hand. 'What a beautiful child,' he said, 'and hazel eyes! hazel eyes!' He kept on saying that about his eyes. 'And this is where you live,' he said, and he went and stuck his head in the door, then just walked away.

I was left speechless. He was the last man I wanted to see. I felt terrible, but I wasn't living there because I wanted to — we had four kids, and steady work wasn't easy to get. Even if you had the money you couldn't just go and find a place to rent — white people had first option there. If you were an Aboriginal family you had to get someone to recommend you for a place to rent.

Anyway, Mr Neville was in town to tell us about the reserve they were building. I think he must have got word from the police to move us all on. I'm just surmising this, but I think it was because the council wanted to build a new suburb there, and all these Aboriginal people were starting to build around the place. Geraldton was only a small town in those days, only around four thousand people, but it was expanding.

Mr Neville was up in town to tell us he was going to build this reserve for us and there'd be housing on it. A lot of people were against the idea; when it was finished and the Sergeant came out and told us to move at a certain time, we didn't take any notice of him. See, a lot of people didn't class themselves as Aborigines and they didn't want to get pushed onto a reserve.

Well, we just went on living where we were, and on Ron's seventh birthday the airport was opened up. Major Brearley was in town for it and my husband wanted to go out and see the flying stunt. So for a treat he wanted to take Ron with him, but when Margaret found out she wanted to go too.

Will had a pushbike for getting around on and he couldn't take them both on it. One of our friends came along and said to her, 'No, don't you go, I'll give you some money and when your father comes back you can go down the shop and buy an icecream.' So she soon stopped crying.

Well, she waited and waited for her father to come home and when he got back they went off to the shop. On their way home this accident happened — she put her foot between the spokes of the bike and grazed her ankle. When she got home it was very bruised. I said to my husband that I thought it needed a doctor, but when he looked at it he didn't think it looked that bad. So I fixed it up the best I could, and we thought she was getting better, but on the Sunday she took a turn for the worst.

We took her into town to the doctor and he put her into hospital. We were at home waiting for news, when a curlew landed on the bank outside and I heard him crying. My hair stood on end and I said to Will, 'Listen...hear that...that's bad news for us.'

'Oh it's only a bird,' he said. 'Don't take any notice of it.' But my mother always taught me to follow the signs and I feared the worst.

Early the next morning I went up to the hospital to see her and the sister told me the doctor wanted to see me. So I rushed around to his house and he took me in and explained that my little girl was very sick and was having convulsions. I told him how on Sunday, after Mr and Mrs Lake had been out to Quarry Street to hold Sunday school, that Margaret said she was hungry and wanted something to eat. I went and got her something but her jaw had locked and she couldn't open her mouth. That's why we'd rushed her up to the hospital. The doctor said she wasn't at all well, but he had two children of his own and he'd do his best.

Well, it wasn't to be. The accident happened on the seventh of March, and on the fourteenth she was buried. She developed tetanus and died in the Geraldton Hospital. I prayed and prayed, begging God for her to survive, but the doctors said they couldn't do anything to save her.

Margaret was such a beautiful little girl, and when I lost her I plunged into a deep sadness. It's not the sort of sadness you can explain in words, it's a sadness very deep inside you that leaves nothing in your life untouched. She was four years and five months old, and she used to have this little bush broom that she'd help me sweep the yard with. She was a happy little girl and she'd sing ' Little Gingerline ', and dance around for us.

The only real comfort for me, and what gets you through a loss like this, was I still had three kids who needed loving and looking after. Margaret left us that day and went to rest, but she'll always be strong in my memories, and I have carried her memory with me always, safe in my heart.

The Reserve

The day that Margaret was buried we moved onto the reserve. They'd been trying to move everyone on from Quarry Street for a while now, and after I lost my little girl I thought, well, this is the time to go.

People still didn't want to leave but nearly everyone was moved to another place. The Rings went out to Bluff Point, the Whitbys to Wonthella, the Ingrams managed to get a house in town because Paddy got a steady job with the Main Roads. Everyone went everywhere.

They'd only built four houses on the reserve and we moved there, along with Doug and Amy Hedlan. After Margaret's funeral we came home to the reserve, put the children to bed, and sat outside our new house with a bucket fire. We were both missing our little girl and still in shock over how it had happened.

Later that evening a very lovely couple, Mick Clarkson and his wife, came to comfort us in our sorrow. They'd missed the funeral because one of their children had been taken to hospital with a broken leg, but they brought the most beautiful wreath with them. It had been a good funeral — the taxi driver, Mr Ted Whitby, offered us his taxi for the mourning car, and he refused any charge for it. All of our friends and relations had come, and I'd had my chance to say goodbye to her.

We'd made the decision to move from our old place and get on with our lives, so that was what I was determined to now do.

When Mr Neville said the government were going to build houses we thought they'd be proper houses. But these were just tin shacks. They built them out of a few sheets of corrugated iron knocked together into two rooms. There wasn't any lining on the walls and they didn't even reach all the way down to the ground. There was a gap of about eight inches between the floor and where the wall began, so the wind used to tear through. The floor had no covering, it was just dirt, and I didn't like the idea of that for the kids.

For water they just put a standpipe about fifty yards away, and there was no fireplace to cook over. Our place in Quarry Street might not have been great, but this was certainly no better. It was obvious from my days working as a housemaid, that what meant houses for white people meant quite another thing for us.

But we were here to stay for a while because Will was out of work and we couldn't afford anything else. It was a real task but we set about trying to make things more livable.

The reserve was very small when we first came and they'd only cleared enough bush to build these four little places. So we had to pull up stumps, clear out scrub and flatten the ground. One of the first things we did was put tin around the bottom to stop the wind coming through, and built up the floor level. That was hard work putting down layers of earth and dampening it down to make it as hard as we could.

Then we got some hessian and sewed it together to put down on the floor underneath the old lino we found at the tip. I think we put about two or three layers on top of each other to make the place comfortable. Then we mixed up some lime and whitewashed the inside walls.

I fitted a double bed and a single bed in and there wasn't room for anything else, so everything we had was in boxes pushed under the bed.

At our place in Quarry Street we'd built a fireplace at one end, but we had no such thing in this one so I used to have to cook outside over an open fire. Then one day my brother-in-law came to visit and he put a fireplace in for me. He made it so I could put bars across to stand my pots and pans on. Having that fireplace made such a difference, especially in winter.

171

I used to bath the kids in a tub in the kitchen until we built a bathroom near the tap. We put up walls around it, and a hessian-lined curtain across the doorway. When that was all set up you could go in there, make a fire to hot up a bucket of water, and have a bath in privacy.

Amy and Doug moved into one of these little humpies too, and they did what they could to make theirs livable. When we first moved there I was carrying my next baby, but when he was born he only lived thirty hours. I don't know exactly what he died of but I think he must have had a heart condition. Another Aboriginal lady had a baby the same night as me and he died too.

I named this little dear Arnold Clive, and he passed away at about six o'clock in the morning. My husband went into town to let the undertaker know I'd lost my little boy and he said, 'Well, why didn't you just bring him down?' Will said to him, 'Because he's only a baby, and because that's an undertaker's job.' When Will left there he got the bloke to promise he'd be out soon.

Well, I waited and waited all day for him to come, and my poor little baby was there in my bed until five o'clock in the evening. It was just me and the kids at home when the undertaker eventually turned up, and he just walked in, picked the baby up and walked out again. He said absolutely nothing to me, just took Arnold away and that was the last of it. I was that upset as it was, I didn't need him to behave like that, like it was all just an inconvenience for him.

A short time later my husband came home and asked me if the undertaker had been.

'Yes, only a little while ago — but I tell you something, Will, his day is coming, and it won't be very long either. Fancy him treating that poor little baby like that! He hasn't got long. He'll be out there before long.'

I should never have done that, cursed him, because a month to that day he was buried, and he happened to be the mayor of this town at the time. Will said to me, 'You shouldn't have, you went too far.'

'I'll ask God to forgive me,' I said. I shouldn't have done it, I know, but I just let my feelings run away with me that time.

172

Well our lives went on, Doug and Amy moved out and other families moved into their place. My oldest son was going to school, and a terrible time I had too, trying to register him. They wouldn't believe that he was my little man. I told them he was born in a camp in Meekatharra and I had Mrs Ingram as my witness. But because I didn't know anything about registering him when he was born, they gave me the real run-around. Eventually, though, after a lot of talking, they were satisfied and he was allowed to start school.

In July of 1940, my daughter Joan was born. When she came into the world it was just the two of us there, her and I. At about ten o'clock that night I said to Will, 'I think I'm going to have the baby tonight, so you'd better go and find Nurse Mooney.'

'Yeah, that'd be right,' he said. 'Always, at night — night, night, night,' and he went off to get her.

While I was waiting for the midwife to come, I went and had a bath and got things ready. I was waiting and waiting, but no nurse. Next minute, little Joan was impatient and she just came along. Will was still away and I delivered her myself. Then I heard the nurse arrive and ask the taxi driver to just hold on for a minute while she found out how long I'd be. When she came in I said, 'You don't have to do anything because baby's here.'

Nurse Mooney came over to the bed and saw this little newborn baby wrapped up in a nappy. I think delivering Joan myself gave us a special bond with each other, and we are very close today. I was going to call her Laurel, but Will wanted Joan, after Joan Crawford, so we named her Joan Laurel.

Around this time, when Joan was a baby, we were finding things pretty hard going and a few times I had to go down to the police station and ask for rations. The police were our protectors in those days and it was terrible going down to the station to ask for help. It was a really hard thing for me to do, to go asking for things, but we were left with no other choice.

The worst thing, aside from the shame I felt, was all the questions they'd ask. They'd ask you everything under the sun, and they'd say things like, 'Why haven't you got a job, plenty of jobs around.' Well this just wasn't true, and besides, I had four children to look after. How was I going to manage another job as well?

Then, when the war broke out, everything started to change in this town. They called my husband up — they called all the blokes up — and he went along to be examined by the doctor. Will didn't want to go away to fight, he said he wasn't frightened to, he just didn't want to go. I don't know what happened at his examination but he wasn't sent, and all the ones who stayed behind had to get a job. With all these blokes signing up there was more chance for work, and Will had a job right through the war at the woolstores.

Lots of Aboriginal boys joined up to fight, but it's not something you hear about when people talk about the war. Boys like the Polands, the Mallards, the Ogilvies, the Isaacs, Ron Kelly (who was a sailor), Sporty Jones and many others were as welcome as anything to sign up. And because they were in uniform, those boys were allowed to go and drink in a bar with the white soldiers. They all reckoned wartime was the only time they ever felt they were equal.

I had to sign up too to be a volunteer worker. I went down and filled out all the forms but I was never called upon.

As the war went on things started getting stricter and stricter. They rounded up all the foreigners working on farms around the place and held them as prisoners. Then they brought in a law that Aborigines weren't allowed in town after dark. We were only allowed to come in freely during the daylight hours, and if we wanted to go to the evening pictures we had to get permission from the police. You'd get that by going down the station and asking if you could go to the pictures that night. If the sergeant was agreeable he'd give you a little card. That was your official permission to be out for the night, and you'd show that to anyone who asked for proof that you were allowed to be in town.

It also got harder to buy food and things in the shops. We all had to have coupons, ration coupons, but we never had the money to buy all the things with anyway. If we went and got our normal rations from the police station, they used to take it out of our coupon book.

Coupons were for everything and different people used to

buy them off of us. One of the storekeepers was especially interested because he loved his tea and butter. He'd say to us, 'Don't give your coupons to anyone else, I'll buy them from you.' We used to do it from time to time because it was a way to get a little bit extra money.

I ran into a girl one day who was working in one of the shops, and she said to me, 'Mrs Nannup, I'm going east and I want some material to make some frocks to go away with. Could I get some coupons off you?' So I sold her a few clothing coupons to help her out and I was able to use the money to buy something myself.

Those coupons were so important because you couldn't buy things without them. One day I came out of the butcher's shop and I dropped my book of coupons on the floor. There was a bloke walking past and he quickly picked them up and put them in his pocket. I knew he'd done it, so I left the kids there and went off after him.

'Excuse me, excuse me,' I said, but he just kept on going. 'Look,' I called out, 'I'm talking to you.'

'Oh,' he said, 'you're talking to me. What's the matter.'

'You picked my coupons up.'

'No I didn't,' he said.

'Yes you did! and I want them back.'

'Well, I haven't got them,' he said, but he wouldn't look me in the eye.

'Right,' I said, 'I know you've got them, and I'll have somebody call on you.'

I started walking back to the shops and I was wondering what I was going to do without those coupons. Well, what do you think he did? He walked back to the shop and put them on the window sill outside the butcher's. When I got back to the kids they said, 'Here's your coupons, Mum. That man put them there.' Well that was a dishonest thing he did, but luckily his conscience got the best of him and he brought them back — otherwise I would have been unable to buy food for my family.

Something else I always remember about the war is those dreadful air-raid sirens that used to go off every so often. I think it was just to keep you on your toes. In town they made all these dug-outs for people to shelter in if the bombs started dropping.

Up where the big statue of John Forrest is now there used to be a thicket of sunflowers, and during the war they dug big trenches along there. Of course there weren't any shelters built at the reserve, and since we weren't allowed in town after dark there wasn't anywhere we could go for safety.

One night, at about nine o'clock, the sirens went off. My husband and my cousin Clarrie were out somewhere and I was the only one home with the kids. Although the Rings had moved onto the reserve they didn't take up one of the humpies, they pitched a tent further into the bush.

Anyway, Joan was only a little baby, so I got Ron and the rest of the kids together, rolled up a couple of blankets, shoved clothes into a bag, plus Joan's nappies and bottles, and got the kids ready to head up into the bush.

Just as we were about to leave, Will and Clarrie came home. They both said there was no need to go and not to worry about it, the sirens were going off all the time. I was right to be worried, though, because these humpies were painted white, and if a war plane was to fly over those places were a perfect bomb target.

A year after Joan was born I had another little girl named Daphne, and in 1943 Lewis came along. I named Daphne after a little baby girl in Mogumber that all of us girls just loved. Her name was Daphne Long and all the girls just loved to bath her and play with her. We never let the poor mother have a hand in, we'd just fight amongst ourselves to have her. At the time, I thought to myself, one day I'm going to have a little girl and I'll call her Daph, so when my own came along I named her Daphne Jean, after Aunty Jean.

When Lewis was born, two years later, his brother Ron was that pleased. See, everytime I'd have a baby Ron would ask, 'What is it this time?' I'd say, 'It's a little girl.'

'Oh,' he'd say, and walk away disappointed. Because he was the only boy he really wanted a little brother.

Well, in 1943, when Nurse Mooney walked out and sang out, 'Will, you there Will?' and told him it was a boy, little Ron was on cloud nine.

He was a funny little kid, Ron. He used to love to play marbles, and it wouldn't matter how tired I was I'd have to go and sit out there and play marbles with him. He'd waited ten years for that brother and when he got him he said, 'Mum, you don't have to worry any more. Two years I'll wait, and then Lew will be ready to play marbles with me.' I just laughed and told him he'd be lucky, and poor old mother still used to have to play those marbles with him.

For most of the war it was only our family living out on the reserve. People had started moving back around the town, and setting up different camps around the place.

One of these camps was called Blood Alley. No alcohol was allowed on the reserve, so people would go down to Blood Alley to drink and gamble. It could get pretty rough there too when fights broke out.

Another camp was set up a bit further from there, where all the coloured women married to whites and people who didn't class themselves as Aboriginal, lived.

Sometimes a group of people would get together and have a game of cards. I used to have my lucky times with the cards, but I never played with anything I couldn't afford to lose. If I was a bit short of money, like I had two and six or whatever, I'd go down to a game and see if I could catch up. If I had a win I'd put it aside and just keep playing with my original two and six.

The Yankee soldiers used to play cards from time to time, too. There was a Catalina, that's a sea-plane, in the harbour with all these Yanks on board. Some of the Aborigines used to mix with these Yanks and play cards or have dances down at the Chapman River.

The Ingrams were living down at the Chapman and we went to one or two of these dances. Although there were black and white Yanks stationed in town, it was only the black Americans that used to come because the white soldiers and airmen wouldn't mix with us. Those Yanks used to bring their own kind of drinks, and some of them used to drink hard. But aside from that it used to be quite good. I was always one for the dancing, I've always loved to dance.

It was around this time that I got some more news about home. There was an Aboriginal lady I knew who used to go cleaning houses in town. Her name was Mary and she was as game as Ned Kelly. She'd knock on doors and ask if the woman wanted any cleaning or whatever done.

Anyway, one day she went to a Mrs Raven's house and did some work for her. Mrs Raven got talking to her and she asked, 'Look, my sisters and I have been looking for this one girl for years. Her name is Alice, and she comes from Roebourne. Would you know her?'

'Yes,' Mary said, 'she's my neighbour.'

'Well then,' Mrs Raven said, 'would you bring her down with you when you come to work tomorrow?'

So that night Mary came over and told me this lady wanted to see me. I was wondering who on earth she was, and I asked Mary for her maiden name but she didn't know. I was very interested to know how she knew me so I went with Mary the next day.

I had Joan with me and when I got to the door this very tall lady came out and said, 'Do you know me Alice?'

'No,' I said, 'I'm sorry, but I don't.'

'Well, you're the same Alice I know,' she said, and she told me she was Gertie Flinders.

Well, I was surprised. I would never have recognised her. The last time I saw her I was only a kid. She was one of the Flinders girls from Roebourne, there were three sisters and a brother, and their parents had a drapery store in town.

'I married Stan Raven,' she said, 'and he's the bank manager here now. We've all been looking for you. Mum's been looking, Laura and Hazel were hunting around for you, and now I've found you. We've got some things to discuss with you, but it'll have to wait until Mum can get here.'

So she got in touch with Mrs Flinders, her sister Hazel, and they were up in about a week to see me.

We all sat around in the kitchen together and Mrs Flinders began, 'You know, your father really loved you Alice, and we saw him the night before he was leaving Roebourne. He came over to our place and told us he was going south to find you and bring you home. He had eighteen sovereigns with him that

178

he'd saved to give to you. But this never eventuated because when he went home that night he met with foul play. I don't know what happened, but someone came to his shack and took his life. He was found a couple of days later and the money he had for you in a little calico bag was gone. I'm sorry Alice, we were all very upset to hear of it.'

'Yes, Mrs Flinders,' I said to her. 'I did know that I'd lost my family. I ran into Mrs Buggenthia in Wiluna and she told me they were all gone.'

'The other thing I wanted to speak to you about, Alice, is, your father made a will for you, and in it he left you four hundred pounds. The money was sent to the Aborigines department. Did you get it?'

When she said where it had gone my heart sank. 'No,' I said, 'I never got it.' The department never even bothered to let me know that my family had died, let alone anything about a will.

Over the years different people tried to find that money for me, but they never had any luck. I've since found out that when this happened, if Aboriginal people received an inheritance, any money left to them became the property of the Aborigines department. I don't understand that, we are all human beings, we should have been entitled to it. I could have really used that money my father left me, and it would have made the world of difference to my family.

When the war finished they had a big parade down Marine Terrace through town. There was a little Chinese lady named Mrs Fong, and her and Billy Marsden decorated a big flat-top truck for a float and went down the street dancing on top of it and waving to the crowd.

I was sick at home in bed with a migraine, but the kids went along and they told me everything about it. Pearl and Joan wanted to go in the parade so I dressed them up as sunflowers. I got crepe paper and stitched big sunflowers on their dresses and I made these big sunflower hats with giant petals. Oh, they looked wonderful, and they were that pleased to be joining in.

Then, when all the soldiers started coming home, a lot of people lost their jobs. The Americans had all left, got in their

179

sea-planes and sailed out of the harbour. Those night-time passes were all finished with, but we were still expected to keep out of town after dark.

When the Aboriginal soldiers came home they found they no longer got the same treatment as during the war. They'd been used to mixing with their white soldier mates but now they found themselves barred from the hotels again. I reckon that really stank, because they were just gun fodder — while they were fighting and getting killed they were good enough, but as soon as they took their uniforms off they were nothing. None of those poor boys could understand why they were treated like that.

Early in the war years the endowment had come in, and that was a big help to me. It was a bit of a battle for me to get it though — I had the problem about Ron's birth not being registered all over again. I had to prove I had Ron in Meekatharra, and I ended up having to write to the doctor who attended to me after he was born. This doctor was Dr Walsh, and he'd ended up marrying Marjory Campbell, so together they helped straighten it out.

We didn't get a lot of assistance then, just five shillings for the eldest child, then two and six for each other child. I used to send to Boans in Perth for parcels of cheap material and things to make clothes for the kids.

From the reserve I often used to take the kids and walk into town pushing the pram. We never had fridges or things like that in those days, so we had to just live one day at a time. The roads used to be quiet to walk along because there weren't many cars in town. There were more pushbikes than motor cars. All the wharfies had bikes and there were racks and racks of them in lines along the wharf.

Taxi fares were pretty cheap then, only about five shillings to the reserve. Funny old cars they were too, but they kept getting flasher and flasher as the years went on. Every year we'd see a new taxi cruising along and we'd think, oh, he must be making some money.

I was going into town one day and it was very hot. I only had two of my kids with me, and by the time we got down to where the Queens Park Theatre is today, they needed to stop in the shade. This used to be the old power-house, and the row of Norfolk Island pines is still there. We made for the trees and walked along while the kids cooled their feet. When we got to the end of the line of trees I said to them, 'Well, there's only one way to do it. We'll dash across to the Queens Hotel.'

We dashed across the road to shelter under the verandah, and when we got there the proprietor of the hotel was standing there whistling. They used to call him the canary. Anyway, he's whistling, whistling, and I was just standing there with my poor little kids trying to cool down.

Suddenly he turned to me and said, 'Excuse me, madam, but you know you're not allowed under these premises.'

I looked at him to see if he was serious. 'Who said?' I really couldn't believe what I was hearing.

'I'm asking you to move because you're not allowed under these premises.'

'Who said?' I asked him again.

'Look, if you don't move I'll get somebody to move you.'

'You get whoever you like to move me. I want to know the reason why. And if you think I want any of your rotten beer, well, you know what you can do with that.' I was that mad with him. I knew what he was on about. Aborigines weren't allowed in the hotel, it was against the law. If an Aboriginal person was caught drinking alcohol they'd get a six month gaol sentence. I wasn't interested in his beer, I just needed a place for my kids to stand in the shade.

'I'll stay until you push me off here,' I said. The kids were a bit worried and they were going, 'No Mum, Mum don't row.' But I said to them, 'Just don't take any notice of him.' Then I said to him, 'You wouldn't deprive your kids of shade when their feet were burning on a hot bitumen road like this.'

'That's none of my business,' he said.

'No,' I said, 'but it's mine,' and I went on standing there.

He went away then and I thought to myself, if he brings back a policeman I'll just tell him the same thing. He'd been gone for about ten minutes when I noticed him peeping around the corner at me. He'd peep at me and when I'd look he'd quickly duck back. So I just stayed where I was and waited until the kids where nice and cool. Then I said, 'All right...

up to Weatheralls.'

Weatheralls was where the shops were, so we ran past the Druids Hall, and down along all the houses that used to be there then. We hopped from one side of the street to the other, catching the shade from the verandahs until we got to the Town Hall.

I left my kids on the Town Hall lawn under a big palm tree and went off to the post office. It was endowment day and I drew the money, picked up the parcel I'd ordered, and went and bought some sandals for the kids.

Money was always tight, having such a big family. Because I was looking after the kids all day I wasn't in a position to go out and get a job. But one day Mrs Parkes, the butcher's wife, was sick and Mr Parkes went all around trying to find somebody to help out while she was in hospital. He'd asked just about everywhere, and at around seven o'clock one morning he came up to our place to see me. He said, 'I'm stuck. My wife was taken to hospital last night and I can't get anybody to come and look after the house for me. Would you be able to come?'

I told him that I'd have to speak to Will first, and I went inside. Will wasn't agreeable — he said I had enough to do at home. But the way I saw it, we needed the extra money, so I told Mr Parkes I would. I got the kids ready for school, put the younger ones in the pram, and we walked down to his residence. When I walked in I nearly fell over. The laundry was packed that high with dirty clothes, and the place was a mess. See, Mrs Parkes must have been sick for a while and unable to do anything.

I stayed the whole day until it was time for my kids to be coming from school. I left his place with a line full of washing and I told George, the yardman, to bring them in when they dried, dump them in the corner, and I'd be back the next day to iron.

So that's what I did, I went there for three days; Monday I washed, Tuesday I ironed and Wednesday I scrubbed and polished the house. Mr Parkes paid me five shillings a day, and each day he gave me something to take home, like a forequarter of mutton one day, sausages and chops the next. When Mrs Parkes came out of hospital she wrote me a note and asked if

I'd keep coming until she recovered.

A couple of weeks later Mrs Anderson wrote a note and asked me if I would go and do washing for her. So I went on a Thursday, washed in the morning and scrubbed and polished her house while the clothes dried. My older kids would be at school, and the youngest ones I'd take with me in the pram.

Then Mrs Holly was coming home from town when she was struck by Marsden's truck. She was an old lady of about seventy and it broke her collarbone, so she had to have her arm in a sling. When she saw me at the Andersons' she asked if I could do something for her, so on Fridays I'd go and work for her.

In the end I was working five days a week at this, as well as doing all my own work at home. I used to be that flat out, because the kids school clothes always needed washing, and I'd be up late at night ironing them with a coal iron so they'd be ready for the next day. We never had any electric lights at the reserve so I had to do all of this at night with a hurricane lamp. It was a lot of work, but having the extra money was too great a help for my family to pass it up.

Living on the reserve had it's disadvantages, but we always tried to make the best of a bad situation. Every Sunday we'd have a hot dinner — even if it was just a hard-up stew. That was a stew I used to make where you just threw everything in — onions, potatoes, rice or barley — and left it to steam. It had no meat so I'd make dumplings to pop in, and flavour it up with a bit of Worcestershire sauce. It used to turn out really nice, too. I'd also make up spotted dog for after. Spotted dog is made from flour, with a bit of dripping, sultanas, some lemon peeling and golden syrup. You mix all that together, then wrap it up in a calico cloth and boil it up for a few hours. I had to put it on at six o'clock in the morning for it to be ready by twelve.

Then after lunch I'd make up some bottles of tea, slice up any leftover pudding, and we'd all march off down to the beach.

They were wonderful times, the kids would be happy swimming around in the sea, we'd have some afternoon tea and go home towards sunset. Then sometimes, on the way home, we'd rob a beehive. If we didn't have anything to take with us on the way down we might rob a beehive then, but it just depended on how anxious the kids were to get to the beach for their swim.

On the Sunday morning, Kath Gregory, myself and the kids used to go to church. The kids would go off to Sunday school first, and then the church service would be after. This was the Church of England church we went to and we were doing this up until they got a new minister.

The new minister was a South African and he didn't like the coloured people sitting in with the white congregation. See, we'd go in, sit down and make ourselves comfortable, but if there was a white person in the same seat he'd come and usher them away to another pew. Also, when the service was over the minister would stand at the door and shake hands with everyone as they left. But when we came along he'd put his hands behind his back and say, 'It's very nice to see you coming along.'

I was getting a bit fed up with all this, but I put up with it because I went there to worship God, not the minister. Then, one day, it was coming up time for the Sunday school picnic for the kids. My kids loved that picnic and they used to go every year.

Well the week before the picnic, the minister said to Gloria and the others, 'You can't come to Sunday school next week.' Gloria came to me very upset, wanting to know why she couldn't go. I wanted to know why too, so I went around and saw the minister. His answer to me was he didn't want any responsibility for looking after our children, so our kids couldn't go. The previous minister wouldn't have dreamt of not taking them, and I was that upset. I said to him, 'Well, if this is Christianity, it's not for me,' and I left.

The Aboriginal kids didn't go on their picnic that year, but he took all the white kids. Although I'd been with the Church of England for many, many years, I never set foot in his church again. I started to send the kids to Sunday school at another church because I didn't want them to miss out, but I decided I'd find something else for myself. I missed having a church to go to but I couldn't go back there knowing we'd be treated like that. So I made up my mind to one day find a true church.

Wells Street

In the time I'd been on the reserve I'd got quite a vegetable garden going. I grew all kinds of vegetables and the kids used to help me cart water to water it.

One day Sergeant Archibald came out looking for somebody when he saw my garden. I had sweet peas growing to hide the fence, and he asked if he could pick some to take to his wife. I told him he could, and when he was out doing that he spotted all the vegetables growing. So he asked if he could have some of them too, and he took a big lot home with him.

It ended up that he'd come out one week and take a load of things home, and the next week he'd bring out some food or clothes for the kids. The sergeant reckoned that the reserve wasn't a fit place for us to live — just a little two-room place for such a large family — so sometime in 1947 he got us a house to rent in town.

I was thrilled to bits to be moving off the reserve, and you should have seen the kids when we moved into this big house. It was a really beautiful house with a big kitchen and plenty of room.

The house belonged to Mr and Mrs Ailing, and they lived next door. Mrs Ailing had a land agent but he was very prejudiced. When she told him she'd let her house to us he was very upset about it. She said to him, 'Well, if that's the way you feel I'll take my business away from you,' and she did too. She went to another agent and put everything into his hands.

185

The rent was seven and six a week and once a month I went down and paid it to him.

We lived there for about four years, and it was really good. I used to get down on my knees and scrub and polish all the floors in the house. Then I'd fill up a corn sack with old clothes and one of the kids would sit on it while another one dragged it around. That was our human vacuum cleaner and the kids just loved it. Pearl and Joan were the ones for making the floor shine — they'd put all the little ones on and whizz around the room, having a good old time. They got that floor so shiny you could see your face in it.

One of my cousins, who was working out on a farm, used to come into town and visit me. Everytime she came she brought something with her, like cake or some eggs. Anyway, this day she brought this beautiful sponge cake she'd made, and when she was walking down the passage she slipped over on the floor. The human vacuum cleaner had just been through, you see.

Well she went up in the air, then landed flat on the floor with the cake still in her hand. I wanted to kill myself laughing but I didn't know how she'd take it. The kids took the cake off her, we helped her up, handed back the cake, and said things like, 'Oh, aren't you light-footed today,' to try and smooth it over.

We all had some good times at Wells Street. Will had a cousin, Josie, who had a house on the hill, and she'd write a note to say, 'How about coming up for a dance on Saturday?'

So come Saturday night, a group of us used to gather at Josie's place. She'd push all the furniture out of her loungeroom, and we'd use the floorboards as our dance floor. There'd be Josie and her family, Will and I and the kids, Harold and Daisy, the Councillors, old Pop Farrell, Ethel Daly, Linda Carnamah and a few others, and we'd all get into the dancing.

The adults would be in the loungeroom and all the kids would have their own party in the bedroom. I used to take up some candles for extra lighting, and for music Josie's dad used to play the accordian. Boy! could old Pop make that squeeze box talk. We'd do all kinds of dancing, then around twelve o'clock we'd finish up and all head off home.

These dances were to have a bit of fun, and somewhere for us to go because we weren't welcome at the white dances. A bit of alcohol used to find its way there, just like anywhere. I've never been one for drinking, myself. I tried it once but it didn't do anything for me — it certainly didn't make my life any better, so I got off that dead-end street very quickly.

I always liked to have a bit of music about the place, and Will and I used to play the mouth organ. He always had an A, but A was too hard for me to blow, so I used to get a G, because that's easier to play. When that song, 'Cherry Pink and Apple White', came out, I just loved it and I learnt to play it on my mouth organ.

About a year after we moved to Wells Street, I had another daughter, Veronica Rose. She was my first baby born in a hospital. This was an instrument delivery and up until then we'd been barred from having our babies in hospital. But it all changed when a white woman had a baby and it died. It became compulsory then for black and white women to have their babies in hospital.

I went into the government hospital, and another Aboriginal lady who'd had a baby and I were in a little room together. We were kept separate from the other ladies — that's the white ladies — and in some ways we didn't mind, because it was privacy for us not being stared at or talked about. But in another way we did mind, and although we used to have a good laugh about it, it still hurt that they thought they were better than we were.

When I went into hospital the next time, when my son Noel was born, we were accepted into the general ward. But even though we were allowed in there we had to be screened off.

It wasn't only the government hospital that screened you off, the St John of God Hospital did too. Once I went in there and the lady in the bed next to me said to the sister, 'Why did you screen Mrs Nannup off?'

'Oh, we didn't think you'd like to be bedded next to a native,' she said. They never used the word Aborigines in those days.

'Rubbish,' she said. 'She's a friend, take that screen away.'

187

So they removed it, but I could hear all the other ladies talking. They didn't like it that I was in full view. They said, 'No, that's not right,' and they wanted the curtain pulled around me. You see, if you were a "blackfella" in those days, you weren't meant to be seen.

I had two more children while we were living there, another little daughter, who I named Beverley Anne, or Bev-anne, and a little boy Kevin. Bev-anne was a lovely healthy baby but little Kevin was stillborn. He was born in hospital in January 1950, but I never got to take him home. It's a terrible thing for a family when that happens, because everyone is expecting a little one to come home.

When we first moved to Wells Street they didn't have an Aboriginal Affairs officer in town, it was just up to the police then. But after the war they got one and his name was Mr Hawke.

One day I'd just picked up my parcel and I was going along past the Town Hall when this Aboriginal Affairs man came up to me and said, 'Excuse me, Mrs Nannup, I'd just like to speak to you.'

'All right', I said. 'What's the matter?'

'I've had a report about you not spending your money properly,' he said.

Well, I just stopped dead in my tracks. 'Where'd you get that from!' I said.

'We just got it, and if you don't spend your money properly, we'll have to take your endowment away from you.'

'Who said that, I'll skin that person,' I said. 'They should mind their own business. You want to see something?' and I put my hand down under the pram and pulled this COD parcel out. 'This is where my money goes. I don't know whoever told you I was squandering my money, but in here are articles I've got for my kids. This money belongs to the kids, and I spend it on the kids.'

'I'm terribly sorry, Mrs Nannup,' he said, because he could see he'd made a big mistake, and he left me alone after that. But that was what it was like. They could just stop you anytime, anywhere, and ask whatever personal questions they liked. Someone might write a letter just to be nasty or something, and they wouldn't stop and think about what they knew of you — they'd just jump to conclusions that you must be up to something.

Getting a bad report about you was something to worry about, in case they got it into their heads to take your children away from you. That was something I was never, ever threatened with, but the worry was always there.

I knew of a lot of women who'd been through Moore River and had their kids taken off them. If they were working girls, and they weren't married, they had no hope of keeping that child. If the mother had her child at Moore River, the baby would stay there and she'd be sent back to work.

I had to learn to stand up for myself well and truly over the years, and it always took people by surprise when I did. This was around the time that I held up all those people at the Radio Theatre, and nearly everyone in town heard about that.

About a week after that incident I went down to the shops for something when I ran into old Mrs Pomeroy. She was a member of the ladies committee in Geraldton and she came over to me and said, 'Oh, you did a marvellous job...where did you get your education?'

'What education?' I said. 'I only learnt off jam tins.'

'Well,' she laughed, 'when you spoke up there you spoke like you had a wonderful education.'

'I never had the chance of school,' I said. 'I was supposed to, but things didn't end up that way.'

'Well look,' she said, 'we've been looking for someone like you to come and join our committee and be our spokeswoman to help people just like you.'

'Well, thanks anyway, Mrs Pomeroy, but no, I had all that I wanted to say in that theatre.'

I suppose she was a bit surprised by my answer, that I didn't want to join her committee, but she left it at that.

Then a few days later I went into the baker's shop and a lady said to me, 'Mrs Nannup, we're so proud of you...where did you get your education?'

'Well, I just spoke,' I told her. 'Just like that, because I've had it up to here, them telling me what we are. All that name calling is not on any more with me. I've had enough,' and I

Alice's children, 1950, ready to go to the matinee. Clockwise from baby Noel in the carriage: Roni (Veronica), Pearl, Gloria, Joan, Daphne and Lewis.

meant it too.

They didn't seem to realise that I didn't just get up there and say those things because I felt like it. I said those things because I had too. I'd just had enough, I'd reached my limit. I've heard Aboriginal people called things all my life and I didn't want my kids to be treated like that. I wanted it all to stop and for us to be treated like human beings.

My kids had a bit of a time of it at school, too. Although there were a lot of lovely little kids, and most of them were good, there were always a few of the bad sort too. I got in to quite a few battles with other kids' parents when they were growing up, just defending my kids' rights.

I remember there was this little Italian girl and she used to give one of my daughters a terrible time. They'd all catch the bus to school, and if my daughter brushed past her, touched her clothing or her hand, this girl used to make a big fuss about brushing germs or dirt off of herself. It was all to upset my daughter and make her feel she wasn't good enough.

One day this girl got on the bus and the only spare seat was next to my daughter, so she started carrying on, brushing down the seat and everything. Well, my girl had had enough, she was really fed up, and those two ended up in a punch-up.

The bus driver stopped the bus and ordered my daughter off, but she told him if she had to get off she was taking this other girl with her, and she'd flog her all the way home.

The next day I was in town with my daughter when across the road I saw the mother of this Italian girl and her older brother. They were looking over at us, and my daughter was really scared — she thought they were coming after her. I had a friend with me, and she said to keep away from them because they were very good with the knives. But I stood my ground and I told them to leave my girl alone. I thought to myself, my daughter has been taking nonsense from that girl for long enough. I taught my kids to stand up for themselves, and not let other people treat them like dirt on account of being Aboriginal, and I always stuck by them over it. I think this Italian girl treated my daughter like this because she was taught to think like that from when she was young.

A few days after I'd run into Mrs Pomeroy, I was walking

along Marine Terrace and there were three little boys sitting in a car. Their mother and father were off at the shops, and the biggest of the kids said, 'Quick, quick, come and have a look. There's a nigger coming up the street.'

Well, I was very close and I heard them perfectly. I went over to the car and I said, 'Excuse me, but what did you just say?' But he wouldn't answer me. 'Well, I know what you said, and I'll tell you what, I'm proud of what I am but I'm ashamed of your mother and father.'

From across the road their father spotted me and he came rushing over saying, 'What's going on here?'

The three little kids looked at him, and I said, 'It's a disgrace to drag children up. You should bring them up to respect other people.'

He wanted to know what had happened so I told him, 'I get it slung off at me all the time. They called the little ones over to have a look because there was a 'nigger' coming up the street. Well, I'm proud of what I am, but I feel ashamed of you. Where do these kids learn these things? They don't just pick it up from nowhere, they get it from you. You teach your kids to call us niggers and not to respect us as people.'

'Well, which one said it?' he asked. See, he hadn't got the point, it's not about belting the kid that says it out aloud. It's about not poisoning their minds to start with.

'Look, don't hit him, just do as I ask. Bring your kids up to respect people who are different looking to themselves,' and I walked off.

See, I believe that — it's the adults that teach their kids how to count, how to talk, how to eat their meals and how to treat other people. When little kids see someone who's darker than them, and they ask their parents about it, the adults say, ' That's just a nigger, a boong, ' or ' That's only a blackfella. ' That's where it all starts from, and they take that with them through their life. So if that's where it starts from, it stands to reason that's where it has to stop.

We would have gone on living at Wells Street for longer except that when Mrs Ailing died the house was sold. If we'd only had the money we could've bought that place ourselves, but we didn't have that kind of money.

The people who bought it were living out at Bluff Point and they wanted to move closer into town. When I found out it had been sold I went and saw Mr Ailing. He said, 'Don't worry, you find somewhere else to move and then they can move in.' But the new owners didn't give us any time, they just turned up and started moving things onto the property. We were taken by surprise and had to quickly get all our belongings together and find somewhere else to go. Because of the way it was done we had nowhere lined up, so we had to move back on the reserve.

I was very upset to lose that place, and I didn't want to stay on the reserve for long, so when Will got a job woodcutting I gladly packed up the kids and went with him.

We went out Northern Gully way and pitched two tents. My eldest son Ron wasn't with us at this time, because he was working up on Mount Seabrook Station. Pearl was out working too, for Dr Royce in town, and she boarded there with them. All the other kids were with us though, and it was very hard going. We had no facilities and all our water had to be carted. It ended up not working out because we sent in for some food but the boss didn't get it for us. Will didn't want to be left relying on him so we moved back to the reserve.

After we'd left the reserve that very first time, another family had moved into the house we built up, so we had to start from scratch again.

I remember I bought a lino from a second-hand shop to put down on the floor. This lino needed a good sweep and wash, and I got down and rubbed some polish into it. Well, I don't know how it happened — whether the dust from it got into my chest — but I had an asthma attack. I was choking for breath and I was in a terrible way for three days. In those days there were very few medicines for asthma and I used to really suffer with these attacks. I'd have to be propped up in bed for a few days and rely on my girls to look after things.

I always remember the year of my first attack because it was at the time of the Queen's coronation. In Geraldton they went mad, they had a coronation party in the main street. The kids all wanted to go, and I remember dressing them from the side of my bed and being too sick to go along.

Anyway, we were only back at the reserve for a little while before we went down to Greenough. Ron had left Mount Seabrook Station, and he was the first of our children to get married. He and his wife Blanche were living in a big house in Greenough that belonged to the farmer Ron was working for. It was one of those old stone cottages that the convicts built, a long bungalow type, and they invited us to come and live with them.

When I was down at the Greenough I met a beautiful old lady named Mrs Rieks, who lived opposite Ron and Blanche. The kids used to be going to school on the bus, and in the afternoons Blanche and I would walk up to the road to meet them. While we'd be waiting this dear Mrs Rieks would come out and talk to us.

One day it was raining and she invited us into her house. We went in and and we were talking when she asked me a few questions about religion.

'Well,' I said, 'I'm a Church of England but I've given it away because I wasn't happy with the minister.' I told her how he wouldn't let us sit with the rest of the congregation, and about the kids not allowed at the church picnic.

We went on talking and I told her how I never set foot in his church after that, and that I missed having a church to go to. I told her how I'd been really searching and she said, 'Then would you like to have bible study with me?'

'Yes, I'd like that,' I said, 'but what religion are you?'

'I'm a Seventh Day Adventist,' she said.

So I started going up every afternoon to have bible study with her, and it got so I just couldn't get out of the house quick enough to go to Mrs Rieks. It was really good, and I felt like I was really finding something for myself.

Then, one Friday, Blanche and I caught a taxi into town, and as we were walking around the government buildings I saw a van go past with VOICE OF CHRIST written on it. I said, 'Look Blanche, just look at that...that's the voice of prophecy.' I was that excited about this and I said to her to tell me if he stopped and parked anywhere because I wanted some pamphlets.

Anyway, we didn't see him again, but when I went up to Mrs

Rieks on the following Monday I told her all about this van. I said to her, 'I wanted to meet that gentleman, but I wasn't lucky enough.'

'Oh did you?' she said. 'Well, you don't have to worry — because he belongs to my church, and he'll be out here tomorrow.'

Well, I ended up meeting Pastor Maberry — he came out and visited me and invited me to come to church on the next Saturday. I took Gloria along with me and a couple of the little kids. We got to this tiny little church and it was packed, people from Dongara and all around the district were there.

The service started up, and everyone was singing the first hymn, when I just felt something tighten up in me. I was standing with Mrs Rieks on one side, and Gloria on the other, and I was swaying from side to side. I had tears streaming down my face and Mrs Rieks asked me if I was all right. 'Yes,' I said, and all of a sudden this feeling came over me. It was like chains had been binding me and they had suddenly broken and fallen away, leaving me free. It was a very emotional experience for me, that whole service, and I have been a Seventh Day Adventist ever since.

Only a little while after that, my last child, Lauraine, was born. I spent a whole month in hospital after having her, because I was really sick with pleurisy. When I came out of hospital we went back to the Greenough for a while, and then we moved back to town. Will knew this old chap who had a property at the back of the cemetery, so we moved out there.

There was no house or anything on the place, so we had to build a kitchen out of sheets of tin and pitch our tents. Although there were no facilities at all, and we even had to cart our own water, he charged us five shillings a week to be on the land.

Out there was where I met Mrs Criddle, who had the bird sanctuary, and I used to do a bit of work in the garden or scrubbing and polishing for her. Both Mr and Mrs Criddle were wonderful people, and I ended up working off and on for them over a number of years.

The first year at Utakarra I worked for Mrs Criddle up at her house. Then in the second year I started doing the pea picking for George Rowe. There was George senior, George junior, and George sub-junior, all in the one family. George senior worked at the condenser making ice, but they had a property of about forty acres, with a great big paddock of peas.

That year George senior asked George junior if he could get some pickers for the season. So George junior, who knew me and Will, came out to our place to see us. We had a big fire going and we were sitting around it talking with him for quite a while. 'Oh, before I go,' he said, 'Will, would you like to pick up a few pea pickers? Dad's looking for some pickers because the peas are all ripe.'

'I can't do that,' Will said, 'but Alice can probably get a few together. She knows quite a few people around here.'

After George left I said to Will, 'Why can't you?'

'Well, I don't want any part of it, but I'll come and pick with you if you get a team together,' he said.

So I went around and asked a few families, and I ended up with fourteen, counting me and Will. We all got in there and started picking, but there were these two fellas who wanted to go to Carnarvon, so they were looking for quick money. I was keeping an eye on them because I could see them filling their bags up quicker than everyone else. So I went over and had a look, and sure enough, they were picking flat ones too, just to fill their bags up. So I had to tell them to finish up, and we finished the job without them.

We did that pea picking for the Rowes every season for a few years after that. I used to walk from our place with all the kids, pushing a pram, out to the paddock. The older kids used to pick too on the school holidays, and Gloria would look after the youngest ones for me. Also during the season I used to clean house for Mrs Criddle because pea picking wasn't every day.

The second season we were there it came Christmas Day and we were down to nothing — no money and very little food. My little son Lewie was very upset, because all the other kids at school were telling him what they were going to have to eat. He was grumbling around the place saying, 'And we, we got nothing! Why haven't we got presents?'

'Look,' I said, 'we haven't even got food.'

Poor little kid, he was feeling that miserable. 'Oh, never

worry', I told him. 'I'll make us a hard-up stew and a spotted dog.' Anyway he went on grumbling about it, so I said to him, 'Look, the Lord will provide.'

"Oooh, you always say that, the Lord will provide," and he wouldn't listen to me.

At about eleven o'clock Christmas morning, George junior came along and sang out, "The boys around?"

"Yeah," I said.

"Can I see them?" he asked, "and you come too."

"All right, I'll be there," and I sang out to Lewie and Noel that George wanted to see them.

At first they were a bit reluctant to go, because George used to get them to do odd jobs around the place.

"Come on," I said, "I'm going too."

So we went down to where he had his ute parked and he said, "Mum and Dad want to wish you and all the family a merry Christmas, and they sent you something in appreciation for what you did with the pea picking."

"Oh, thank you," I said.

"That's why I'm calling the boys over, so they can carry in this stuff," he said.

Well look, there were two big boxes, one was full of food and the other had cool drinks, nuts, tomato sauce, everything you could imagine. There were Christmas crackers, Christmas lollies, just about every luxury you could think of. My two boys picked up these boxes and they ran off to show their father.

I thanked George and wished him a merry Christmas too, then I went off to find the kids. They were all just that happy, there was ham and everything. Well the hard-up stew never got made that year, and Lewie had to think twice about the Lord providing. See, we got paid sixpence a pound for the peas, and I wasn't paid anything extra for organising the team. So the Rowes sent this gift over in appreciation for all the work, and that year, I tell you, it was very appreciated.

When we first moved to Utakarra, Joan, Daph and Gloria were all still going to high school. But as each finished their education they got jobs at Saint Pats College in town, and they used to live in at the college.

197

One day, on Saint Patrick's Day, Joan and Daph came out to visit me for the day, then headed back to the college just before sunset. I asked them before they left if they'd come to church with me the next day, and they went home early to give themselves time to prepare their clothes for church.

On the way back home they were riding their pushbikes, and Daph rode at the front because she had the head light, and Joan was behind her because she had the tail light.

Well, this car came pelting along the road and Daph sang out, 'I don't like the sound of that motor car, let's pull over.' So she jumped off, but poor Joan was just a little bit too late and she was hit by this car full force from behind. She was laying on the road and poor Daph was panicking. She looked over and saw the bloke in the car pull up and get out to have a look. He didn't come across to help or anything. Then as soon as he saw it was an Aboriginal girl that'd been hit he just got in his car and took off.

During the war all the cars had little shields over the head lights to stop the beam from going up high. Well, this car still had those and that was what hit her leg and broke it, cut it on a slant, just like trimming a rosebush.

Anyway, Joan and Daph were both just left there when another car came over the hill and saw Joan laying on the ground, and Daph crying. The chap got out and came across to them, and in all the excitement he picked Joan up instead of getting an ambulance and took her to the hospital. Well, that was the wrong thing to do, because she shouldn't have been moved — only an ambulance officer should have moved her.

I was home at the time ironing clothes for church when I heard this BANG. I didn't know what it was but it was so loud I walked out to see what was going on. Noel was with me and he said, 'What are you looking at, Mum?'

'Oh, I think there's been an accident up on the hill.'

I went back inside and I said to Will, 'Look, there's been an accident up there, and I've got this terrible feeling it's one of the girls.'

'You're always full of imagination,' he said. 'If there's anything wrong somebody will let us know.'

I still had this awful feeling, but I went back to finish the ironing when I heard this whoosh whoosh noise. It was Daph pushing her bike through the bushes. When she got close I could hear her crying and screaming.

'Is that you Daph?' I called out to her.

'Yes mum — Joan's in hospital, she's been hit by a car.'

Well we just tore into town to the hospital, and poor Joan was in a very bad way. She was in terrible pain, and all she could say was, 'I want to see mum, I don't want to see anyone else.'

So I stayed with her while Will went up to the police station to report the accident. Although the bloke who'd hit her had taken off, Daph had seen him, and she knew who he was. But while all this had been going on this man had gone into the station himself and said he'd knocked a black girl over on the road, and bribed the policeman. See, we found all this out later, and the reason for the bribing was it was the man's son driving the car and he didn't have a license.

Will had no luck at the station. They reckoned they didn't know anything about it and no charges were ever brought against the driver or his father. Well, something like that is just not right.

We were very lucky Joan lived through all this. She had a terrible time. The doctor stitched her leg up but blood poisoning set in and we nearly lost her. The specialist came down from Northampton and cleaned all the bad tissue out, and she had this great big dent in her leg. That dent was so big I could have put my arm in it and it would have fitted in nicely.

I used to walk in to sit with her and take Bev-anne with me. Joan would say, 'Keep talking to me, Mum, don't let me go to sleep.' And I'd talk and talk and talk until I just couldn't think of another word to say. She ended up being in hospital for nine months, all but a day, and if it wasn't for the medical fund we would never have been able to pay for it.

We all used to be in a medical fund in those days, and I always say it was a great thing. All Aboriginal people paid into it, and it was about three pounds a quarter. Then, when somebody got sick, there was a fund of money to cover all the expenses. Well, for Joan it was about four hundred pounds for Dr Crook, and six hundred or eight hundred for the hospital bill, so without that medical fund we would have never been able to afford it.

The man who was in the car that hit Joan was a tomato gardener, and when the Aboriginal Affairs man heard about what happened he went around to see him. Well, this fella pulled a knife on the department officer and chased him off his property. His attitude was, she's only a little dark girl so what did it matter.

When I heard about the way this man had behaved I said to the department man, 'My daughter is suffering and I hope he suffers the same punishment. And another thing, I hope his tomato garden is wiped out.' Well, lo and behold, that tomato season the frost was very bad and his garden was the only one in the entire area to be wiped right out. And that man's leg just withered up and he had to have crutches. My husband said, 'You don't want to keep going around and cursing people.' So after this one, and what happened to the undertaker when Arnold died, I vowed to never put a curse on anyone else again, and I never have.

It was while we were living at Utakarra that I met Mr Gare. Mr Gare was with the Native Affairs and he was building new houses on the reserve. There were more Aboriginal families moving into Geraldton then, and the reserve was expanding. Mr Gare wanted us to move back to the reserve and into one of these new places. Will didn't want to go at first, but eventually he came around and we moved back.

These houses were much better than the ones built in Mr Neville's time. They had two bedrooms, one up each end, a kitchen in the middle, a big verandah along the front and hot and cold water for the shower recess. They didn't have their own toilets, though — there was a communal block, separate ones for men and women. These houses were certainly an improvement, but a bit too small for my large family.

Mr Gare's wife, Nene, was a writer and she was very friendly with a friend of mine, Mary Forrest. Mrs Gare was writing a book and I think Mary must have been helping her out with some of the stories around the place. That book was called *The Fringe Dwellers*, and today it has been made into a film.

Family group, Geraldton Reserve, 1956. Back row: Lewis, Will, Alice, Daphne. Front row: Roni (Veronica), Noel, Bev-anne, Lauraine.

Mary didn't live on the reserve because her husband had an exemption. That meant you weren't classed as an Aborigine and were supposed to have the same privileges as whites. You've got to remember that it wasn't until later, until citizenship, that we were permitted to vote in this country.

After we'd been on the reserve for a while, the Native Affairs brought two houses down and put them on the reserve. These were two workers' houses from when the Howatharra Railways closed down. Kath Gregory got one and I got the other. Our house was on top of the hill, and Kath's was opposite. We paid one pound a week rent, and it was really good to have a bigger house.

We stayed in this house for quite a few years, and I got back into my gardening and had a lovely garden again. In 1957 the laundress at St Pat's College left, and I took over her job. When I first started there a woman named Annie was working there too. I heard her name was Annie, and I asked one of the other ladies there if her surname was Williams. It turned out it was Annie Williams from the boarding house in Meekatharra, so it sure is a small world.

In those days showtime at Mullewa and Geraldton was a big thing. At Mullewa they'd have these boxing tournaments, Blum's Boxing Troupe, and the Alabama Kid used to come up for it. The Alabama Kid was young Thomas Bropho, and he was Will's nephew. Young Tom's father was Tommy Bropho senior, who used to hold the services at Mogumber, and his mother was Nana Leyland's daughter, Bella. Tommy and Bella were married at the settlement and they used to live down at the camps.

The Alabama Kid and Tom Calvan were pretty good boxers. Come showtime those two would be up in Geraldton and sometimes they stopped with us for the night.

I never went to these boxing shows much, but Will used to be the one for them. I didn't like them, even the ones they had at the police boys' club. I went to one of those once, and there was this young, skinny Aboriginal boy fighting this big white kid. I went along because I knew this Aboriginal kid, and I wanted to barrack for him. I went into where the ring was and everyone was standing around calling out to the boxers. There was this lady and she was eating peanuts and shouting out with her mouth full for this big lug of a white kid to kill this little dark kid. She was shouting, 'Go on, get 'im, get stuck into 'im.' The big kid downed this little kid, and it was really awful. I was shouting out, 'It's one-sided, it's one-sided,' but nobody seemed to care.

I was standing behind this woman and I was that mad with her and the things she was shouting out. Just after she'd taken a big mouthful of peanuts I lifted her. I gave her such a surprise she started choking on these peanuts and making funny noises.

Will saw what happened and he just got me and pushed me outside and said, 'I'm never bringing you here again!'

'That's all right,' I shouted. 'I never want to come back here again.' I'd shocked that woman, and I'd shocked myself. But I just couldn't stand it, I couldn't bear seeing little kids getting knocked around.

Will and I stayed together until 1963, then we decided to go our separate ways. We'd been together for thirty-one years and reared up a family of ten children. We'd been through some really difficult times together, and losing Margaret had been very hard. Now that most of the kids had grown up and left home we knew it was time for us to live apart. Mr Beharell was in charge of the Aboriginal Affairs then and he got me a job as senior assistant domestic at the Aboriginal Children's Hostel in Cue.

I went up to Cue with Lauraine, my youngest daughter, and took my granddaughter Jennifer, to keep each other company. There were thirty-six kids at the hostel when I first got there and it was run by a white couple, Mr and Mrs Clarke. But they were only temporary and Mr and Mrs West came to take over.

I loved those kids there, and they used to call me Aunty Alice. By the start of the next school year, the number of kids got bigger because people started sending their kids there. Some of the kids were sent by Mr Beharell, and they'd been taken away from their parents.

It was while I was working there that I had to apply for my citizenship. There was another Aboriginal lady working there and we both had to go for it. The reason was, if Mr West and his wife had visitors or a social evening and they had beer, we weren't allowed to associate with them. We had to have this certificate to be in the same room. So Adeline and I both put in for it and got it, and then we could join in on the darts nights and things at the hostel.

It ended up I decided to leave there about a year later, because I was accused of leaving the door to the boys' dormitory open for them to get out. It wasn't me at all — I knew who was responsible but he never owned up. Anyway, it made me look like a liar, and when the committee came up and had a meeting I had my say. I told them how upset I was being blamed for something I hadn't done, and they believed me too. But after that happened I decided to leave there and go and stay with my daughter and son in Mullewa.

I went off to Mullewa with Bev-anne and Lauraine, and I looked after a house of seven boys. Two of them were mine, and the others were boarders. Three of the boys were working on the wheat bins and the other four had jobs with the

Alice and Mrs West at the Cue Races, 1964.

railways.

I did this for a while — until Joan was expecting another baby and she needed me to come and help look after her boys. So I went back to Geraldton and lived there until her daughter Dianne was born.

In all I had thirteen children, and I was blessed with ten to rear up. By now most of them had married and had families of their own. They were scattered all over the place but we always kept in touch. I still had Bev-anne and Lauraine with me, and I probably would have just stayed living in Geraldton if it hadn't been for Amy coming to find me.

I had always wanted to go back home, but I'd never been in the position to be able to. It had been my secret dream, and I used to think of my family all the time. They might have taken me away from my home, but they didn't take my home away from me. But if it hadn't been for Amy, my niece, finding me when she did, I might never have got back there to see my people.

When The Pelican Laughed

Amy came down to Geraldton in 1965 with her husband to buy a new ute. Her and I had never met, but she'd heard through the grapevine I was living down here. So she asked around two or three different people and she accidently ran into my daughter Joan.

Joan came home and told me, 'This lady wants to meet you, she's from Port Hedland. If you go down on Saturday you can meet her out the front of Jack King's.' That was the barber's shop then, on the corner where Betts & Betts is now.

I thought about it and I thought to myself, yeah, I'll go and meet her. So Saturday came, and I was standing there waiting for this person to come along, when the next minute, this brand new ute pulled up.

A young woman got out of the car and I said to her, 'Are you looking for me, Amy?'

'Are you Aunty Alice?' she asked.

'Yeah, that's me,' and we had a bit of a cry and a bit of a talk. Then she said, 'Aunty Minnie is very sick. She said for me to try and find you and ask you to come up and see her.'

'When the opportunity knocks I'll definitely go,' I told her.

'Well,' she said, 'the opportunity is knocking right now. You can come with me.'

I was really excited. 'When are you leaving?' I asked.

'Tomorrow at ten and we want you with us.'

Well look! This was Saturday, Sunday was when they were

leaving. I was shocked, but I was pleased at the same time.

'Well, you want to come with us?' Amy asked. 'We've got a new ute with plenty of room.'

'Right!' I said, and I just jumped at it.

I had to get some washing done before I could leave, but first of all I had to let my daughter know what was going on. Joan was visiting her sister-in-law in Augustus Street, so they took me off to find her. I pulled up in this brand new ute and walked over to Joan and said, 'Joan, I'm going to Port Hedland tomorrow.' Well, she just looked at me and just about fell over.

'Are you?' is about all she said.

'Yes, love,' I said. 'My Aunty is very sick and Amy is taking me home.'

It had come as a bit of a surprise to her, but she was pleased for me. 'That's good, Mum,' she said. 'I'll take care of things here for you. Daph and I will look after Lauraine.'

So the next day at ten o'clock I had everything packed and ready to go. I had my bible in my purse on the fridge ready to pick up at the last minute. It only had about four pounds in it, but still, that was money, aye?

They came and picked me up and we got along the road to just out of Glenfield. They wanted to take some tomatoes back with them, so I took them out along the road where they were for sale. We went down this avenue with trees on each side. They got their tomatoes and I thought I'd get some for us to chew on the road. And that's when I found that I'd forgotten my purse — I'd left it sitting on top of the fridge. I was upset about it but Amy said, 'Don't worry about money, Aunty. We'll see you right.' So off we went again.

There were two cars of us that travelled up. Because this ute was brand new we had to travel at about thirty miles an hour. Just imagine that! The car in front would have to pull up every now and again to wait for us.

Just before you get into Carnarvon there used to be this old tracking station, and because it was so late we slept on the side of the road there. We got up early the next morning and went into Carnarvon to have breakfast.

Then it was 'on the road again.' We slept on the road that night, and got into Roebourne about one o'clock the following day.

As you come into Roebourne there is a creek near a big hill. We went around this hill and the first thing I spotted was this paperbark tree. 'Oh no,' I whispered, and my tears began to flow.

'What's the matter, what's the matter,' Amy was saying.

'Oh, Amy,' I cried, 'is that a Cajuput tree?'

'Yes,' she said, 'yes Aunty, that's a Cajuput.'

After forty-two years I still remembered those trees.

I remembered when I was only little they were my favourite, and we all used to sit under them. My father used to make troughs for the animals out of the older trees. It was amazing to see this tree and all the memories it brought flooding back to me. I drove along feeling a mixture of great joy and deep sorrow.

We got into Roebourne, and went to Amy and my mother's relatives' place for a shower and that. They were my people too, but I wasn't yet feeling like I had come home. Going to see my Aunty Minnie was coming home for me. We went down to a cafe and bought a chook for lunch, then left there and got into Port Hedland at around eleven o'clock that night.

As we had been travelling along, more of the memories were coming back to me. When we got towards Munda, Amy looked across and said, 'See those lights? That's Munda Station over there.' I felt terribly sad as I stared across, because my mother, my two sisters and little nephew are all buried there.

My mother and Ella had died a long time ago, and Myrtle had been left behind. The people who owned the station took her over and she worked as a house-girl for them. She was about fourteen years old when there was this big electrical storm. She got ready to go up to the house to serve afternoon tea, but as she walked along the lightning struck her and she fell down. She laid on the ground for a few minutes, then she got up, but walked straight into the line of the lightning again. It struck her, but this was for the last time, and the poor little thing died. It's one of those things I suppose — I had always feared electrical storms, and then my little sister had to be killed in one.

It was so sad to pass them all by in the night, and it really rang home that I was never, ever, going to see any of them again.

When we got to Port Hedland we went to my Aunty Elsie Brockman's place to sleep. Over night, the message that I was in town spread like wildfire, and the next morning a few people turned up to see me. At seven o'clock the next morning, as we were having breakfast, a tall gentleman came to the door. He looked at me and said, 'By joves, you're a different girl to what you were when you left home.' It turned out his name was Lennie Houghton and he'd known me when I was only little. He asked me if I remembered my pony Clay, and told me that he was the one who broke him in for me.

Lennie stayed for a while and then my two uncles, Uncle Sam and Uncle Ernie Mitchell, turned up. We all had a good old talk, and a few tears, and I was starting to feel a bit more like I'd come home.

After breakfast I felt ready to go down to see my Aunty Minnie. Jack Coffin came along and Aunty Elsie asked him to run me down to the Two-Mile.

Jack took me to Aunty Minnie and Uncle Bill's place, and I asked him not to say a word. He understood I wanted to surprise them, so he took my case from the car and put it on the ground. 'I'll be back for you later,' he said, and drove away.

I walked up to the door with my heart in my mouth, and I could see Uncle Bill. I couldn't see Aunty Minnie, but he must have told her somebody was coming because she was behind the door just peeping around. I was thinking to myself, well Wari, this is it, this is finally coming home.

When I got up close to them, I said, 'Good morning.'

'Good morning,' they said back, and just looked at me.

'Do you know who I am?' I asked.

'No,' they said.

'You don't know?'

'No.'

'Well then,' and I just let out this great big cackle. I know I shouldn't have laughed, but I was so pleased to see them, I'd been waiting so long for this, but I didn't know what to say.

When Uncle Bill heard my laugh he looked at me closely.

'You wouldn't be Alice, would you?'

'That's me,' I said, and then the game was on. They couldn't get hold of me quick enough. Aunty Minnie just shot around the corner, and we held one another and cried and cried.

I cried the whole day that day, just talking about Mother and everybody, you know. It was so sad. I had always wanted to come back home. When I went out to work and I had my first break from Mrs Larsen's, if I'd only been able to go back then. I wish I had tried, but of course, they weren't about to let me. But if only I'd found somebody that could have helped me to find my way back. But there had been nobody, no one who could.

Aunty Minnie brought out the photos and showed me some of my mother and her working on the stations. It was hard to cope with the way I was feeling. I felt cheated, like deprived of so much, but there was nothing I could do about it now. It had all been out of my control, and there's no turning back the clock, it had all gone, and I was too late.

So her and I had a crying session, and a talking session, and a crying session, and a memory session. Aunty Minnie said that she'd written me a letter not long after I'd left.

'Yes,' I said, 'and I asked Mrs Campbell to write back.' But she'd never heard from me and they'd been worried. She was sad too, because she'd been down to Perth a couple of times and hadn't known how to find me.

After I spent the day with them I went over to see my poor old Uncle Paddy. He was the one who had given me the tin of peaches when I was leaving home. He was blind now, so he couldn't see me, but he could hear my voice. He was with some other of my relatives, talking in our language. It had been so long I couldn't speak to them, but I could understand most of what they were saying. I'd listen to them, to their questions, and I'd answer yes or no.

Uncle Paddy had this big long stick, and he was hitting it on the ground and crying as he spoke to me. He said, 'This is the only one girl that went away and come back. Mobs of girls been away from here, and they never come back yet. We are proud of you, proud you've come back.'

After I'd been with Uncle for a while I went back to Aunty Minnie's. In the evening, Jack Coffin came and picked me up and took me back to Aunty Elsie's. I was staying with Aunty Elsie, but during the day I'd go over to Aunty Minnie's. We had a lot of catching up to do and there were still lots of people for me to meet. But, although a lot of my relations were there, not many of my close family were still alive. I met my half-brother, though, Ronald Captain — he was Myrtle's brother. My mother and Captain had him after I'd left. I was also pleased to see my cousins, Uni Parker and Girlie Lockyer, because as girls we all used to dance together. A lot of people remembered me, but I couldn't remember them because I was only a kid when I left.

I was at Aunty Elsie's place when Uncle Bill came over to tell me that Aunty Minnie had gone back into hospital. She was in her seventies now and had been very sick for a while, going in and out of hospital.

I had only planned to be away for three weeks on this trip, but with her so sick I had to re-think what I was going to do. Elsie and I went up to visit her and when we got back home I said, 'I'm not going back to Geraldton until she's out of hospital.'

I had decided to stay for the time being, but I didn't want to be there doing nothing, so I looked around for some work. There was a job going at the North Star Laundry, so I went off and saw the manageress and started work there.

Now I was able to stay and be near Aunty Minnie, and have some money coming in. After I'd been at the North Star for about a month I ran into Aunty Jean. Aunty was working out on Hillside mine, and she'd come in for the day with one of the working men's wives.

At lunch-time I used to go to Snodgrass's Cafe and buy a roll, then go over to the Pier Hotel for a big glass of lemon squash. On this day I went over there and was sitting in the garden when who should come along but Aunty Jean. She had one of her daughters with her, and she nearly fell over when she saw me. She asked me how long I was going to be around for, and I told her I was here until Aunty Minnie was well enough to leave hospital.

Then, about a week later, I got a letter from Aunty Jean asking if I would relieve for her while she went on her holidays.

She was cooking on the mine, and I wasn't sure I could cope cooking for all those men. But she said she was sure I could, and she was only going to be gone for a few weeks. Aunty Minnie was out of hospital now, so I went and met with the manager and went out to Hillside to relieve.

Like I said, when I left Geraldton to travel up with Amy, I had only planned to be away for a few weeks, but it ended up being three years. Aunty Jean stayed away longer than she said, and when she came back she went and worked on another mine not far from where I was.

The mine wasn't very far out of town and I used to see Aunty Minnie as often as I could. While I was up there, my son Noel and my daughter Bev-anne both came up to stay with me and got to meet Aunty Minnie, and a lot of family on my mother's side. I was very, very, pleased they met their relations, and I think they were pleased too.

It had taken me forty-two years to get back to my family and so much had happened in that time. The old life of the stations had gone, and people had to move into towns like Port Hedland and Roebourne. Of course, that was going on everywhere in the North, and it was very hard for the old people to do — leave their life and their land behind.

I never spoke much about what had happened to me after I left with the Campbells. It was just enough for me, and for them, that I'd finally been able to come back. Aunty Minnie reckoned Amy bringing me back was the best thing that could have happened. She was pleased to see me grown up with a lovely family, and to have met two of them herself.

Three years later I finally returned to Geraldton. I might have stayed working on the mine for longer, but I suffered a heart attack and decided to go back to Geraldton.

It was when I was back there that Aunty Minnie passed away. I was heartbroken to hear she'd gone. But I am grateful that I was able to get back to her for those last few years that she lived.

Somedays, when I think about things, there is a lot of grief and sadness in my heart. It's then that I realise how much I was denied when I was taken away. But then, there are other days, when I think, well I wouldn't know what I know today if I had been able to stay. That's just how it is for me, thinking over the past. It's a lot to do with how I am feeling at the time, because sometimes, I miss my mother, my father, and all of my family so very, very, much.

PART FOUR

NAN, a great-grandmother

1968–1991

Yinda Ngurra

I left Port Hedland in 1968 and caught the plane down to Geraldton. Joan, her husband Aub, and the kids were living in Rangeway, and I went to live with them. After that I moved to a place in Fitzgerald Street.

When I was in Fitzgerald Street Aunty Jean was still up in Port Hedland, and she used to come down and stay with me for a couple of weeks at a time. Her hair was that red I'd say to her, 'Aunty, what's the matter with your hair. You been dying it?'

'No,' she'd say, 'it's the iron-ore, it's all over everything.'

That's the mining that did that, all that tearing up of the earth to get to minerals. When they first talked about getting the iron-ore and putting it on Finucane Island, the Aborigines up there were very upset. That island was a ceremonial ground, it was only five hundred yards across from the mainland, so when the tide went out those Aborigines would go there to have their rituals.

I was up there when that iron-ore first started, when they started loading it on to the boats, and the dust kicked up was terrible. It was really red and it blew from west to east, all over the port. Hedland used to be such a beautiful town but it's ruined now.

Even when they could see how the dust was choking the place they didn't stop, they just kept on going. They even tried putting hoses and sprinklers to stop it from blowing around but

Alice and Aunty Jean Hill, Geraldton, 1990.

it didn't work. When I used to come in from Hillside I couldn't believe it, everything you touched was red. Even the poinciana trees lost their beauty, and they used to be the pride of Port Hedland when they were flowering.

All that mining and destroying of the land is something that worries me a lot. It's not only happening in the Pilbara either, it's everywhere, the world is off it's axis, they're destroying everything just to make money.

To me, Australia is a big country, and it's crying poverty today, all through people being greedy. Greed is a terrible thing, and I think everyone should be equal.

It makes me very sad to say this but I don't think I'll see a time when there will be true equality in this country, because to me it's too far gone. I believe there is a time when Jesus comes back and they say then there will be a new heaven, and a new earth. But until then I don't think it will change. That is, if people don't develop a respect for one another, and a respect for our land, and stop tearing this beautiful country apart.

I saw some people on the telly the other day, trying to stop these bulldozers from going through and destroying a forest. I felt sorry for those poor people, because they were the ones getting arrested and made to stand aside. The people who were behind it, the greedy ones who don't care what they're destroying, they were allowed to keep on going.

Sometimes I think we were better off in the 1920s and 1930s when we never knew this kind of life, because today there's too much machinery ripping up the country and putting nothing back into it. It really makes me wonder what's going to be left for future generations.

Anyway, I stayed at Fitzgerald Street for quite a few years then I moved around staying with my family and into a flat in Spalding before moving to where I am today.

My place is a little duplex and I tried for this place three times, but the first two times the State Housing kept knocking me back. So I kept on trying, and third time lucky. I really wanted to live here because Joan lives across the road, and now that I'm on my own I know there's always someone close by. I don't know why the State Housing made it so hard for me to be near my family, and I doubt they have a good reason either.

I suppose health problems is something that was always going to catch up with me. That, and being older, has pretty much slowed me down today. Not that I see myself as a real old lady, I know women older than me. Aunty Jean is here in a nursing home now, and she's just turned eighty-eight. But even though I can't get around like I used to I still keep myself very busy. I think you're never too old to learn, and I find something new every day, some new experience, or something I didn't know.

Ever since that time on the reserve I've had trouble with asthma. Then, in the early 1980s I got pneumonia and was admitted to hospital. I was very sick in intensive care for four days. The doctor came and said to me, 'Do you smoke Alice?'

'No,' I said, 'I don't, and I never have smoked.'

'Why don't you pull the other one,' he said, and he just didn't believe me.

'Look doctor, I wouldn't say I haven't if I had, and I'm telling you NO I've never smoked.' I told him I was a God-fearing person, and wouldn't lie. He just grabbed my hand, patted me on the head, and walked away shaking his head, talking to the sister.

See they'd found out I had emphysema, and that's usually associated with smoking. Well I don't know how I got that one — since that time on the reserve I'd always suffered from asthma but I have never touched cigarettes.

Today I rely on puffers for my chest and tablets for a few other things. But when I was a kid living out in the bush there was no such thing as medicines like these. My people always cured themselves with eucalyptus leaves, goanna fat, and other bush medicines. If we were really sick we'd go and see one of the Marban men, who were special Aboriginal doctors. The women knew about healing too, and of course my mother had to know a lot of bush cures looking after me. She was one for the goanna fat and the emu oil. She used to make up the emu oil herself, right from hunting the emu through to preparing it properly and bottling the oil in jars.

It's very good medicine, emu oil. I have a friend who says when she's got a cold she gets a tablespoon of it and puts it in her mouth, and down the hatch. She hates the taste of it, but the next morning she wakes up as good as new. Nowdays it's not just an Aboriginal cure either, it's recognised for how good it is, and you can buy bottles of it at chemists.

I know my kids worry about my health, but I always say to them, 'Don't worry, I'm like a rubber ball, I'll always bounce back.' I think writing this book has been really good for me, like medicine of a different kind. In many ways it has given me a new lease of life, and I think it's been important to get all my stories down into the one book. That way my family, and their family, and their family, and so on, will always have them.

Mainly these are the stories of my single life, and just how hard I had to work in my day. Over the years I've been told by that many people that I've got so much to talk about, and I should never let it go to waste. See, when I go, the stories go with me, and then nobody benefits by it.

I've told my family some of these stories, but when they see them all together in one place I think they'll be surprised. There are things I've told that will make them sad too, but I had to tell those things because they are the truth, and part of doing this is the hope that all people, young, old, black, white, will read this book and see how life was for people in my time.

I turned eighty this birthday, and I couldn't begin to tell you all the changes I've seen. One of the biggest changes is, in my day, white people had all the power and we had no say, no say at all. Like when I went out to work, I had no choice about that, and I had to stay in that job for twelve months before I could even think about leaving. It didn't matter to the Department how much trouble we might have had, we were there to do that job, whatever happened. That's something young people don't realise today, they have no idea how little freedom we had. Some of the girls that were sent out to work had a really rough time. You won't find anything about the hell we went through in history books, but it happened, every little bit of it is true.

I think too, there's a lot more opportunities today than when I was a kid. If I'd had a choice when I was taken away I would've got that education they promised me, and I would've liked to have been a hairdresser. I said that to Mrs Larsen once, that if they would accept us I'd like to go for hairdressing. She agreed I would've been good, but we didn't have the choice, we had to scrub, polish, cook, or work out in the fields like a man.

That's why I drilled my kids from when they were knee-high to a grasshopper. I told them I didn't want them to grow up and have to fight their way through life like I had to. I wanted them to do better for themselves. 'Whenever opportunity knocks,' I said, 'don't knock it back, grasp it with both hands, because it's your future, and you're not going to have me all your life to defend and take care of you,' and they have done just that.

All of my kids have done well, and I'm very proud of these kids of mine. Not long ago Lauren asked me to count up all the people who have come from me, like my children, my grandchildren, and my great grannies. Well I had thirteen kids, they had forty children between them, and their kids have had forty six. So all together that makes ninety nine. I have another great grandchild due in February 1992 which will make it one hundred, — and maybe I'll get a telegram from the queen!

Today my children live in all parts of the country; I've got three daughters in Geraldton, one in Northam, one in Canberra, one in Perth, and another in Darwin. My sons are spread out too — Ron works on the rabbit-proof fence, Lew's out on a mine but his family are in Perth, and Noel, who is a national park ranger, is studying in Canberra with his family.

I don't get to trip around and visit them like I used to, but they still come home to Geraldton to see me and one another. I see my three girls that are here; Joan pops in after work sometimes, and she cooks tea on week nights and sends a meal over to me, Daphne comes every Friday and does the washing and tidies up around the house, and Bev-anne comes to visit and we have lunch together. All my other kids keep in touch, they ring me up from time to time, and my grandchildren are good like that too.

Nowdays I keep busy with my family, my church and Grannies club on Mondays. The Grannies club meets down in the Community Welfare place in Diosma Street, Rangeway. It started up because there were all us old ones living around the same town but we never saw one another. We all knew each other from places like Mogumber, living in Quarry Street, or from living in Geraldton for all these years. Anyway, this lady named Pat Leigh worked for the Community Welfare, and everyone got together and thought they'd get a Grannies club for us. That was so we could have one day a week just for the Grans, to go for picnics, or for drives, just things like that. Different Grannies come and go, but there's about nine of us regulars, and we have a great old time together. We make things too, and some of the Grans are very clever.

In 1990 they had the Moore River handback and I was very keen to go. The handback was held at the old settlement and it was the government leasing the land back to Aboriginal people to run as a farm. All the Grannies were going to go down together, but when my girls heard about it they wanted me to go with them instead.

We went down by car, and as I was travelling along with my girls I was feeling like, how am I going to cope seeing the old place again. I had five daughters with me and I made them laugh. I said, 'I'm just like an old mother cat, went away, and now I'm coming back with my kittens.'

When we got there, to my amazement, there was nothing much left of the old part of the settlement. When I'd first come there from the North, the pine trees were only saplings. When I went back to get married they were a bit more grown, but coming back this time, I tell you, I was amazed at the size of them. I just couldn't believe my eyes.

The old buildings were all gone. The only things left were the new hospital, other newer buildings around it, and some buildings on the side of the hill. The only old buildings were the old church, and the real old hospital, which was all overgrown with trees and things. Its windows were all broken and half the stones had been pulled out. The old laundry was sort of standing, with its ribs knocked out. All that was left of the girls' dormitory was a pile of little stones from the wall they'd put up to stop the boys. Where the sports ground was there's nothing there now, just plain white sand. Even the second boss's house was gone, and the Big House had been burnt to the ground.

When I looked down to the camps it was just bare ground. There were a few York gums still standing, and the one where Aunty Jean and Uncle Jack had their camp is still there. When the mission was going it had been like a little village on it's own at the bottom of the hill, but now all the humpies were gone.

I saw all this and I had mixed feelings about seeing it so different. In one way I was glad the buildings weren't there, and in another way I wanted to go back there and stand at the top of the street and see it all again.

When we arrived we got out of the car and went straight down to the old church. There were two chaps standing there and I said to them, 'Good morning.'

'Good morning,' they said back. Then I said, 'You don't mind if I ask you who you are?'

One of the men said, 'I'm Tom Corbett,' and the other one was Arnold Franks. I knew Tom from when I was in Mogumber, but I'd never spoken to him. He's from North, from Marble Bar, so of course we made a fuss of one another. He'd come back with his family too and he introduced us to them. The other chap, Arnold, is much younger, but I knew his mother from when I was at the settlement.

My girls went off taking photos and walking around everywhere, but I couldn't go with them, because I couldn't walk the distance. I met up with some people and I went off to have a look at all the photos they pinned up on the church porch. They had this great big board there with lots of old photos on it, and some people found their wedding photos, but I didn't see any from my time.

There was quite a turn out too, lots of people had come up for it. There was a big marquee set up where they had the hand-over ceremony. We stayed and Sister Eileen had her say, she worked as a nurse there after my time, Neddo (Ned Mippy) said a few words, and so did a couple of others. They had a big cake but we didn't stay for that.

Driving home I thought to myself, if the buildings had still been there I'm sure I would have broken down and not been able to take it. I'm really glad I went, I'm glad I saw the old place for the last time and it is finally put to rest. All the people are gone from there now but it still has a real feeling. I think my girls felt it too; being there, seeing where all us kids were sent when we were taken away from our mothers had an affect on them.

I suppose you could say I've gone back and visited all the places in my past. Like going to the old settlement and getting back to see my family. To me, going back with Amy is my true going home story, but there is another part too, and that's going back to make my peace with my country.

In 1987 my son Noel was working as a national park ranger at Fitzroy Crossing, when he got transferred to Millstream, which is my country. They'd only been there a week when he rang me up and said, 'Mum, how would you like to come up and have a holiday with Cheryl, me and the kids.'

'Oh I'd love that,' I said. 'Really and truly I would love it.'

'Well then, you just come up.'

'All right,' I said, 'when do you want me up there?'

'As soon as you can get here, Mum.'

I talked to my girls about it and Joan said, 'Yes, Mum, but

221

you can't go on your own.' So my daughter Bev-anne volunteered to take me up on the bus and we left Geraldton in May.

I was really looking forward to seeing Millstream Station because it was one of the stations my mother's family worked. When we were kids mother used to take us there from time to time and I thought I knew a lot about it. But when I got there I was surprised to find that the only thing about it I recognised was the kitchen.

But, I had a marvellous time up there with them. Noel was wonderful, he had intentions of taking me back to Abydos where I was born, and of visiting all the places of my childhood.

Cheryl's brother lived in Karratha and once a fortnight we'd go in there to stay the weekend with them. The word spread that I was back, so all the old folks came out from Roebourne to see me, and we had some great old yarns. I had a really good time catching up with my relations, and I met some I'd never seen before in my life, from my father's side, the Bassett line.

I saw quite a few of the old places while I was there, and I even got back to Pyramid Hill. It was on the road out of Millstream and we stopped there one day so I could have my photo taken. There used to be a stock camp near there, and when I was a kid I'd run off to the hill with my cousins playing. There was a great big snappy gum on the side of the hill and we used to try and get up there to reach it. We'd get as far as we could, then we'd race down the hill and nearly crack our knees. I think that's why I've got this bad leg now, because once we got on the downhill we just couldn't stop, and we'd go almost half way across the flat. To think of it now it's a wonder we never broke our legs, but we used to just love to do it.

One day, when Noel was taking us into Port Hedland to have lunch with Aunty Jean, we drove past a sign saying Croyden. I said to Noel, 'No, this can't be Croyden. Croyden is miles away.' I asked him to go back so I could have a better look because I just had this feeling. So he turned around and we drove past the gate and down towards the main house. When we were about three quarters of a mile away I knew exactly where I was.

'Croyden!' I said. 'No way — it's Mallina.'

I could see the old windmill and I remembered how us kids used to climb up and look for dust rising to see if anybody was coming from Whim Creek. We pulled up at the front gate and the manager came out to us. He and Noel got talking and he explained that Mallina and Croyden were one now. I sat in the car gazing around at the old place and how it had changed. Although there'd been a lot of changes made to the old station over the years, being there I could just picture everybody again — my mother, Aunty Minnie, Ella, Doris, the whole lot of us. I was crying very quietly to myself thinking back over the past and my two little grandchildren were just watching their old grandma, wondering why she was so sad. It meant a lot to me to see Mallina again, and my only regret is I wish I'd asked Noel to give me a handful of soil, so I could've held it tightly then just thrown it back.

One very special trip we did was out to a place called Deep Reach. Noel had decided he wanted to take us out to see this place, so the next day, after he'd done his rounds, he drove us out there. This is the place where the old snake lives, and I'd always been told by my mother that we mustn't go to a pool without making our peace. If you've been away you can't just go back there and walk around or do what you like, that's the law.

Bev-anne, Cheryl, Noel, and my two little grandchildren were with me, and I said to them, 'I can't reach down there, but just cup your hands and give me the water.' Then I told them, 'You've got to tell me if you see a rainbow when I blow.'

When we got to the edge of the pool Noel went down and got some water, put his hands into mine, and I took it. I put the water in my mouth and I blew hard towards the sun. As I blew this big rainbow came, and I said, 'Yinda ngurra — I belong.'

I looked over at them and they all had tears in their eyes, and I said, 'I've made my peace with him, the rainbow is a sign that he's accepted me.' I felt good then, I felt I was back.

The next morning, Bruce, who's one of the Aboriginal rangers, went out with Noel to do their rounds. They went to the place where I'd made my peace, and they saw him, they saw the snake. He was stretched out on top of the water and they just couldn't believe it, because that old fella hadn't been back for as long as they could remember. As they went towards him he must have heard them walking, and he started sinking down into the water. But they got a look at him, and they said he was so big he was like a porpoise, and he had a mane along his back. They both just stood there and watched him sink down deep, back into the pool.

Well, you wouldn't believe it, but that news was flashed around Roebourne and all over the place. People heard about it for miles around and two of the old tribal men came to see me. They were really happy to think that I did the right thing, and I told them that I'd always been told by my mother that I mustn't ever go to a pool without making peace.

There are pools all over that country and you're not allowed to go near them unless you make your peace, that's the Aboriginal law. As soon as you do that, and you're accepted, you can have a drink. But if you don't do it, and just take from the pool, then anything can happen to you. That's beautiful isn't it? To keep your tradition and never let it go.

I feel really good about going back, because although they tricked me when they took me away, in my lifetime I was able to get back some of what they took from me. You see, forty-two years later I got back to my family, and sixty-four years from when I left Point Samson, I got back to make my peace with my country.

POSTSCRIPT

Nan decided to tell her story in *When The Pelican Laughed* primarily to pass her stories on to her family. She was, however, genuinely surprised and pleased at the wide interest in her story, and in the way her candour had affected so many readers. Many people wrote to her, and Nan called these her 'fam mails'. She kept the letters in an album which she personally cherished, and which provided her with an important window into what the wider community wanted to learn; about the lives of Aboriginal women like Nan.

On the morning of Tuesday 7 November 1995, Alice Nannup passed away in Geraldton Regional Hospital. Hundreds of people came to her funeral; both black and white, and it was a testimony to who Nan was that we all came together to share in our collective loss. Nan has left behind an important record of her life, and it always gave her private pleasure to know that even after she left us, the Old Pelican's stories would live on.

Lauren Marsh and Steve Kinnane
August 1996.